Esperanza's
Way

CINDY BURKART

MAYNARD

HISTORIUM PRESS

Library of Congress Cataloging-in-Publication Data on file
Library of Congress Control Number: 2023909513

First Edition 2023

Standard Images by Shutterstock & Public Domain
Main cover image copyrighted and protected © Cindy Burkart Maynard
Cover designed by White Rabbit Arts

Visit Cindy Burkart Maynard's website at
www.thehistoricalfictioncompany.com/cindy-burkart-maynard

Hardcover ISBN: 979-8-9883817-0-9
Paperback ISBN: 979-8-9883817-1-6
E-Book ISBN: 979-8-9883817-2-3

Historium Press, a subsidiary of
The Historical Fiction Company
2023

CONTENTS

ESPERANZA'S
WAY

PROLOGUE

NAPOLI 1300

I know my days are few. When I sleep, my loved ones come to me, whispering, beckoning me to join them. My mother, my saviors Mateo and Amika, the good Master Cohen, Signore Adolfo, and the complex, enigmatic Dolores, and our children, they promise they will help me cross over. The next life now seems more immediate to me than the present.

I am sitting in the loggia, the setting sun warming me, as I inhale the tantalizing aroma of the olive and lemon groves below, as I am serenaded by church bells drifting up on the breeze, and the wavelets in the aquamarine Bay of Napoli dance like fireflies in the fading amber sky.

I am like a set of bowls nested one inside the other, each one holding more and more of my story, until the largest bowl overflows with the accumulated experiences of a lifetime. My story began long ago in an obscure corner of northeastern Spain at the foot of the Pyrenees, where ancient Basque traditions collided with the onslaught of Christianity.

A vision of myself as a young child swims into view. What a sight I must have been, sitting in the rain, my mother's dead body, ravaged by leprosy, lying across my lap. My poor mother bequeathed to me an uncanny intuition to sense people's ailments, and a promise that I would be saved. And I have been saved, many times. First, Amika and Mateo who found me and gave me a start in life. We three pilgrims, thrown together by circumstance, entwined like vines winding across a garden wall, joining, diverging, then joining once again until fate set me on another, more dangerous path, my own Way.

1

PONFERRADA

SPRING 1259

A mangle-eared mutt cocked his head toward the sky sniffing the breeze, sensing the approaching storm. The dog lowered its head, hunched its shoulders, and sidled into an alley. A concussive boom tore the clouds open, and torrents of rain sluiced over the stone-built town of Ponferrada. Up and down the street people scurried for shelter.

"Amika, help me haul this table up against the wall out of the rain." Gabriela, stocky though she was, struggled to muscle a heavy oak table under the covered walkway that lined the street. The two women were fortunate their apothecary shop lay along the ancient pilgrimage route, the Camino Santiago de Compostela. Road-weary pilgrims, always in need of remedies to assuage their aches and injuries, walked past their shop every day.

"I'll be right there," Amika propped her broom against the wall. Like the dog, she turned a weather eye to the skies. *This rain is going to be hard enough to drown fishes,* she thought.

"Esperanza, take these jars and bottles inside." A waif-like girl scooped their wares into a well-worn wicker basket. Her serious demeanor and small size belied her twelve years.

Inside their stone house on the ancient cobblestone street, an apothecary cabinet, burnished by age to a rich mahogany patina, dominated the room. An intricate warren of compartments and drawers held ointments, elixirs, and infusions. Bundles of herbs hung upside down from the ceiling. A symphony of spicy, citrusy, fruity, and minty smells harmonized like a fragrant orchestra. When customers entered and inhaled the aroma, their spirits lightened, buoyed by the aromas of nature. With their wares safely inside, the three companions settled on a bench, warming themselves before a capacious open hearth.

"This is the third downpour we've had this month," Amika said. "It will be a good wildflower season, after it warms up a bit. Esperanza, you, and I will scour the hillsides for herbals to replenish our stock. Wild garlic and sorrel mature early, and we might find rosehips that survived the winter. We'll have a lovely time roaming the hills, won't we, Esperanza?" Amika placed her work-hardened hand atop the girl's soft, delicate one.

The girl turned her smokey grey eyes toward Amika and nodded. Roaming hillsides too steep for the farmer's plough was the greatest pleasure Amika and Esperanza shared. In the two years since Amika discovered the girl curled next to the body of her dead mother along the Camino de Santiago, the two had grown as close as any natural mother and child.

"You're a good student. Think of all you've learned since you've been here." She beamed at the girl affectionately pinching her ear.

"I'm too old for that!" Esperanza protested. "I'm twelve years old, almost a young lady!" She raised her chin defiantly.

Amika's cupid's bow lips stretched into an amiable smile. "Alright then, no more pinches. I wouldn't want to annoy my little mountain goat. What would I do without you scampering over the hills for me, when all I can do is limp along behind? I need you."

At twenty-four years old, her childhood living rough as an orphan in the wild hills of the Basque country had made Amika wise beyond her years. Her knowledge of plants, learned at the side of a Wise Woman of the old tradition in her Basque homeland, could fill volumes. The two had ranged over the hills, among the feral grasses and wildflowers, until the antagonism of the Catholic church toward her mentor's traditional ways cost her life and forced Amika to flee. Her flight ended here, in Ponferrada, at the foot of the Cantabrian Mountains, after an injury crippled her left leg. But all she had learned still lived within her, and she was eager to pass it along to Esperanza, the orphan with stormy grey eyes and an ineffable power to perceive illness.

Amika limped along as she taught Esperanza the uses of every plant that grew.

"God did not create a single plant without a purpose," she instructed the girl. "You just need to learn the virtues of each one. Where others see grasses and flowers, I see foods and medicine." Amika grew passionate tutoring her young protégé. Under her wing, Esperanza learned quickly, growing from orphaned stray to beloved daughter.

Gabriela mumbled, gripping her woolen shawl tightly around her shoulders as she retreated into the house. She said nothing as she plopped down heavily on a wooden bench facing an open hearth so large it spanned the room. A tripod hanging over the fire supported a heavy iron pot. When her stomach was empty, as it was now, her disposition soured, and she could focus only on satisfying its insistent grumbling. Amika and Esperanza followed her in and took their places next to her on the bench.

"The farmers and herders will be happy with the rain," Amika explained. "They can expect bountiful crops, and fat sheep with pelts so thick wolves will get a mouth full of wool rather than a meal when they catch one."

Esperanza smiled at the vision of sheep so fat and woolly that they were impenetrable.

"I expect we'll see many customers coughing and wheezing," Esperanza predicted. "We will need plenty of mustard greens for poultices, and catmint for fevers."

"Alright then, I'll cook up some onion tea and hearty bone broth to comfort the pilgrims along their way to Santiago," Gabriela added.

"Speaking of cool, wet weather, I have just what we need."

Gabriela heaved herself up off the bench and trundled into the kitchen, emerging with three wooden bowls. Dipping her ladle into the cooking pot, she filled them with a thick stew of beans, onions, and lentils. A smile crinkled the corners of her blue eyes as she handed Amika and Esperanza their bowls, then carved thick slabs of barley bread to fill out the meal. The three companions huddled together like birds in a nest. The warmth of affection enfolded them like a well-loved quilt. Gabriela was plump as a partridge, Amika tall, lithe, and still beautiful with acorn-brown eyes, and Esperanza, defiant and serious, with springy mouse-brown hair erupting from her head, and gray eyes peering out from under a wide forehead. In the years since their unlikely meeting, they had settled into an amicable partnership that did not require words.

* * *

Gabriela had not realized how lonely she had been after her husband's death. Without the money he earned as a stone mason, she had resorted to doing what she did best - cooking. Her husband had not been good company. Taciturn and gruff, he was often hard to live with, but she had loved him, nonetheless. When he died, he left her with nothing but this ancient stone building. Its dark and joyless interior reflected the gloom of lives together. Its one redeeming feature was that it faced the well-traveled route of the Camino de Santiago.

Every day, an assortment of pilgrims shuffled past her doorway - threadbare penitents, aimless vagabonds, and wealthy grandees riding richly caparisoned horses.

"Have a cup of hearty broth!" She called out to the peregrinos, the pilgrims, as they passed her door. "Look at these! Wouldn't you love some of these vegetables, picked fresh from the garden this morning?"

Despite her humble circumstances, Gabriela was generous to all. To those who could drop a coin or two into her bowl, she gave thanks. To those who could not, she gave encouragement. "Ultrea!

Onward!" she called out to the weary pilgrims.

One day a young woman with a pronounced limp blew in on a gust of wind.

"Do you remember the day you arrived on my doorstep?" Gabriela mused.

Amika and Esperanza exchanged knowing glances. The story of her arrival had been repeated so many times it had attained the status of legend. It was the glue that held them together.

"Of course, I do. You took one glance at me, realized I was not going to buy anything, and you couldn't wait to be done with me," Amika chuckled.

"But you didn't leave, did you? I don't think I had ever met a young woman as bold as you. How old were you? Fifteen?"

"Seventeen." Amika murmured, lost in reverie recalling the fate that brought her to Gabriela's door.

"You walked right up and made a proposal. You were certain you could improve my business. What gall! We hadn't even met yet." Gabriela smiled with delight.

Amika glanced down at her malformed knee, so twisted that she would always be a cripple. "After my fall I couldn't finish my pilgrimage to Santiago. The sisters at the convent nursed me back to health. But after I was healed, they asked me to leave."

"I understand that now, but that day when you showed up at my stall, you were as strange as a beard on a baby," Gabriela chortled. "Now, look at us. You were right. Thanks to your boldness we have a fully functioning apothecary." She flung her arms wide encompassing home, hearth, and self-made family.

"As if having you in my life was not enough, two years later this Mateo friend of yours dropped off this homeless orphan girl." One meaty arm reached out to squeeze Esperanza's shoulder, sending the soup bowl in her lap sloshing. "And I resisted taking the girl, didn't I?" She winked at Esperanza.

"Mateo is your sweetheart," Gabriela's elbow shot out nudging Amika's ribs. Amika raised a palm in the air, ready to argue, but quickly gave up the pretense of innocence. Her friendship with

Mateo was as complex as intertwined rose petals, layered with desire, disappointment, and love.

"You know our story perfectly well!" Amika's voice twanged defensively. "I would marry him the moment he asked. He has been the love of my life since I met him along the Camino," her smile turned sour. "I was never going to be enough for him. He had ambitions. And now he is a successful, educated man with excellent prospects."

"He still loves you; you know." Esperanza stretched across Gabriela's broad lap to squeeze Amika's hand.

"Ah, well." Gabriela chose to see the rainbow, not the storm. "He is a kind and generous man. You could do worse than Mateo." She winked conspiratorially. Amika smiled demurely.

Esperanza sat silent. She also harbored a story of how she came to this place, but she had shared it with no one. A single tear seeped from her eye remembering her mother's last words before she died in her arms.

"Esperanza, child of my soul, you will not be alone. I will send two others to you, and they will care for you as their own." Her mother had closed her eyes and breathed a long, rasping breath, then fell silent. When Esperanza was sure she had crossed over to the life beyond, her mother took one last gulp of air and whispered. *"You will have powers of intuition far beyond those of ordinary people. You will know it is real when your eyes burn and your ears buzz. This is my gift to you."* Then she was gone - no last gasps, no more final words. Esperanza's heart was too broken with grief to ponder her mother's strange prophecy.

Before Esperanza's mother's body was cold, Amika and Mateo found the girl sheltering under a rock ledge cradling the body of her dead mother. *Here they are. The others who will care for me. Just as mother told me.*

The three women settled into a comfortable silence on the bench before the fire, each one reminiscing about their shared history. Gabriela and Amika believed they would live in harmony forever. Esperanza however, sensed change marching toward them as surely as the mangle-eared dog sensed the storm rolling in.

"Listen!" Esperanza said tilting her head upward. "I think the rain is letting up." She gathered their wooden bowls, brought them to the kitchen, walked to the door, and drew a deep breath. The air smelled like freshly cut hay. "Today will be special. I can feel it. "

Gabriela and Amika no longer questioned Esperanza's remarkable intuition. It was clear the orphan girl with eyes like thunder clouds and hair as wild as a storm at sea had a rare gift. They had seen it often when she diagnosed invisible ailments. She seemed to see behind the curtain of everyday life to a realm where past, present, and future blended into a continuous rhythmic flow, like the confluence of three rivers.

"That's wonderful," Amika stood, gathering her herbs, preparing to go back to work. "I would love to have a special day. Days have been so dismal this spring."

The three of them wrestled the heavy oak table back into the street. Within minutes an old woman approached, tugging a sunken-eyed child by the hand.

"She has a cold with a nasty cough," the old woman declared. As though on cue, the girl unleashed a spasm of uncontrolled hacking. By the time the fit subsided the child's ragged breath came in short, wheezing gasps. Her cheeks flushed red. Her narrow shoulders crumpled. The episode had exhausted her.

"Poor dear." Amika bent over the table to pat the child's head. She placed the back of her hand against her cheek. It was warm and swampy to the touch. "Stir a spoonful of honey into warm water. Add a little radish juice and a pinch of salt. Do this three times each day." Amika prepared a packet with a small square of honeycomb and a vial of radish juice. She pressed it into the old woman's hand and curled the woman's fingers around it.

The old woman opened her other hand. Lines like dark rivers scored the valley of her open palm. She dropped a single copper coin into the offering bowl. "Thank you. I would hate to lose her to the coughing disease as I lost her mother. She is all I have left."

As they walked away, a burly man of middle years who had

been lingering in the shadows approached the table. He did not raise his eyes but looked forlornly at the ground, kicking his toe in the dust in embarrassed silence. Eventually he spoke.

"I can't explain what's wrong. I don't even know why I came here today, but I just don't feel right." He appeared to be in excellent health with the muscular build, and ruddy skin of a hard-working man in his prime.

"Are you getting enough sleep? Do you and your wife have a crying baby disrupting your nights? Are you eating enough?" Amika peppered him with questions.

"No, our son is almost grown. My wife sleeps the sleep of the innocents as I lay awake turning from one side to the other like a hare roasting on a spit."

Amika's questions shed no light on the cause of his vague symptoms. She paused, cradling her chin between her thumb and forefinger. When she could think of nothing further to help the man, she pulled open a drawer and sprinkled a palm full of willow bark chips into a cloth bag.

"Simmer these. Wait until the water cools. Strain the leaves out and drink the tea. It may taste like chewing wood, so you might want to add a little honey."

"Willow bark tea," he mumbled. "My wife has made this for me many times. Do you have anything else I might try?"

Esperanza moved to the front of the table to examine him more closely. The man was a giant compared to the slight girl with unkempt hair and large eyes.

"Please show me your ankles," she said. The man looked sharply at the girl, shocked by the cheeky request, then pushed his leggings up a few inches to expose swollen ankles.

"Give me your hand."

Reluctantly he extended his arm toward her. Esperanza turned his hand over several times. The skin under his fingernails was a purplish blue and there was a blue tinge to his lips. She laid her fingers lightly on the veins radiating from his hand up his arm. She closed her eyes as she held his palm upward.

"You are exhausted, aren't you?" Not waiting for an answer, she continued. "Yet you have trouble sleeping. You are short of breath. You have moments of confusion."

The man was stunned. "How did you know?"

She ignored his question. Esperanza could not explain how she came by her knowledge, and the man would not have believed her in any case. It came from a place of deep, inexplicable insight. She felt something more - a vibration emanating from the patient. She could not define it, but it was as real to her as his beating heart.

"Your heart has grown weak," Esperanza told him. "It is working too hard. You must eat less meat and more asparagus, peppers, squash, and onions. Strenuous physical activity will overpower your heart. You must rest more."

"How will I do that?" He protested. "I have crops to plant, rocks to remove from the fields, animals to butcher."

Esperanza ignored his excuses. "Your son is coming of age. You love him too much. You have allowed him to become lazy and selfish. You must train him to work as hard as you do. If you do not do these things, your family will be fatherless, and your son will be unable to support them."

Her blunt words struck him like a hammer blow. How could she perceive these things? She was just a young girl, not old enough to marry, yet she spoke with authority. He turned to go, his stomach churning with dread.

"Don't worry." Esperanza's tone softened as she tried to offer the startled man some comfort. "Just train your son to do the work. Refrain from the heaviest labor, and eat mostly vegetables, only a little meat. If you do these things, you should live long enough to see your grandchildren."

Amika called after him. "And don't forget your willow bark tea."

Gabriela and Amika looked at each other, incredulous but not shocked. Ever since Amika and Mateo found Esperanza that rainy night sitting next to the body of her dead mother, haunted by horror, the forlorn girl seemed to grasp things of which she could not possibly have knowledge. When asked, she insisted she heard her mother's voice instructing her. Now, at twelve, her discernment of illness complimented Amika's herbal treatments. Amika was a master of folk remedies, her knowledge passed down through generations of healers. Esperanza saw maladies through the lens of her brilliant intuition. Their combined talents, along with Gabriela's nourishing bone broth, attracted many visitors.

By evening, the rain had wrung itself out leaving the dry fabric of filmy clouds hanging in the western sky. Amika and Gabriela gathered up their wares and brought them inside. Esperanza did not move but sat staring toward the darkening horizon. When it was almost too dark to see, someone approached from the west. A black cloak enveloped the person's entire body flowing seamlessly from hood to hem. Back lit by the setting sun, it looked like an ominous apparition emerging from the twilight. *Here he is,* Esperanza thought. *I knew he would come.*

"My girl!" the man exclaimed as he approached. "I haven't seen you since last summer. How you have grown!" He bent over to hug her as he would a child but stopped himself. "You are a young lady now. I must treat you with dignity - no hugs." The man stood erect and leaned over to kiss her hand.

"Nonsense!" Esperanza squealed. She threw her arms around Mateo's neck. "I will never be too old to welcome you as a father."

"What's going on out there?" Amika emerged from inside, wiping her hands on her apron. She stopped abruptly. Her eyes softened; her lips parted; her shoulders relaxed.

"Mateo," Amika's voice caught in her throat. "You're here. I didn't expect you."

Esperanza released him from her embrace, and Mateo straightened to face Amika. He had not changed since she last saw him. Though only of average height, his broad shoulders and regal bearing made him appear powerful and significant. Thick, black hair swept back from his forehead reaching almost to his shoulders. His deep-set black eyes beneath a brooding brow were hypnotic.

Six years had passed since Mateo and Amika met along the Camino. Since that meeting, fate had braided their paths together. But as a braid eventually needs to be untangled, the two were not destined to remain entwined.

"I am coming from Salamanca." Mateo was almost breathless with excitement. "I'm sure you remember our friend, Samuel the Jew?" Without any preliminaries, Mateo dove into the conversation. "When we met him along the Camino, he was on an important mission as an emissary for King Alfonso."

"Yes, of course I remember him," Amika tossed her hair back in a gesture of mock arrogance. "I was the first to make his acquaintance, if you recall. He was delivering important documents from the School of Translators in Toledo to King Alfonso in Burgos. If I hadn't rescued the document that dropped from his saddlebag, his important mission would have failed."

Mateo smiled indulgently. "Of course, Madam." He bowed and swept his hat from his head. "You saved his priceless parchment." He rose smiling. "Samuel has been my great ally in establishing my Academy of Classical Learning in Salamanca. Our students are becoming true scholars. Samuel sent me word that the King has granted our school permission to teach an innovative curriculum meant to prepare our students for the University of Salamanca, and Pope Alexander has approved our charter. Ours will be the first true university preparatory school in the kingdoms of Castile and Leon. I am traveling to Leon to meet Samuel, so we can complete the official documentation," Mateo explained. "I came to share the news with you."

When she met Samuel, Amika had not encountered many Jews, sheltered as she had been in the forested hills of the Basque country. Yet she apprehended immediately that Samuel was unique, not only in his high rank, but also in his open-heartedness. He was a distinguished scholar at the School of Translators in Toledo and an aristocrat, but had treated Amika and Mateo graciously, without the slightest trace of arrogance. He was grateful for Amika's quick action in saving his precious document.

Samuel insisted that the pair of shabby pilgrims join him for dinner. Without asking permission, the three of them showed up unannounced at the home of Aaron Cohen, Samuel's cousin, and invited themselves to dinner. Though they were dirty and disheveled, Aaron and his wife, Johanna, welcomed them wholeheartedly. Never had Amika seen such opulence as graced Aaron's home in the Jewish quarter of Burgos. Mateo, with his patrician background, felt entirely comfortable in such luxurious surroundings, but Amika was shy, self-conscious about her grimy clothing and disheveled appearance. Once Amika and Mateo were properly bathed and given clean tunics and woollen cloaks to replace their tattered clothing, they joined the family for dinner. Mateo shared with Samuel his dream of establishing a school of classical learning, independent of the monasteries, and unfettered by the narrow world view of clerics. It would be a school like the Muslim madrassas he had attended in his childhood in Andalusia, modeled after the schools of ancient Greece, dedicated to pursuing philosophy, mathematics, astronomy, and natural history. His graduates would learn the languages of scholars - Latin, Greek, and Arabic.

At the time of their visit to Samuel's home, the dream of opening a school for young scholars seemed unattainable, but here he was, four years later, his vision about to become reality. He could scarcely believe his luck.

Amika pulled her mind away from her memories of the Camino. She was delighted by Mateo's news, but his words swirled around her head like a swarm of bees, buzzing but not landing. The whirlwind of emotions that stirred her had nothing to do with Mateo's school. Her feelings were visceral. Her heart swelled to overflowing, not with pride for his accomplishments, but with an aching need. He had risen so high in the world, she worried he would slip away from her altogether. Her accomplishments were ripples in a stream compared to the waterfall of his success. She knew he would never marry her; their differences were too great. Nevertheless, from the moment she met him on the Camino, she understood he would always be her first and only love. He had ambitious plans that did not include an uneducated peasant girl. Though he loved her in his way, he would never tether himself to her side. She put her disappointment aside as Mateo threw his arm around her shoulder enveloping her in his cloak and led him inside.

Tonight, at least, he will belong only to me, she thought.

That night Amika and Mateo climbed the shaky ladder to the loft above the kitchen, leaving Gabriela and Esperanza to lie on their straw mattress next to the fire.

The next morning, Gabriela and Esperanza arranged their wares outside on the oak table without Amika's help. When the sun rose past the roof lines, Mateo and Amika had not yet emerged from their nest in the loft. Esperanza rifled through the drawers and compartments of the apothecary cabinet, deciding which remedies she would need for today's customers - sweet violet for cloudy eyes, mugwort for sick intestines, spring sage harvested just last week to make a tincture to relax muscle spasms. The last herb she selected was a sprig of a black nightshade, called belladonna; she tucked it into the pouch at her waist. She did not often suggest it to customers except in cases of chronic sleeplessness, and then only in tiny amounts. Her fingers twitched and her stomach clenched as she dropped a small sprig into her drawstring purse. Part of her resisted, but today she would need it whether she liked it or not.

As the sun rose into a waxy yellow sky, the trickle of bleary-eyed morning pilgrims swelled to a steady stream. At midday, a sumptuous palanquin stopped in the road in front of their table. A coat of arms with gold flowers against a startling red background decorated the door of the enclosed litter. The bearers carefully lowered it to the ground and an elegant lady parted the curtains. The lead bearer hurried to her side, bending his ear toward her as she whispered her instructions. He straightened and marched, sober faced, toward the apothecary table.

"The lady wishes to purchase belladonna," His tone was terse, imperious.

Esperanza hesitated, and extracted the sprig of belladonna, her most precious and deadly medicine.

"Are you sure this is what you want? It is very potent, and can be dangerous if you take too much," she said, starting to tuck it back into her waist pouch.

"Stop!" the bearer commanded. "Her ladyship knows quite well the properties of this herb and how to use it." He flicked the back of his hand toward her dismissively as if swatting away fly. "Things will not go well with you if you deny the lady her wishes." He tossed the vague threat at her as someone would throw a stone at a mangy street dog.

"Fine." Esperanza responded, bristling at his arrogance. "But you should tell the lady it is very fresh, at the height of its potency. She may make tea from the leaves, but she must drink only a small amount."

Esperanza stared at the man. He lifted his chin and swiveled his head to avoid her suddenly uncomfortable gaze.

Ignoring her words, he added. "If she wants more, she will send me. The herb is popular among the ladies at court. It dilates their pupils making them more beautiful. They are quite charmed by the effect."

"Please. Be. Careful," Esperanza emphasized each word separately. With that, Esperanza handed over the sprig of belladonna. The lead bearer dropped two gold dinars into her hand, an extravagant amount for such a tiny twig. Then they were gone. She felt suddenly queasy. The ringing in her ears grew to a steady hum. Her tingling eyes grew hot. She stood immobile in the street taking slow, heavy breaths.

Amika and Mateo at last emerged from the house in time to watch the palanquin disappear down the street.

"Who was that?" Amika asked.

"I have no idea. I have never seen her before. I expected someone unusual would stop at our stand today, but I did not expect anyone like her. She insisted on taking the belladonna." Esperanza's voice was a dull monotone, but her heart raced, and her face drained of color. Her eyes followed the palanquin. "I had misgivings, but her bearer assured me she was quite familiar with it and knew how to use it appropriately." Esperanza paused; unease spread through her body like a winter chill.

"I recognize that lady's palanquin," Mateo broke in. "She is not a local. You would have no reason to be familiar with her. But I would recognize that design on the door anywhere. That was Lady Consuelo Miranda, Conte Fernando de Asturia's current favorite courtier. She is quite well known at court for her excesses. Perhaps she is on pilgrimage as penance for her many sins." Mateo laughed as though it was an inside joke. "You are well rid of her. She has a reputation for being temperamental. Perhaps she has fallen out of favor with the Conte and is trying to win back his good graces by dilating her eyes to beguile him. I will probably hear all about the incident at court in Leon. How the ladies love to gossip." Mateo tugged at the hem of his elegant, embroidered vest. He rattled off aristocratic gossip with stunning nonchalance. Amika stared at him uncomprehendingly. Esperanza's blood ran as cold as ice melt in spring. Her hand flew to her throat. A choking sensation gripped her. The bitter smell of belladonna lingered on her fingertips.

"Come, have some breakfast," Gabriela came out to see what was going on. She offered the kind of comfort that appealed to the stomach. "Mateo, a good porridge will fortify you for your trip to Leon."

Mateo bent to kiss her hand. "Thank you, Gabriela." Gabriela blushed furiously. "I apologize, but I am off to a late start." He glanced over his shoulder, winking at Amika who smiled coyly. "I suppose I will see you again after I finalize the details of my school proposal."

2

FLIGHT

SPRING 1260

The three women watched Mateo disappear down the maze of morning streets, not expecting to see him again for many months, so it caught them by surprise when a few weeks later he burst in on their sedate breakfast.

A bleary morning sun shone through wispy clouds when Mateo, frantic with haste, loped up to Gabriela's house. He burst through the door and swept Esperanza off her feet. There were no greetings, no affectionate hugs, no hesitation, only a muscular arm encircling her waist and a hand clamped over her mouth. Her bowl clattered to the floor spattering porridge. Amika, still in the shift she had slept in, rushed into the room.

"What are you doing? Mateo, this is outrageous. Stop!"

"The Lady Consuelo Miranda has died." The words spilled out. "The Conte Fernando de Asturia is furious. He has sent his knights to capture the culprit who sold her the belladonna. The bearer told them exactly where to find her. They are on their way. They are seeking Esperanza. She is wanted for murder."

"You're smothering her. You can't do this!" Amika's distraught cries filled the space between them. "She is just a child; the Count can't blame her."

"Do you think the Count cares about the girl's age? If she is old enough to sell herbs, she is old enough to die for her crimes."

Mateo pulled Esperanza out the door and swung her up behind him on his saddle. Sensing the girl's tension, the horse danced excitedly, reared up then dropped heavily to the ground.

"We have no choice. I will send word when we reach safety."

He spurred his stallion and sped away from town at full gallop. Behind him Esperanza gripped his waist, her face pressed up hard against his quilted vest. He smelled of sweat and dust. Clinging to his tense body was like hugging a tree trunk. The horse was slick with sweat when they finally slowed to a canter. Instead of traveling the main route out of town, Mateo turned down a muddy sheep track coming to a stop at a shady pond surrounded by a dense thicket of green alder. Mateo slid off the winded horse with the girl still clinging to the horse's neck and pushed through the dense shrubs to the shallow water. The sheltered retreat reverberated with emerald hues of dragonflies dancing on a mat of verdant duckweed floating on the shallow pond. Green frogs leaped from lily pad to lily pad. Even the sky reflected the verdant chartreuse of the oasis. After the horse had drunk its fill, Mateo re-mounted and turned south, away from the Camino. For a long while neither of them uttered a word. When their breathing calmed, and their hearts slowed, Mateo laid out his plan.

"If we stay on the sheep paths and country tracks, they will not find us," Mateo said. "They will be searching for us along the Camino."

Esperanza nodded. "Are we going to find the Jew, Aaron?"

"Yes, how did you know?"

She did not answer his question. "I have heard Amika's stories of his gracious hospitality many times. He lives in Burgos. Is that right?"

"Yes, in Burgos. He treated us with great generosity when we needed it most. Since then, I have visited him many times when I travel between the king's court in Burgos and my school in Salamanca. Burgos is far from here. If we keep to the country paths, our progress will be slow so we will be traveling for many weeks."

"Weeks . . ." she sighed. The enormity of what had just happened began to seep into her consciousness. She felt as helpless as the ball shot from a catapult as it hurtles into an unknown future.

* * *

For the next several days they walked as much as they rode. The horse, bred for beauty and bursts of speed, tired easily trudging long miles across rough terrain. Every evening Mateo cleaned its hooves and rubbed down its flanks with circular strokes to loosen the day's accumulation of dirt, and detritus of the road. Day by day the landscape changed. Steep hills thick with oak forests, and carved by rivers cascading down every valley, began to flatten, replaced by a high, monotonous mesa. The horizon flattened; the hills shrunk to gently rolling slopes. The sun intensified, sapping their energy and water grew scarce, as they trudged across the high table land called the meseta. This vast plain of central Iberia stretched out ahead of them like an undulating sea. On the far shore was the city of Burgos. Between them and their destination the path appeared, disappeared, and reappeared as it draped itself over the rolling landscape. The hilltops wore castles, like crowns, on their peaks as they looked down upon the land below. In the fields, sleepy-eyed oxen pulled wooden harrows across newly sown fields, depositing precious seeds for the year's crops. Peasant farmers trudged behind them no more introspective than their beasts. Heads turned as Mateo and Esperanza tramped through unwalled stone villages whose cobbled lanes deteriorated into wagon ruts that tapered to dirt paths then shrank to sheep tracks.

Their route ran parallel to, but a bit south of the Camino. They might as well have been trudging through an entirely different country, as much as it contrasted with the vibrant energy of the Camino. Dark stone villages huddled with their backs hunched against the outside world. Unused to seeing strangers, the townspeople were surly and suspicious. Gone were the Camino's roadside stands offering sustenance to pilgrims, gone too were the monasteries with open doors and straw-strewn dormitories promising pilgrims a dinner and a night's rest.

Esperanza and Mateo were soon mud spattered and hungry. They wheedled food from the few soft-hearted peasants they encountered. The sight of a thin girl trailing after a stalwart aristocratic man puzzled them, but they asked no questions. The peasants had little to offer, a heel of bread or a few of last year's mealy apples. The farther they walked into the heart of the treeless plateau, the more forlorn and poor the villages became, and the less likely they were to find peasants willing to feed strangers. After a week of tramping off the beaten path, they were hungry and disheartened, ready to take the risk of returning to the Camino.

They discussed their predicament hunched together over a small campfire under the cover of a dense wood lot. Mateo wracked his brain, trying to envision a different solution to the danger of being recognized.

"The Conte's men are no doubt still searching for us, but they are looking for a high-born man riding an elegant horse with a long white mane in the company of a nondescript girl. Perhaps we can leave those two behind and become ordinary pilgrims."

Esperanza winced at Mateo's description of her as a nondescript girl, but he was right. There was nothing to distinguish her from any other peasant girl her age other than her remarkable grey eyes, and no one looked closely enough at them to notice. For several moments they said nothing, each of them spinning imaginary webs of deception to throw the Conte's men off their trail.

"The horse, does he have a name?" Esperanza broke the silence.

"Yes, I call him El Jefe because he likes to take charge. He is highly intelligent and brave; responsive to the smallest cues."

"Yes, he is beautiful, but easy to identify. He needs a disguise too."

Esperanza rose and approached the horse as it calmly nibbled sparse meseta grass. She curled her fingers around his bridle, and gently pulled his face down until their eyes met. The two stood, gazing at each other peacefully. Esperanza rested her forehead against his. His heavy jaw relaxed, his eyes softened and drooped; he looked as if he might fall asleep. She placed one soft hand on his jaw and stroked his neck. El Jefe's tail swished from side to side as the girl and horse leaned into each other.

"He approves of my plan. He will not be dishonored if we make him less beautiful."

"Did he tell you that?" Mateo chuckled. "He's smarter than I thought."

Esperanza's enigmatic smile softened her features. "Actually, yes he did."

That evening the transformation began. Mateo hacked away at El Jefe's beautiful white mane and tail with the blade he carried tucked into his waistband. They doused their campfire fire before it burned itself out and used chunks of blackened wood to transform El Jefe from a beautiful Andalusian steed with a flowing hair into an unremarkable, badly cropped plug. Then Mateo curried him down with an ash-encrusted comb giving him a coat as dull as ditchwater.

In the next dreary stone town, they found a stable that housed the short, sturdy ponies peasants used to work the fields. Mateo rousted the stable boy from an empty stall where they found him napping. The boy who was about Esperanza's age jumped to his feet rubbing his eyes, stems of hay poking out from his hair like a scarecrow come to life.

"I would like to make a bargain with you." Mateo ran his eyes up and down the boy's slight body, assessing his prospects as an unwitting accomplice to their little scheme.

"I will trade this fine saddle pad for two simple wool blankets," Mateo dove into the conversation with no formalities.

The boy's mouth dropped open, tongue protruding like an old dog's, "I don't understand," he said.

"Here," Mateo removed El Jefe's saddle and pulled an opulent, embroidered saddle pad off his back. He draped it over his forearm and held it out to the boy. "I will trade this for two woollen blankets," he repeated.

The stable boy gaped wide-eyed at the sumptuous saddle blanket.

"And I want your clothes," Mateo added off-handedly.

"No! You can't take my clothes." Now the boy came to life, fully awake and squinting skeptically at the stranger. "You must be mad. What will I wear? I don't have a trunk full of clothes as you probably have." His eyes fixed on Mateo's knee-length tunic, not an undyed hemp shift like his, but fine linen bleached to a brilliant white and laced at the neckline with a leather thong, and his form-fitted quilted doublet, covered by long cowled cloak. There could be no doubt this stranger was an aristocrat.

"The clothes are for her," Mateo gestured toward the girl.

"For her? But, but . . . " he stuttered.

"Here, take it." Mateo extended the arm holding the saddle blanket toward the boy, his outstretched fingers almost poking the boy's ribs. "You can trade it next time you go to town for market day. It will certainly bring more than enough money to buy a nice new set of clean clothes. If you drive a sound bargain, you might even have money to spare." A smile crept across Mateo's face. "Have you ever had any money of your own?"

The boy shook his head, baffled at the prospect of having money.

"I thought so. Don't accept less than five silver reales for the saddle blanket. Act like you have been bargaining at the market since you were old enough to talk."

The boy's face transformed from that of an old dog to sly young fox. Glimmers of greed lit his eyes.

"Wait a moment," he said ducking into a horse stall. He emerged wrapped in a feed sack; two coarse woolen blankets clutched in his arms. He handed Mateo the blankets and his clothes - a coarse wool tunic, a rope belt, baggy leggings, and a simple cap with long, narrow ties that dangled down next to the ears. He pulled the splendid saddle blanket from Mateo's arm with reverence fit for a golden chalice and fingered the embroidery with a lover's delicacy. His bewildered eyes followed as the man who behaved as if nothing unusual had happened.

"How will you like being a boy?" Mateo winked at Esperanza, handing her the stable boy's clothing.

The prospect of living as a boy, even one dressed in these pathetic clothes, tickled her imagination. What would it be like to walk the streets freely without the protection of a male companion? What fun it would be to run around town unsupervised, playing kickball, or rolling barrel hoops down the street. She would love knowing she could aspire to a life outside hearth and home. The fantasy of living with a boy's freedom quickly dissipated when the overpowering aroma of horse, hay, and manure flooded her senses. She bound her mouse brown hair into a tight knot, and tucked it up inside the cap. She ducked into a stall and emerged looking as humble as the peasants who worked the fields and faced Mateo in her new incarnation as a boy. She threw her shoulders back, held her chin high, and planted her feet wide, with the knuckles of her balled fists pressed firmly into her hips.

Mateo let loose a full-throated belly laugh. "No one will recognize you! You make very convincing scruffy stable boy. Can you take care of horses? Of course not!" He answered his own question. "You've never been around horses."

"No. I have not. But I know this horse." She reached out to stroke El Jefe's forehead. The horse lowered his head to meet her outstretched hand. "He will teach me all I need to learn."

Mateo removed his padded vest, folded it, along with Esperanza's smock, wrapped them into his cloak and tied them to the saddle. He assumed his bleached linen tunic would soon be dirty enough to hide its fine workmanship. By the time Mateo and Esperanza ambled out of town, they were different people - a peasant man and his boy leading a gray horse with badly cropped tail and mane. When the grim little village was well behind them, they stopped in the dirt track and faced each other.

"I feel as devious as one of those dice throwers in the market, swindling unsuspecting victims," Esperanza laughed.

"People will give us a wide berth because of your odor alone. The transformation is complete." Mateo chortled, happy with their ruse. "Tomorrow we will return to the Camino. There is little chance Le Conte's men will recognize us now. At least traveling along the Camino, we will be able to find food and a place to sleep until we reach Burgos."

3

BURGOS

SUMMER 1260

For the next two weeks the expansive green plateau called the meseta rolled on beneath their feet leading them through one unremarkable stone village after another. The tranquility of the rural landscape, dotted with grazing sheep, interspersed with tidy farm plots outlined by stone fences, added to the monotonous rhythm of their footsteps, inducing a trance-like calm. The hostels and monastery dormitories that sheltered and fed them blurred into one dream-like impression in the same way early-morning fog obscures the edges between earth and sky.

When they finally reached Burgos, the abrupt contrast between the placid countryside and the jangling urban furor unnerved Esperanza. The press of crowds entangled her in a distracting web of confusion. Ramparts of a rancorous castle crowned the hilltop above the city like a bully aching for a fight. The crenelations of its stone walls protruded like rows of bared teeth. Its highest bastion grew straight from the rocky crag on which it sat as if the rock had transformed itself into a fortification. Below the castle's promontory, thick stone walls reached out to embrace the town that spilled down to the river. Inside the walls, buildings crowded out open spaces. Any unused plots that remained were pressed into service as kitchen gardens.

Mateo and Esperanza paused to admire the symmetry of the bridge spanning the Rio Arlanzon protecting the entrance to the town. Sixteen graceful arches reflected a mirror image in the slow-moving water creating the effect of perfect circles. For over a hundred years, donkey carts, royal armies and thousands of pilgrims had worn soft depressions into the walkway.

"I wonder how many feet it takes to wear down the stones this way?" Esperanza mused.

For many minutes Mateo remained mute, pensively scanning the scene. "The bridge has spanned the river for over one hundred years. Uncountable thousands have entered the city this way."

Standing midway across the span, they saw a massive cathedral dwarfing the surrounding neighborhood. From the bridge, the gargoyles and saints adorning the façade were still too far away to see clearly, but their silhouettes protruded ominously. Two huge bell towers loomed from the enormous red tiled roof. Residences and businesses crowded at its base like supplicants kneeling at an altar.

Once inside the gate, Esperanza felt the city's imposing presence bearing down on the surrounding streets. Buildings crowded so close to each other that Neighbors could reach across the narrow streets touch a hand extended from the other side. Clothing and under garments hung shamelessly on lines strung across the gap. The tumult of people pursuing their daily business shattered the calm of the meseta like glass trampled by horses.

Esperanza clung to Mateo's hand. Unable to see beyond a sea of chests or shoulders at her eye level, fear began to overwhelm her. Sensing her rising panic, Mateo reached down for Esperanza hefting her onto El Jefe's back. He shortened his grip on the horse's reins to keep his movements as confined as possible. El Jefe pranced excitedly, eyes wide and nostrils flaring, snorting his displeasure at the unfamiliar smells, and cramped quarters of the city streets. But he did not bolt or balk.

A cacophony of smells, sounds, and sights pummeled the senses of both girl and horse. The smells of dung, unwashed bodies, and the aromas of cooking nearly took her breath away. Ineffable emanations of health and illness that only Esperanza perceived poured over her from every direction like a bully browbeating her into trembling submission. After a few minutes she closed her eyes, laid her head on the El Jefe's neck, and synchronized her breathing with the horse's, calming them both.

Esperanza discerned no pattern to the maze of streets leading from the entry portal to the gates of the Jewish Quarter. Once inside the Juderia, the streets narrowed even further. The buildings appeared even more ancient than the houses outside the walls of the quarter. Stone walls of the ancient buildings were crumbling; shutters with flaking paint hung at odd angles. The entire Jewish precinct seemed exhausted by the effort of persisting.

"There has been a town on this site for almost four hundred years." Mateo explained. "And Jews have lived here almost from the beginning. This Jewish quarter is one of the oldest in all of Castile," Mateo's voice took on the tone of a school master teaching history to his students. "The king tolerates, even encourages the Jewish presence here because their businesses are profitable, and they create a reliable flow of taxes into the king's coffers." He paused before an ancient door. "Ah, here we are."

He stopped before the unadorned façade. Affixed to the doorpost a cylindrical silver tube with an ornate carving of the tree of life hung at an angle. Mateo reverently touched the mezuzah, meant to remind all who entered that this house belonged to God, and pulled the bell cord. Inside they heard faint chimes echoing down a corridor. A small door slid open revealing tiny eye hole, then quickly closed again. With a groan, the massive door swung open. A robust man in his middle years stood rooted to the tile floor, glaring at Mateo and Esperanza. In the next moment, his icy expression melted into warm recognition. He threw his arms wide in welcome.

"Mateo, what a delightful surprise. We were not expecting you, but you are always welcome," Aaron greeted him.

Another, more melodious, voice resonated from down the colonnaded hallway. "Aaron who is that? Not that street musician again. Tell him we . . ." Aaron's wife, Johanna, stopped midsentence when she spotted Mateo. "Mateo! We were not told you were coming. Is something wrong?" Knitted brows replaced her delighted smile.

Then she caught sight of Mateo's companion, a peasant boy who looked like a homeless street urchin and smelled like horse manure. She lifted the hem of her silk mantle to her nose.

"And who is this?" she asked gesturing toward the youth. She had a hundred questions for Mateo but forced herself to remain cordial and calm.

"Where are my manners? You two and that horse of yours look like you've been dragged through a muddy field. You all need baths." She looked at the sturdy Andalusian whose mane and tail were mottled with charcoal. A slender youth, attracted by the excited voices, walked toward them.

"Benjamin, please take the gentleman's horse to the stable. Make sure he is fed, cleaned, and curried. And take this stable boy with you." She then turned back to Mateo.

"I see you have risen so high in the world that you have your own groom." She gave Mateo an ironic, crooked grin, and glanced at his odoriferous companion.

Mateo performed a well-practiced ceremonial bow, balancing his weight on his back leg, extending his front leg far forward and sweeping his arm in a wide arc before him.

"Let me introduce Esperanza." He straightened up and plucked the cap from Esperanza's head. Her curling brown locks tumbled in disarray around her shoulders.

"What is this?" The woman took a step back. Her eyebrows rose almost to her hairline as she registered both surprise and revulsion.

"Now Johanna," Aaron spoke up. He patted his wife's shoulder. A smile tugged at the corners of his mouth as he struggled to resist laughing out loud. "Remember four years ago when Mateo brought an inquisitive, wild-eyed Basque girl with him?"

"Of course, I remember," Johanna replied. "Mateo, how is our Amika?"

Before Mateo had a chance to answer, Aaron stepped toward the girl and lifted her chin with his thumb and forefinger. A complex medley of conflicting emotions flashed through her smokey eyes. A swirling stew of humiliation, defiance, arrogance, insecurity mingled in them, and his heart went out to this evil smelling, confused creature.

"I'm sure this unlikely apparition will have an equally captivating tale to tell." Aaron bent forward and addressed the disheveled girl directly.

"Amika entertained us with her fascinating stories. She told us of the perilous events that brought her to us. She explained her origins as a Basque peasant, daughter of a healer, her mother's fiery demise, her pagan foster mother, and fleeing from witch hunters. Quite a story! Tonight, at dinner you will regale us with yours."

"Yes, I know Amika's story well. She is my foster mother." Despite being treated like a side show, Esperanza held herself erect and spoke coolly.

Aaron and Johanna's eyes flashed toward each other in astonishment.

"My dear girl." Johanna gingerly patted the girl's dirty hair. "You are as welcome as daisies in spring. We will have you smelling like one in no time." A dazzling smile lit her face.

With this, Johanna ushered the girl inside. "Come with me. We will show you to the women's bath." She waved to a girl lurking in the hallway. "Rebecca, come take this girl to the baths." A girl, about Esperanza's age emerged from behind a column where she had been surreptitiously snooping.

Rebecca straightened, threw her shoulders back, and raised her chin in a gesture quite familiar to Esperanza. The smelly urchin and the patrician young lady locked eyes. Rebecca's eyes, black as obsidian, never left the girl's face. Esperanza turned her own dusky eyes toward Rebecca. A flash of undefinable emotion rippled through both girls. In that moment, a bond of friendship was born.

That evening, Aaron installed himself at the head of the dinner table as if it was a throne. Johanna laid her hand on his arm as she seated herself on his right side. Aaron's hand tenderly covered hers with practiced affection. Mateo, clothed in his newly cleaned vest and smelling of lemons and sandalwood, took the chair next to Johanna.

Rebecca marched Esperanza into the room as if proudly displaying a pedigreed puppy and they sat down next to Mateo. The bedraggled stray had vanished like a dream upon awakening, and in her place a young girl on the brink of adolescence materialized. She and Rebecca were dressed identically, wearing blue tunics, embroidered at the neck with delicate purple flowers sprouting from undulating vines. Finely woven muslin veils as blue as flax flowers tumbled down their backs. Rebecca had woven a purple ribbon into Esperanza's thick brown braid.

After the others were seated, a pair of youths sauntered into the dining room with the entitled air of those accustomed to a life of wealth and privilege and settled themselves at Aaron's left.

"Mateo, meet my sons, Benjamin and Ariel."

Esperanza gawked at the long-limbed youths. They were identical - tall and slender with narrow shoulders and curly black hair.

"How do you tell them apart?" Esperanza whispered into Rebecca's ear.

"Oh, there are differences," Rebecca said loudly enough for everyone to hear.

Esperanza shrank with humiliation, mortified her inquisitiveness had been exposed. In unison, the boys turned to scrutinize her, unperturbed by a question they had heard countless times before. Their faces registered mild curiosity. They wondered if Rebecca was trying to create a copy of herself so she too might have a twin. But the new girl resembled Rebecca only in her attire. Though Rebecca was as tall as the boys, she was broad-shouldered and squarely built like their father. The twins, on the other hand, had inherited their mother's slim, delicate frame, glossy black curls, and renowned beauty.

"Benjamin has a stork bite high on his forehead, just below the hairline," Rebecca explained.

Esperanza stared at the two faces. There it was - a small

irregularly shaped pink spot on one boy's forehead.

"And he is a little taller." She went on. "Ariel is second born and a bit shorter. It's too bad that their intelligence does not match their beauty," she scoffed.

"Now Rebecca," Johanna broke in. "Show some kindness toward your brothers. Let Esperanza form her own opinions."

"Please excuse my daughter's rudeness," Johanna turned her radiant smile toward Mateo.

"Don't concern yourself" Mateo replied. "I once had a sister, so I understand." A somber shadow flashed briefly over Mateo's face remembering his beloved sister. He recovered his smile as he turned toward Rebecca. "You remind me of her," he said. "She was also strong and vibrant, as you are."

Rebecca's face flushed with embarrassment, and she bowed her head. "Thank you, sir" she whispered.

It was clear to Esperanza that Johanna had been a beauty in her younger days. Though no longer in her prime, the years had treated her kindly. Only a few strands of gray threaded through her sable hair. A lifetime of smiles had etched fine lines at the corners of her eyes and beside her mouth. Though the skin at her jaw had begun to soften, her unblemished complexion still glowed with a youthful blush. Kindness was etched into every feature.

When everyone was settled, Aaron broached the subject on everyone's minds. "Now, my friend, tell us how you came to visit us in this unceremonious way."

Mateo explained how the death of the Conte's lady, and the subsequent murder charge against Esperanza had precipitated their panicked flight from Ponferrada where Esperanza had been working at Amika's side.

Johanna and Aaron exchanged worried glances.

"The lady's death was not my doing," Esperanza spoke up, reading their expressions. "You see, Amika had trained me in the healing arts and herbal medicines. The Lady insisted on buying my last sprig of belladonna and refused to heed my cautions about its use. I had a feeling when I sold it to her that something terrible would result. But I was trapped. I was only a simple shop girl advising a noble courtesan! I could hardly defy a direct order from le Conte's favorite lady." She looked down at her hands clasped tightly in her lap.

"We bargained a stable boy out of his clothes," Mateo grinned, deftly changing the subject. "We left him wearing only a feed sack." Aaron and the twins guffawed. Rebecca reached out and squeezed Esperanza's hand lightly, sensing that Esperanza's humiliation equaled that of the poor stable boy.

"Well, you are here now," Aaron concluded. "And dinner is served." With this, the kitchen servant, Lisbeth, brought out a plate of fruits, fresh cheeses, and salty hard sausage, followed by cabbage rolls stuffed with aromatic rice, a sweet stew of carrots and turnips, and thinly sliced white fish. Esperanza watched in silence as the platters of food were passed around the table.

"Eat." Rebecca nudged her with her elbow. "It's alright. No one is judging you. No one is even looking at you. Don't be shy."

Esperanza picked at her food watching in disbelief as the family proceeded to enjoy their meal as if this abundance were no more remarkable than spring rains.

As the days passed, Rebecca continued to treat Esperanza with welcoming kindness. She familiarized Esperanza with the spacious portico surrounding the interior courtyard landscaped with a reflecting pool, flowers, and an ancient well. Mateo spent much of his time behind closed doors in Aaron's study. One day he drew Esperanza aside. He knelt on one knee to look her in the eye, and cradling her hands in his, he explained what the next chapter of her life would hold.

"I am going to return to my school in Salamanca," he explained. Esperanza drew a sharp breath. "No, listen to me," he stopped her objection before she voiced it. "I have spoken to Aaron and Johanna. They are willing to welcome you into their home as a companion for Rebecca. I have explained your intelligence and your precocious understanding of people's ailments. They will care for you and educate you as one of their own."

Esperanza understood that this was undeniably generous of them, and she genuinely appreciated their willingness to take her in, but Mateo was the last cord that tethered her to the happy life she had known for the past four years as Amika's ward and protégé. Now she would be set adrift yet again, sailing unfamiliar seas, this time into the complexities of family life. She had never had a proper family with both father and mother caring for their children, all living under one roof. From the time Esperanza was an infant, she and her mother had only each other. When her mother died walking the Camino in search of a miracle, Esperanza had no one, not a single human being, until Amika and Mateo rescued her. She had certainly never lived amid the opulence and privilege enjoyed by the Cohen family. She riveted Mateo with her intense gaze. No sobs, no moans or wails accompanied the lone tear that trailed down her face. She knew she should be grateful. And she was. But she also suffered the familiar sinking sensation of abandonment. She nodded and said nothing.

The day after Mateo's explanation, Master Cohen called the rest of the family to join him in the courtyard. One by one, they bade him farewell. The twins shook Mateo's hand awkwardly, Rebecca dropped her eyes and performed a small, graceful curtsy, Johanna planted a chaste kiss on his cheek, and Aaron embraced him heartily.

Mateo tore his gaze away from the others and embraced Esperanza. "Never too grown up for a hug." He wrapped her in his strong arms. "I will visit whenever I can. You can write to me. If you need me, I will come."

Then, Mateo turned, crossed the courtyard, strode through the heavy oak door, and was gone.

4

EDUCATION

SUMMER 1260 to 1262

The familiar rhythms of life in the Cohen family proceeded as predictably as the tolling of the Cathedral's massive bells. Each morning, by the time the bells had rung nine times, the twins Benjamin and Ariel, Rebecca, and now Esperanza, were in their seats in the oak-paneled library. There they found Rabbi Ezra Beneviste hunched over, studying ancient texts and scrolls, whose pages were as creased and desiccated as the old man's papery skin. His deep-set brown eyes squinted as he bent so low that his grizzled beard brushed the pages like a frizzed white whisk.

Aaron Cohen had been lucky to find Rabbi Beneviste. He had recently retired from the famous School of Translators in Toledo, where, for decades, he had immersed himself in translating the works of Greek luminaries like Aristotle, Hippocrates, Galen, and Ptolemy into Latin, Arabic, and Hebrew. His reputation as a linguist was unparalleled. Within the Jewish community he gained great notoriety as an authority on the esoteric tomes of Jewish philosopher, Maimonides.

When Aaron Cohen heard of the Rabbi's retirement, he sought out the esteemed old scholar hoping he would agree to tutor his children. The Rabbi agreed reluctantly, lured by the generous salary and luxurious accommodations Aaron Cohen offered. The enticement of wealth and stability in his old age was irresistible, so he put aside his fear that the position tutoring children was far beneath his ability as a scholar.

The quill of old age had written its signature on every part of him. His shoulders were rounded from years bent over his rostrum at the scriptorium. His hearing was so muffled he could not follow a conversation unless he and the speaker were face to face, and his weak eyes could see no further than the length of his arm. But his mind was as clear as cut crystal.

The curriculum he designed for Cohen's children was strenuous, based on Greek and Roman traditions, and balanced by the wisdom of the Torah. In the morning they studied the liberal arts: grammar, rhetoric, logic, mathematical arts, arithmetic, astronomy, geometry, philosophy, and logic. In the afternoon they shifted to in-depth study of the "the law," the five books of the Torah, the Pentateuch. The library's books and scrolls stood in their alcoves along the walls, queued up like the king's bodyguards. Even by his exacting standards, these were the perfect surroundings to transform the Master's children into serious scholars.

Esperanza was an apt and enthusiastic student, quick and perceptive, but in comparison to the Cohen children, she was woefully under-educated. Her schooling consisted of two years at the convent school in Santiago de Compostella. She was able to read and write basic Latin and, because of her everyday immersion in Hebrew was becoming fluent. She could compute simple sums, skills deemed adequate for running a household or performing clerical duties. But among the Cohen children she was like a squirrel running with wolves, always struggling to catch up. In the evenings, in the dim light of their shared sleeping quarters, Rebecca drilled her in mathematics, Greek, and Arabic.

"How did Aristotle define empiricism?" Rebecca quizzed Esperanza.

"The Rabbi makes these ideas sound complicated, but to me it's simple." Esperanza reasoned. "Empirical evidence is information you understand by means of your senses - seeing, hearing, smelling, or touching. Amika, my adopted mother, practiced this type of learning every day as a healer. For untold ages, Wise

Women and healers knew which plants could treat which illnesses." Esperanza grew quiet, considering her next words carefully.

"But Rebecca, aren't there other ways of knowing?"

"What do you mean?"

"For example, take the story of Noah. God told him to build an ark because the world would be drowned. Noah had no evidence that this would happen. Why was he so sure this God even existed, much less that the world was on the verge of cataclysm? Yet he built his boat exactly as he was directed because in his heart, he knew the flood was real and would happen just as it was revealed to him."

"Yes, of course he did, because all of us, including Noah, must follow the word of God." Rebecca's unquestioned acceptance of the teachings of the Torah was as uncomplicated as the turning of the seasons. The scripture was true because God had dictated it directly to the Jewish people – his chosen ones.

"Exactly" Esperanza interjected. "Noah had faith. He believed the rains would come because God told him so. He had no empirical evidence, but because of his faith, Noah simply *knew* what would happen. To him, it was self-evident; why would anyone question God's word?" Esperanza grew silent, then almost in a whisper, she continued. "There are times when I know what will happen, just like Noah, because the voice of my mother tells me. She bequeathed to me the ability to know the sufferings and illnesses of people and how to relieve their afflictions."

"Esperanza, you sound like a lunatic. Do you think you are a prophet?" Rebecca had not intended her reply to be so tart, but Esperanza's comparing herself to Noah verged on heresy.

Esperanza's heart chilled. The icy realization that 'normal' people would never understand her enveloped her like a blanket of snow covering a mountain meadow.

"You're right, I suppose. But I sometimes have a sense . . ." Her voice trailed off. "I can't explain it. I just *know* things."

Rebecca set aside the tract they had been studying, Plato's

"Theory of Soul." The conversation made her as uncomfortable as ill-fitting clothing.

"Let's blow out the candle and sleep now. We can't know what tomorrow will bring, but we can be certain it will be here soon enough."

* * *

While the children were in their classroom each day, Johanna and Aaron Cohen tended to their separate responsibilities. Johanna settled herself behind her oak desk, its sturdy legs sculpted with carvings of fat-leafed foliage. She was businesslike and efficient as the household's chief administrator, making sure everything ran smoothly.

Her first task of the day was to meet with her servant, Lisbeth, an unassuming young woman, as bland as porridge. With her unremarkable black hair, black eyes, and dusky complexion, she was indistinguishable from the laborers and farmers in the field. Though Lisbeth was only sixteen, she was capable and compliant, taking orders and making sure she completed her tasks efficiently. Having been in domestic service since she was ten, she was well aware of what was required of a good helper, and she took her duties seriously. Though she came from a good family, like most young women of her class, she could neither read nor write. Her greatest strength was her facility with numbers. She need not be able to read to tell a dinero from a maravedi. She had long ago worked out how much each coin was worth, and what were reasonable prices for vegetables, spices, or grains in the market. The merchants respected her knowledge and shrewd bargaining skills.

When Johanna dictated the menu for the upcoming week, Lisbeth accurately committed the list to memory and scampered off to the market with the coins Johanna doled out to her. After Johanna had waved Lisbeth off, she turned her attention to the long columns in the ledger where she logged each item purchased and its cost. Her long, slender finger slid down the page searching for any errors or omissions.

Each morning Master Cohen made his way down to his medical office where a variety of patients, from wealthy tradesmen to destitute beggars, formed a queue that snaked down the street. He treated everything from acne to 'sweating sickness.' After assessing the urgency of his patients' needs, he dispensed remedies and advice. If the patient required simple procedures, like lancing a boil, removing cataracts, or cauterizing a wound, he ushered them into a back room where he performed simple surgeries. His back room also housed his medical library, a collection of works from many traditions. The wisdom of Maimonides, rested side by side with works of the famous Islamic physician, Ibn Sina.

The patients who came through his door each day could not have known nor appreciated that they would reap the benefit of Aaron's lifelong study of the greatest medical traditions of the world. From this panoply of knowledge, Master Cohen had synthesized his own coherent approach to healing. His reputation as a learned and attentive physician earned him the trust of patricians and paupers alike. The town's elites often summoned him to their bedsides and compensated him generously for his services.

After their evening meal, the family gathered before the hearth in the great room to relax and converse. Sometimes Rebecca and Esperanza entertained themselves with sedate games of backgammon or huddled together fashioning grass-filled poppets, clothing them in dresses made from scraps of fabric. Their favorite game was an exercise in imagination they had invented, dubbing it "how about."

"How about your doll and my doll play backgammon," Rebecca would say. Or "how about our dolls play school. My doll will be Rabbi Ezra, and you can be Benjamin, who can't learn anything." Giggles ensued at the mention of either of the twins. Or she would say "how about we have a spitting contest. We'll see who can spit the most olive pits into the ash bucket."

The boys preferred to wage mock combat, staging surprise raids, leaping out from behind columns as the girls walked through the portico. The girls retaliated and the chase was on. The girls pursued the boys, threatening to lash them to the pillars if they were caught. Often, when their games became too raucous, and their squeals and shouts interrupted her work, Johanna had to call a halt to their games.

Whenever she could break free from her lessons, Esperanza wandered into Master Cohen's offices. Aaron did not banish her if she promised not to distract him. Esperanza tried to make herself useful, fetching tinctures and potions, grinding powders with the mortar and pestle, cleaning and preparing strips of fabric to bind wounds. Her time in the dispensary was sweet with learning and bitter with the pangs of loss when she remembered her treasured days with Amika.

Each day was unique, and Esperanza was never bored. She observed Master Cohen skillfully treat a steady stream of patients. Before long, she anticipated the treatments he would prescribe. There were simple diagnoses, like the woman who came in with a girl of about six years whose face and arms were marred by patches of dry scaly skin that the girl scratched continually. Without being asked, Esperanza stood on a wooden stool, reached for a jar, and handed the Master the stalk of aloe vera preserved within. He sliced it open and spread its oozing jelly over the girl's inflamed skin. Her relief was almost immediate. Only later, after the daily bustle of activity, did he marvel at Esperanza's ability to anticipate his diagnoses and treatments.

"Wash your hands and hers too. Make sure she doesn't scratch." Esperanza called after the mother as she walked out the door. "Something on your hands may be making her sensitivities worse, and hand washing is beneficial for most skin problems." Master Cohen sat back in stunned silence as she doled out unsolicited advice, but he did not stop her.

Master Cohen's skill was the culmination of years of study and practice. But when it came to diseases and maladies specific to women, he had gaping blind spots. Personal reticence and religious taboos prevented him from examining their bodies. He apprehended very little about their complaints. He believed Jewish women healers and midwives were best qualified to deal with "women's problems."

One day a respectable woman of middle years queued up with the others at the door to his office. A narrow belt accented her slim waistline, and a fur-lined surcoat draped her narrow, sloping shoulders. She stared at the ground, not meeting the Master's eye when he asked her what brought her to see him that day.

"I have a . . ." she hesitated, too deeply ashamed to describe her symptoms. She stopped. "I should not have come here expecting a man to help me. But I have already consulted the midwives and their remedies have been useless to me. I don't know where else to turn." She gazed steadfastly at the ground. Defeated even before she began, she turned to go. "I'm sorry. I shouldn't have bothered you."

A foul odor emanating from this respectable woman clearly testified to her need for medical care. "I'm sorry my dear lady, I cannot help you. I can recommend a good midwife." Master Cohen said. The lady shook her head despondently, ready to give up hope.

"Don't go," Esperanza called out. "May I talk to her privately?" she asked Master Cohen as she emerged from a shadowed corner where she had been eavesdropping.

"Yes, certainly." Master Cohen replied, relieved to be rid of this woman.

Esperanza drew her into Master's back room while he returned to his other patients. The woman looked skeptically at Esperanza. *Who is this child dispensing medical advice? What could she possibly know of the intimate complications of a woman's body?*

"It's alright," Esperanza reassured her. "I understand that I do not look the part of a healer." The woman's eyes widened. Her eyebrows lifted. Had this girl read her thoughts? "I have been helping Master Cohen for quite a while. And before that, when I was just a sprout, I worked at the side of a noted healer for several years."

The woman softened. Her shoulders slumped and her face slackened. Though it was foolish to talk to this slip of a girl, what choice did she have? She was desperate. She resumed her explanation. "Though I am not having my monthlies, I have a . . ." Her voice wavered as she searched for the right words. "I have seepage. It's not red like blood, but viscous and yellowish, almost like the discharge from the nose when one has a cold. I don't know how to say it," the woman whined hopelessly. "I'm oozing. I can think of no other word; I'm draining like an infected wound, but I have not been injured."

"Please sit," Esperanza pulled up a chair and sat facing the woman. She reached out to hold the woman's hands. For many moments they just sat, not moving, not talking. *What is this girl doing? This is ridiculous. I should go.*

Esperanza closed her tingling eyes, and her ears rang. She felt a great surge of revulsion. She envisioned a disturbing image like a waking dream. In her vision, a snake wound higher and higher up the woman's leg. When the serpent reached the top, it reared back and struck directly into her womb.

Esperanza startled out of her reverie. "Your husband, is he faithful in your marriage?"

The woman dropped her head. One by one tears dripped into her lap. "He frequently goes out at night, after the evening meal. Sometimes he doesn't return for days. When he returns, he looks and smells like he has been cleaning a pig sty - covered in grime, reeking with an awful stench. If I demand an explanation, or even gently chide him, he explodes, chastising me for stepping out of my place as an obedient wife."

"You fear his anger, don't you?" Esperanza murmured. Esperanza's heart cried for this poor woman and the hopelessness of her situation. The woman would starve if she left him. She had nowhere else to go, and she could not defend herself from his advances. The sins of the husband are visited upon the wife.

"I don't have a treatment that will cure you. But don't despair. I will search through Master Cohen's books to see if I can find some relief for your symptoms. Give me three days to see what I can concoct."

Three days later, when the woman returned, Esperanza presented her with an aromatic paste in a small wooden box. The woman gingerly lifted the lid and held the mixture to her nose. The jarring scent sent a tremor coursing through her.

"What is this?" she asked, holding it out at arm's length.

"This is compounded of ingredients used by ancient peoples to fight infections," Esperanza said. "The people of the far east used sarsaparilla; the Greeks and Romans used raw garlic, and herbalists have used oregano for ages. I have combined them with tallow to create this paste. It may not cure you, but your symptoms should lessen, and you will not suffer so much."

"What do I do with this?" The woman eyed the tin box suspiciously.

"As distasteful as it may be, you should apply it to the affected area."
The woman gulped air like a downing man returning to the water's surface. "Must I do this? Really? This is repulsive to me."

"I'm sorry," Esperanza reached out to retrieve the box, but the woman quickly snatched it back.

"No, I'll take it. I must." The woman squeezed her eyes shut and gripped the box.

"Whatever you do, you must not become pregnant. If a baby emerges from your womb, it too will become infected." Esperanza said.

"What can I do when my husband demands his rights? I can only comply. If a baby comes, I cannot prevent it."

"I understand. Many women have similar misgivings. A God-fearing woman such as you would not want to end a pregnancy. I anticipated this, so I visited our best Jewish midwife, and she gave me this." Esperanza withdrew an herb-filled gauze pouch from her pocket. "You are not powerless. Generations of women, good women like yourself, have used this remedy to prevent unwanted children. Steep this in boiled water to make a strong tea." The corners of Esperanza's lips curved into a half smile knowing what the next question would be. "You want to know what it is, don't you?"

The woman's chin dipped slightly in a nod.

"It is a mixture of ground pennyroyal, parsley, and wild carrot. It will cleanse your womb when you have relations with your husband. If you do not wish to bring a child into the world, this is better than trying to rid yourself of an unwanted pregnancy. No child will die if none is conceived; this will prevent it."

The woman's mouth turned down. Lines appeared between her eyebrows.

"Ask yourself this," Esperanza said. "What is better, to bear a child only to see it suffer from your awful disease and die a horrible death? Or is it better to prevent a new life from taking hold inside you? Which fate is kinder, more loving?"

The turbulence that had been brewing in the woman's eyes settled. Her shoulders relaxed. She tucked the small box and the tea bag into her waist pouch. "Thank you. The hand of God guided me to you today." She dropped a generous donation of two maravedis into Esperanza's hand, straightened her spine, and resumed her mask of imperturbability, as she walked away.

Esperanza's eyes followed the departing lady, knowing her steps were sending her back to an unhappy marriage. How many women, she wondered, shared a similar fate? How many suffered from the ignorance of male physicians or the limitations of midwifery? In that moment, Esperanza saw her own path; it led her toward caring for unwanted children.

* * *

"Tonight, we have an honored guest." Aaron Cohen stood at the head of the dinner table as erect as a palace guard. He had planned a grand introduction for their guest of honor. "My dear cousin, Samuel, joins us for dinner tonight," he announced, gesturing to the red-cheeked, rotund figure next to him at the head of the table.

Johanna smiled, amused by her husband's affinity for formality. The family twittered with pleasure, happy to see Samuel again after a year's absence.

"Aaron, I appreciate the introduction," he said scanning the faces at the table. "I am honored to share a meal with you and your family."

"What Aaron means to say," Johanna steered the tone of the conversation into placid waters, "is you are most welcome here and we are delighted to see you again. What brings you to us tonight?"

"I am here on an errand for the king, as I was the last time we met. King Alfonso is a very wise and studious man. As you may know, he is ever vigilant in defending his realm of Castile and is constantly patrolling the frontiers. He has recently returned from his latest skirmish and is resting at court in Burgos. He has ordered me to acquire a book of oriental fables for him. Originally written in Sanskrit, then translated into Latin, our wise king has commissioned a translation into Castilian. He would like more Castilian scholars to be able to learn its wisdom. I am honored to once again to be his emissary on this mission. I understand that he is working on his own poetic work that he will name 'Songs to Holy Mary'."

"We are honored by your visit, my cousin. I can imagine nothing more noble for a scholar than to unlock the knowledge of the ancients. I have a small library which I cherish, but to work with some of the most important books in history as you do, well, that would be a sublime honor."

Aaron locked eyes with Johanna. In that moment, an unspoken understanding passed between them, as they both eyed the twins. Earlier that day, they had a serious conversation about the futures of Ariel and Benjamin. They had recently reached the age of thirteen, had studied the Torah, and were ready for their Bar Mitzvah, making them adults. Aaron and Johanna could think of no higher purpose for their sons than to study the classics at the most illustrious school in Iberia - the School of Translators in Toledo. Such a prestigious education would bring honor to the family.

"If you approve, Samuel, we would like our sons to return with you to study at the Toledo School of Translators."

Samuel looked at the boys, dubious of their chances of success. Two such handsome aristocratic youths, used to a life of privilege and pampering, might find the study regimen too rigorous, and the temptations of the city too distracting.

"The school curriculum is demanding, suitable only for the best, most dedicated scholars." His eyes drilled into the boys, gauging their reactions. Ariel and Benjamin looked at each other, stunned that their futures were being decided in the time it took to eat a meal. Though they knew their carefree life in Burgos would not last forever, the suddenness of its conclusion was shocking. The weight of their parents' expectations sat on their shoulders as heavily as an ox's yoke. There was no escaping their fate. They nodded mutely in unison.

"Well then. It's settled. You will be a credit to our family," Aaron crowed. He fairly burst with pride just thinking of his sons studying in Toledo. Not only was this the place where translators labored over priceless works of ancient wisdom, it was also the seat of Iberia's most esteemed school for Talmudic scholars. What better opportunity could Aaron give them?

Samuel's visit to Burgos lasted only a fortnight. The hasty decision to send Ariel and Benjamin back to Toledo with him precipitated a mad flurry of preparation. Johanna, Rebecca, Esperanza, and Lisbeth scurried about planning for the boys' trip, trying to anticipate their every need. The journey would be long and would require two sound horses apiece. Johanna tried to keep the preparations organized, assigning tasks to each of the three girls - cleaning clothes, gathering personal items, assembling the notes the boys had accumulated during their lessons with Rabbi Beneviste. She reserved for herself the task of packing their trunks. She lovingly stowed each item into their trunks as if performing a sacred ritual. Before she finally closed them, she wrote each of them a heartfelt farewell message and tucked it between the folds of their favorite garments. When would she see them again? She felt as though her heart was being crushed like wheat between millstones. On the day of their departure, she stood tall suppressing her pain, embraced them, and gently nudged them away, smiling into their excited faces. Only when they were gone, did she retreat to her chamber and allow herself to mourn.

5

THE TRADER

SPRING 1262

Esperanza habitually took the measure of everyone who came through Master Cohen's door. She soon recognized his regular patients and anticipated their needs. On some days, unfamiliar faces enlivened the routine, but most often Master Cohen's clients were familiar and predictable. They had grown accustomed to Esperanza forecasting their needs and preparing the perfect treatments. One day, a man unlike anyone she had encountered strode to the front of the line ignoring all the others. Tall and broad, with swarthy features, he moved with the assurance of a man who commanded obedience. The regular clients instinctively made way for him.

A red striped turban wound tightly around his head as if it had sprouted there. A long cloak, with wide blue stripes, lined with silk the color of lupines, draped gracefully over a spotless white linen tunic. A colorfully embroidered band encircled a waistline grown thick with prosperity.

"Aaron, friend, how are you?" he called out in a sonorous voice as smooth as melted honey.

Master Cohen rose and welcomed this strange man with open arms. "Ibrahim, how nice to see you again. I pray Yahweh has smiled on you since I last saw you. And I hope your voyage has been successful." He brusquely dismissed the patients who stared at the two men, curiosity painted all over their faces.

"Come in, come in. Have a seat." He gestured to the one upholstered chair in the corner of the room. "You bring good news? Let me clear my office of clients so we can talk privately."

Aaron rose and ushered the patients out the door, telling them to return tomorrow, then returned his attention to his visitor.

"Shalom, Aaron. It is good to see you again. Yes, our voyage was quite successful. You invested your money wisely when you decided to finance this venture. We made a tidy sum, my friend." A smug smile blossomed on his unshaven face. "I traded Merino wool from Castile for silk that came all the way from the orient. The silk is of the highest quality and the merchants of Valencia paid a generous price for it."

"Good, good. Now I suppose you have a new venture planned?"

"Yes indeed. I intend to visit the ports of Palma, Cagilari, and Palermo, then sail on to Napoli. With your support and Allah's blessing, this should be another lucrative trip."

"Wonderful, I look forward to discussing the details with you later. I see we are being observed." Aaron tilted his head toward the doorway of the back room.

Esperanza, overcome by curiosity, peeked around the doorway. Ibrahim, sensing eyes resting on him, turned and saw a slim adolescent with smokey eyes and a solemn expression peering at him.

"Could this be your daughter? She has grown into a beauty." A sly smile lifted one corner of his full lips.

"No, no. This is Esperanza." Aaron waved her forward with a flick of his hand. "Esperanza, come out from behind the door. You are behaving like a curious child."

Esperanza stood before the two men. Though she felt as exposed as a sheep after shearing, she squared her shoulders and looked directly into Ibrahim's eyes, boldly meeting his gaze. She took a few paces toward him. He smelled of sandalwood and myrrh. Teetering between attraction and aversion, she could not quell the churning in her stomach. He was compelling, and brazenly manly, with such an authoritative air that she would not have been surprised if he could part the waters like Moses at the Red Sea. But something about him was off. Perhaps she was repelled by his swaggering smugness. Her stomach twisted and a rush of warmth splashed her cheeks pink. *Why am I reacting this way?* She wondered, trying to pinpoint what she found so disturbing about him. Maybe he was simply more worldly and exotic than any man she had met.

Ibrahim saw her struggling to disguise her uneasiness and took it for attraction. His eyes ran over her, judging her quality as dispassionately as he would judge a juicy Valencia pomegranate. The girl was a beauty, no doubt, but her blatantly frank demeanor, looking at him straight in the eye, was unladylike in the extreme. A young lady, with a fearless, independent streak presented a challenge, like a horse needing to be tamed.

"Esperanza is our ward." Aaron broke the tight band of tension between them. "She came to us as an orphan, and we took her into our household as a companion to Rebecca. The girls have become inseparable. I don't know what we will do with her when Rebecca marries."

Esperanza bristled. It was humiliating to be talked about as though she was a loaf of day-old bread. It was unlike Aaron to be so dismissive of her. He had always shown her tolerance and respect.

"She is an excellent student, better than my sons. And her healing powers are quite extraordinary. She seems to know a person's malady before they even open their mouths. Her knowledge of herbal remedies is impressive. With a little more training she would make a first-rate physician. But of course, that's quite impossible, being only a girl."

"Maybe not impossible," Ibrahim said. He did not explain, just left the suggestion hanging in the air like an exotic scent. "Impressive," Ibrahim said, prying his eyes away from Esperanza and turning his attention to Aaron. "And how are your sons?"

"Benjamin and Ariel are doing well. They are in Toledo completing their education at the Talmudic school and the Toledo School of Translators under the tutelage of renowned Jewish scientists and doctors. I will be looking for appropriate positions for them when they are ready. My daughter is turning into a woman before my eyes. She will soon become marriageable, and I am negotiating with a matchmaker who has found a suitable mate for her. Her mother, however, is reluctant to have all three of our little birds fledge the nest in the same year, so we will wait until the boys are settled in Toledo before marrying Rebecca off."

"You have done well raising your handsome children, my friend." Ibrahim clapped a strong hand on Aaron's shoulder. "We will talk more of this. But now, down to business." He shrugged off thoughts of Aaron's family as easily as he would shrug off his cloak.

"Esperanza, if there are any remaining customers in the street, go tell them to return tomorrow. I will be unavailable for the rest of the day." Aaron summarily dismissed her and turned back to Ibrahim. She could hear their voices receding as they walked toward the house.

"Tell me Aaron, who has the best wine available for trade this season? I have sellers who would trade textiles, carpets, and paper for your best Rioja wine. Do you know a vintner who can offer good prices? I will take as many barrels as will fit in my vessel. I plan to return to my ship as soon as my negotiations are complete."

Ibrahim cast one more glance over his shoulder at the smoky-eyed, enigmatic almost-woman, then slung one arm over Aaron's shoulder like a brother as they walked away. An aura of change swirled around them like fallen leaves in autumn. When their business transaction was finished, the mysterious Ibrahim was gone.

* * *

May transformed the orchards into an ocean of blooms. The weather warmed, and grapevines blanketing the hillsides burst into bloom, bathing the air in their seductive smell. The shimmering pond in the courtyard reflected the blues, pinks, and yellows of pampered hydrangeas, begonias, and dahlias. In the years since Esperanza arrived, she and Rebecca had blossomed like the flowers in the courtyard.

The daily rhythm of family life ebbed and flowed as before, but the sly fox of change stalked the sedate hallways. One morning, seemingly the same as all the others, the calm façade of the household was broken. Rebecca suddenly bolted up from her chair in the classroom and fled down the colonnaded hallway like someone chased by ghosts. Rabbi Ezra's nearsighted eyes, squinting at a scroll he held inches from his nose, did not even see Rebecca fleeing the classroom. Esperanza stood and slipped out unnoticed, following her friend into the courtyard. She found Rebecca huddled in a corner cowering behind one of the pillars. Rebecca's veil slumped over her shoulders. Her hair hung loose hiding her downturned face. Though she tried fruitlessly to muffle the sound, great sobs wracked her body as she buried her face in her hands.

"Rebecca, what is the matter?" Esperanza asked, kneeling next to her friend.

Rebecca turned toward her and laid her head on Esperanza's shoulder.

"I'm dying,"

"No, you're not. You are as healthy as flowers in spring." Esperanza laid a gentle hand between Rebecca's shoulders. "I'll go find your mother."

Johanna wasted no time attending to her daughter.

"I'm dying" Rebecca repeated. Her mother's face furrowed with concern. "I'm bleeding, hemorrhaging. My stomach is cramping. I will die soon."

"Don't worry, child. You are not dying. You have started your monthly bleeding." Johanna smiled and smoothed Rebecca's tresses. "This bleeding will happen with each moon cycle. It is a sign that you have become a woman and can now bear children."

"Nooo!" Rebecca shrieked. "I am a child myself. I am not ready to be a woman. I want everything to stay just as it is."

"Don't worry. Your future is bright. Your father and I love you. We have found a good husband for you. Within a few years you will be a mother yourself. When the time comes for children, you will be ready." Johanna knelt before her daughter wrapping her arms around the girl's sturdy body. As Esperanza watched, she sensed a shadow descend over Johanna. The air around her smelled vaguely rotten, like meat gone bad. Rebecca would be fine, Esperanza thought, but Johanna . . . Esperanza tried to chase the intuition from her brain, but her eyes burned, and her ears vibrated with insistent buzzing. She was certain Johanna was not well.

"Noooo" Rebecca wailed again. "I don't want a husband. I am happy here with you. And what will become of Esperanza?"

Johanna's eyes flicked toward Esperanza. This was a problem she and Aaron had not fully considered when they agreed to take the girl into their family. Since Rebecca and Esperanza were about the same age, Esperanza would soon become marriageable as well, but her prospects were murky. Though she had studied the religious texts, she was not Jewish. Though she was well-educated, because she was not Jewish, she could not teach in a Jewish household nor tutor Jewish children. Though she was beautiful and eligible, she could not marry a Jew. She and Aaron would need to seriously consider her future, and soon.

Any thought Aaron and Johanna had of Esperanza's future disappeared as abruptly as a shooting star in the light of dawn. Johanna's health took center stage. For almost a year Johanna had hidden her grim discovery from everyone, hoping the lumps in her armpits would go away. Rather than disappear they multiplied until, by the time she confessed her concern to her husband, they had spread to her breasts.

Master Cohen had dealt with this before. Several women had come to him with breast lumps, but he had found no treatment that would cure them. He referred them to a midwife as he did all "women's problems." Now he wished he had schooled himself better in how to treat them. He searched Johanna's face, looking for the young beauty he had married, not the doomed woman who now stood before him. His heart abandoned its normal rhythm, first sinking to his stomach, then racing wildly. A blinding headache stabbed his temples, and nausea overwhelmed him. Watching his face blanch, Johanna realized instantly the prognosis was grim. Yet his well-trained instinct for healing insisted he try something, anything, to save his beloved wife. Next day, he jettisoned his pride, put aside his skepticism of Esperanza's inexplicable gifts, and called her to his office.

"My wife," he choked back tears. "She has the breast disease that kills so many women. Johanna needs both of us to bring all our resources together to save her. I have never treated a woman who had breast lumps such as hers. I have always referred them to a midwife." He looked at his hands, as furrowed as a fallow field, resting on the desk before him. "It defies logic, but I must admit that your power to intuit a person's maladies and prescribe treatment almost always rings true. I never imagined that I would enlist the help of an adolescent with an unusual gift of insight to help me fight this disease. It verges on sorcery. But I have seen the efficacy of your treatments with my own patients." He raised his eyes from his hands to Esperanza's face. "All I know is that Johanna will have a better chance if we work together. I am open to your suggestions."

"What if there is no cure?" Esperanza's wondered out loud. "What if nothing helps?"

"Then we will all suffer her absence. She is the glue that holds this family together."

Over the following months, the young woman and the old Master worked side by side, trying every treatment they could find. They rifled through Master Cohen's books, desperate to fend off the invader overtaking Johanna's body. They dressed the lumps with damp cloths infused with black nightshade. Esperanza created a poultice of nettle, mustard seed and moldy bread and laid it against the invading tumors. Among his books, Master Cohen found an ancient Egyptian remedy - an ointment that combined bull bile, fly droppings, and ochre. They prepared gallons of marjoram tea and forced her to choke it down. They spooned a powerful mixture of heartsease, marigold, and yarrow into her mouth. Nothing worked. By the time the courtyard flowers drooped in their pots, and cold winds stripped the trees of their leaves Johanna's condition had worsened to a critical stage. She thrashed back and forth on her pallet, insensible to anything but the pain that enveloped her.

"Please, husband," she rasped. "Please end this torment. You must have something to release me from this agony." Looking toward Esperanza standing at her bedside she begged. "Esperanza, you once killed a woman with belladonna. If you love me at all, please, please do the same for me."

Esperanza lifted her eyes to Master Cohen's. He squeezed his eyes closed and nodded almost imperceptibly, giving her tacit permission to end Johanna's suffering. Esperanza's blood turned to ice in her veins.

That evening, sequestered together in Master Cohen's anteroom, Esperanza confronted him. "Please don't ask me to do this. I know she requested it, but I can't," Esperanza begged. "Please, I can't."

"I understand if you cannot deliberately end her suffering. As much as I love her, I cannot not do it either. But seeing her agony is as painful to me as it is to her. If we do not intervene, nature will take its course, and nature is a cruel master. It may take many months to finish the job. I cannot bear to watch her endure this brutal torment."

Nothing more was said about the deadly alternative, though the undercurrent of their conversation tainted every bedside visit.

Through endless winter nights Aaron, Rebecca and Esperanza never left Johanna's bedside. Watching her in an unending rotation of nightly vigils, each of them hovered over the suffering woman, enduring their own personal misery. Esperanza believed it would be a mercy to end her suffering, but she had read in Hippocrates' treatise that the first obligation of a healer was to do no harm, and she could not face the act of murdering her beloved benefactor."

She asked herself what she would do to relieve her own pain if she was writhing in agony. She must at least do that much. If she could not cure the lumps, perhaps she might find something to make Johanna sleep. Esperanza searched for herbs that caused drowsiness and relieved pain; she struck on the idea of combining equal parts of opium, mandrake, and henbane. When it was her turn to sit with Johanna, she soaked a rag in the mixture and held it to Johanna's nostrils. Johanna calmed almost at once; her breathing slowed, her face, previously contorted in pain, relaxed. She no longer struggled. A profound sleep descended softly on Johanna, like an autumn leaf falling on a still pond. Esperanza could hardly hear Johanna's heartbeat or feel her thin breath on the cheek she put to Johanna's mouth. But when the sun crested the horizon next morning, the pain was back. Day after day the pain returned, worse than the day before. The cold dark months stretched out as endless as a boundless sea, wave after wave of brutal misery lapping at Johanna's bed.

When winter's icy fingers loosened their grip, making way for the warm caresses of spring, Johanna's condition worsened. Esperanza's anesthetic elixir no longer induced sleep. One uncommonly cool, rainy night in spring, Rebecca took her turn at her mother's bedside. A cold, damp draft seeped in around the window frame. Exhausted from months of sitting at her mother's death bed, she prayed, she wept, and finally wished only that Johanna's agony would end. Around midnight, Johanna regained consciousness.

"Rebecca," she whispered, hardly moving her dry, papery lips. A shock rolled over Rebecca, standing her neck hairs on end. Her head jerked up, and she reached for her mother's hands. She had given up hope of ever again seeing her mother clear-headed, free from tormented pain or drug-induced oblivion. On this night, Johanna opened her eyes, seemingly lucid and rational, though as fragile as a snowflake in spring. Johanna tenderly placed her hand atop Rebecca's.

"Rebecca, heart of my heart." Johanna's eyes fluttered as she struggled to maintain consciousness. "My time has come. I had a dream. My own dear mother, gone for many years, sat at the foot of my bed. She told me all would be well, and she would help guide me to the other side." Johanna's breath shuddered. "I can go now. My pain will not last much longer. I will be free. I am not afraid."

"Mother, mama!" Rebecca mewled like a new kitten. "Don't go. You are getting better now. Our prayers have been answered. Look! You are awake and talking. Don't go."

Johanna patted her daughter's hand, laid back against the pillows, closed her eyes and rocked her head side to side. "No, it is my time." With those words, she subsided once again into unconsciousness.

Johanna's respirations came in fits and starts. Long moments passed without her taking a breath. At times the pauses lasted so long Rebecca was sure her mother had breathed her last. Then a convulsive inhalation rattled Johanna's chest followed by another long pause. Rebecca was horrified. The cycle of long lapses followed by violent gasps continued for long, dark hours. Rebecca's heart wrung itself out, twisting and untwisting like a wash rag. Rebecca held her own breath as she waited for her mother's next convulsive gulp. It felt to her like she was witnessing her mother's death, not once, but over and over. In the hour just before dawn, Johanna's breathing changed. It gurgled and rattled in her throat. She let out a soft moan, then nothing - no more jagged inhalations, no more groans, nothing. Rebecca waited for what seemed like hours. She stared into Johanna's face as her color faded to a sickly gray. Her slightly opened mouth slackened, and yellowish bubbles seeped onto her pillow. Her skin drooped from her bones, sagging like a burlap sack. Her body was an empty vessel. Johanna no longer lived there.

When the sun peeked over the horizon, Master Cohen tip-toed

into the sick room to begin his morning vigil. Johanna lay as still as stone, her face a gray mask, her lips blue. He found Rebecca at the bedside, her head resting on Johanna's cold hand. He soundlessly pulled a chair up next to the bed and lightly shook Rebecca's shoulder. She turned her swollen, red eyes to her father.

"She's gone." Rebecca's face was vacant, expressionless, lost.

One look at the Johanna's slack skin and he recognized the face of death. Only an empty shell remained. He slumped in his chair, unable to contain his grief. He howled in pain like a wounded animal. Rebecca roused herself and laid her head in his lap.

Hearing their agonized cries, Esperanza hurried into the room. She paused at the door, paralyzed by the tender scene between father and daughter. Rebecca's long tresses draped themselves across Master Cohen's knees as she sat with her head in his lap. He caressed her black mane as he did when she was a young child. His face was a mask of despair.

"It's only us now." Rebecca said to her father. "Just you and I."

Esperanza's heart skipped. 'Only us now.' The words might as well have been an eviction notice. For Rebecca and her father, the two of them were the only 'us' that mattered. As close as she and Rebecca had been, she was not one of them. She was an outsider. She saw a great rift opening between her past life as part of a family and her new life as an interloper hovering at the periphery of the household.

Master Cohen noticed Esperanza clinging to the door frame, peering into the room. "There you are, Esperanza, good. Go find Rabbi Ezra." His voice was hoarse and cracked. He looked at her briefly then turned his back and continued weeping.

Esperanza disappeared down the corridor and hurried out the door into the winding streets of the Juderia to the house next to the synagogue and pounded the door with her fists. She could hear the old rabbi chanting his morning prayers. His wife of forty years came to the door to chase away the source of this rude interruption.

"The rabbi must come right away." Esperanza's words gushed from her mouth.

The wife's demeanor softened at the sight of this distraught young woman. "No, my dear, you must wait until he has finished his prayers. Come sit down. It will not be long."

Esperanza sat demurely on a bench in the entryway as the rabbi's wife disappeared down the hallway. The singer's nasal chanting voice faded, followed by two voices murmuring. Then the rabbi appeared, as his wife carefully removed his tallit, the tasseled prayer draped over his shoulders, and left him alone with the girl. His watery brown eyes filled with sympathy as he listened patiently to Esperanza.

He straightened his yarmulka and hurried to Aaron Cohen's house, where the servant, Lisbeth, ushered him in. He approached Johanna's body reverently and, with thumb and forefinger, closed her eyes. He turned his head and brought his white-bearded cheek to Johanna's lips making sure no breath remained in her. Knowing that the family's grief would be profound, and that Rebecca would be ill-prepared to carry out her duties as required by tradition, he summoned Lisbeth and the Jewish matrons of the community to help Rebecca prepare the body for burial. They guided her through the ritual bath, washing the body thoroughly, then dressing it in a white shroud. Rebecca fumbled through the procedure, embarrassed by the intimacy of the acts she was performing. Johanna's long ordeal had transformed her once-beautiful body into an emaciated, tumor-ridden vestige.

Esperanza was not included in the preparations; she could only step aside and watch, knowing that she was not one of them and never could be. She felt as hollow as a drinking gourd. She stood by, unable to participate but unwilling to leave, clinging hopelessly to the shreds of her adopted family. She was trapped between two locked doors, one barring her from the life she had known with the family, and another obstructing any vision of the future.

Two days later, under an incongruously bright sun, dozens of friends and acquaintances stood silently as four strong men lowered the simple pine coffin into the grave while Rabbi Ezra recited the kaddish. Each mourner tossed a handful of dirt into the pit. Though not invited to do so, Esperanza was the last to approach the grave and sprinkle a clot of damp, spring soil on Johanna's body. *Goodbye, sweet Johanna. You taught me how a kind, gracious woman leads her life. I will not forget you.*

Word spread that the good Master Cohen's wife had died, and the house filled with friends and neighbors from the Jewish community who had known the master and his kindly wife. They brought food - enough food to feed visitors and family alike for a week. They remained with Master Cohen and Rebecca, praying with them and consoling them so they were never alone. Two days after the funeral, Esperanza sat with Rebecca who was crippled by grief, holding her hand in quiet sympathy. Lisbeth took charge, making sure the family was fed and the household continued to function.

For the townspeople life went on as before. But for Rebecca, Aaron, Esperanza, and Lisbeth a great chasm opened, separating the past from the future. Over the next twelve months of mourning, the pain of Johanna's death ebbed to benumbed listlessness. Master Cohen still ministered to the people who lined the street outside his office, but his attention drifted, his feet shuffled, and his back bent. He looked like he had aged ten years. As painful as it was, the time had come to move forward. The time for fasting, keeping candles burning, and wearing black arm bands came to an end. Master Cohen visited the homes of some of his poorer patients and bestowed thoughtful gifts on them in remembrance of Johanna.

During the year of Johanna's decline, the twins, Benjamin and Ariel, continued to pursue their studies at the great synagogue Ibn Shoshan and labor in the scriptorium at the School of Translators in Toledo. When she died, they were too far away to travel home in time for the funeral. Though they were not in Burgos with the family, they realized their world had shifted too. As students, they had enjoyed their freedom in Toledo, but knew their father monitored their activities from afar. Master Cohen corresponded regularly with their teachers. He had read with great interest reports detailing the twins' progress. He allowed them more freedom than most students.

For a while, they had tested their limits, roaming the streets, missing classes, meeting people not a part of their sheltered community. But after a few sharp missives from their father, they settled down, and pursued their academic interests. Benjamin drifted toward medicine and hoped to follow in his father's footsteps.

Ariel's future was murkier. He found the vibrant markets of Toledo exhilarating with their heady aromas of spices, perfumes, and leather. Gems of every color, gold ingots, and delicately crafted jewelry sparkled under Toledo's blistering summer sun. He observed elegant, aristocratic ladies examine brilliant white cotton, fine taffeta, velvet, and damask fabrics. They fingered tapestries brocaded with gold thread that came from as far away as Hindustan. As Ariel ambled through the markets, his imagination wandered to distant lands imagining outlandish architecture, unfamiliar landscapes, and exotic people. Bargaining with the vendors, stirred his blood; the more spirited the haggling the better he liked it. In the markets he honed his aptitude for business and fed his hunger for adventure.

Johanna's death slammed the door on Ariel and Benjamin's freedom. Aaron Cohen called his sons back to Burgos.

6

DIASPORA

WINTER 1262 to WINTER 1263

The midsummer sun warmed the office where Rebecca worked at her mother's desk. Exhausted from endless complications of administering the household, she pored over the ledgers until the columns of numbers blurred and her head ached. Receipts and invoices littered the desk, and discarded, ink-soaked ledger sheets accumulated in drifts around the ornately carved table legs. As regular as rain, at the same time each day, Lisbeth knocked on the jamb of the open door. Rebecca lifted her head, rubbed the back of her neck.

"Do you have the day's shopping list for me Senorita?" Lisbeth asked.

Rebecca groaned quietly. "I haven't gotten to it yet today, Lisbeth. I don't know how my mother did it, managing the household, supervising us children, coordinating the menu. I simply can't keep up."

Rebecca, despite her knowledge of Greek classics, philosophy, and literature was ill-prepared to assume household management and Lisbeth knew it. Lisbeth didn't dare criticize, but she recognized she had far more practical experience than the new lady of the house. Not wanting to appear boastful, yet sincerely wishing to help Rebecca and possibly improve her own standing as well, Lisbeth carefully broached the sensitive topic of handling household oversight.

"I can help you if you'll let me." Lisbeth began. "If you teach me my letters, I would be able to read the menu you devise and do the marketing. I have been handling money and marketing for several years. Your mother simply told me what she needed, and I memorized her list. I know the merchants and they know me and appreciate my ability to haggle for good prices. But letters make as much sense to me as a deck of cards thrown down a flight of stairs. To me they are a meaningless jumble. If I could read, I would be able to plan the menu as well as do the marketing."

Rebecca lit up at the prospect of Lisbeth taking more responsibility. But where would she find the time to teach her to read? She dropped her eyes to the chaotic mess on the table and shook her head.

"That's a very good idea, Lisbeth, and I'm sure you are fully capable of the added responsibility, but learning to read takes time and dedication. I am already swimming in deep water with all my duties."

"If you cannot do it," Lisbeth continued, undeterred. "Perhaps Esperanza can teach me. She knows how to read, and she would be a good teacher."

Rebecca brightened. "Excellent idea! Tell Esperanza I told her to tutor you in writing." Rebecca knew Esperanza deserved the respect of being asked personally to teach Lisbeth, but she was too overburdened to worry about Esperanza's feelings. Rebecca cared only that it meant one of her problems would be solved. Learning to read takes time, and although beneficial in the long term, it would take months for her to learn enough to lighten her burdens. In the meantime, Rebecca's responsibilities threatened to sweep over her like a giant sucking wave at high tide and drag her into deep water.

After Johanna's death Esperanza carried on as before, helping Master Cohen with his patients, surreptitiously offering diagnoses and dispensing remedies. But for Rebecca a much larger issue loomed, and it was approaching fast.

Many months before her mother died, Johanna and Aaron had arranged a marriage for her. Before her father and the prospective groom's family could finalize the agreement, Johanna had died. The groom's family had respectfully waited until the mourning period for Johanna ended. Now, a year later, the black cloth draped over the front door had been removed and the black armbands were gone. It was time to move on with their lives and settle the marriage contract.

Final negotiations could be sensitive, but Master Cohen hoped both families would benefit from the arrangement. Rebecca, wrung out by grief and worry, succumbed to the proposed match with passive acquiescence. Though not strictly necessary, both families agreed it would be helpful if the betrothed couple met before the ceremony. Their first encounter would be perfunctory. Rebecca and the young man were expected to submit to the will of their families regardless that they were strangers, but at least they would have an opportunity to meet each other before the wedding day found them together before the Rabbi.

After the marriage, Rebecca would be expected to pull her roots up from the warm soil of her loving family and transplant herself into a new household, dominated by the groom's mother. The thought of leaving her father pained her, filling her with anxiety and fear. She was riddled with questions. Would her new mother-in-law treat her kindly or jealously guard her power over her son and the household? Would her new husband help her adjust to her new situation and treat her with respect, or abandon her to the established clique of his mother and his sisters? Would her anxiety for her future stunt her ability to open her heart to her new family? Any thoughts about how Esperanza would fare after she was gone faded into insignificance.

The dreary winter months passed quickly with Esperanza, Lisbeth, and Rebecca each immersed in their new roles as teacher, student, and household manager. When the day of the young couple's first meeting finally arrived, the potted plants in the courtyard bloomed again, awash in the buttery spring sun, and with a light breeze rippling the water in the reflecting pool. Lisbeth filled vases in the great room with pomegranate blooms, suffusing the room with a sweet aroma. Although she had never counted pomegranate seeds, Master Cohen told her pomegranates were sacred because they had exactly 613 seeds signifying the 613 commandments of the Torah. Lisbeth could think of no better way to signify the importance of the first meeting of the soon-to-be bride and groom than with pomegranates.

While Lisbeth bustled about dusting, arranging vases, and lighting scented candles, Rebecca sat listless, waiting for her groom to appear. A gauzy veil covered her face as she sat perched on the edge of the upholstered sofa. The groom's family had arrived two days before the meeting, but Rebecca had been kept out of sight, confined to her quarters. The day of the first meeting, Lisbeth and Esperanza dressed Rebecca in a tastefully modest pale-yellow dress, brushed her dark hair until it shone like sable, and pinched a pink glow into her cheeks. Then they sprinkled her with water scented with rose, orange blossom, jasmine, lemon, and lavender.

"You look lovely," Esperanza cooed. "How could he resist instant affection for a wife who smelled like the Elysian fields?"

"What if he is repulsive, or stupid, or acts like a spoiled boy? Father is interested only in his family's wealth and reputation, not the personality of the groom."

"Your father wants only the best for his Rebecca," Esperanza reassured her. "You can be sure of that. He loves you and I'm sure he has chosen your groom with utmost care."

Rebecca looked unconvinced. Esperanza didn't know what the boy would be like any more than Rebecca did but thought it best to encourage Rebecca to keep a positive attitude.

"Just open your heart; make no judgments before you meet the young man," the ever-practical Lisbeth advised.

The time had come, Rebecca would soon know what fate had ordained for her. The groom's mother escorted Rebecca's prospective husband into the room. He settled tentatively on the edge of the couch separated from Rebecca by a long stretch of brocade upholstery. The adults exited the room, leaving the couple alone. Rebecca lifted her veil and the pair snuck wary, side-long glances at each other.

"My name is Daniel." His mellow, soft-spoken voice broke the silence.

"My name is Rebecca," she replied. He was in his mid-twenties, older than her by several years, but he was not an old man. His thin hair was drawn back into a slender tail drooping down his back. He could not be considered handsome with his round cheeks, thin lips, and narrow shoulders, but he was not loathsome, and he seemed almost as nervous as she was. Her eyes slid sideways, taking in his finely woven tunic, dyed with costly indigo, and edged with gold embroidery. He surely must be a wealthy man indeed.

"I am a money lender." It was an awkward way to begin a conversation and he instantly regretted it. At a loss for any other way to begin, he forged on. "You could say that I make the wheels of commerce turn smoothly. My father taught me his profession, but with him gone, I have taken over the business."

"Oh, I'm sorry you lost your father. I too have lost a parent. You have my sympathy," Rebecca's natural compassion rose in her breast. If nothing else, they shared the pain of a lost parent.

"It was three years ago," he continued, comforted by the kindness of her response. "The pain has lessened, but I still miss him. I understand you lost your mother recently. Your grief must be new and still sharp."

Having found a sliver of common ground, they looked directly at each other for the first time. Rebecca managed a small smile. At least Daniel had a good job and would be able to support her and the many children everyone expected her to bear.

Rebecca was not beautiful, Daniel thought, but she was not homely, and it was obvious she had a good heart. They relaxed a bit. He turned toward her and gingerly slid a bit closer.

"I understand your father dabbles in lending money also."

"Oh no, not really," Rebecca replied. "He works as a physician – a very good one. There are patients lined up outside his door every day except Sabbath, but he has a long-time friend who is a trader, and my father finances his voyages."

"I have no experience financing traders. My business is mainly with the merchants of my town, Valladolid. But one day perhaps your father could educate me on the subject." Daniel fidgeted, uncomfortably.

"We never talk about that aspect of his business. I have my own household responsibilities to worry about." Wanting to appear capable and self-assured she continued. "I am learning the intricacies of managing a household and aspire to be as competent as my mother was."

The desultory and erratic conversation stumbled on. Though awkward and self-conscious, it was a start.

After an appropriate amount of time, Master Cohen and Daniel's mother re-entered the room. Daniel rose and bowed slightly to the elders. He reached down and gently touched Rebecca's hand; the simple, affectionate gesture felt surprisingly intimate. She raised her eyes to his and smiled sincerely. Rebecca and Daniel parted, taking their first impressions with them to sort through like buttons from beads.

During the months that followed her betrothal, Rebecca drew farther away from Esperanza. Household details consumed most of Rebecca's day, and she had little extra time to spend with her friend. Resigned to her fate, Rebecca focused on the road ahead, allowing her youth to recede into the past along with her friendship with Esperanza. For her part, Esperanza worked at the apothecary and spent her remaining free time teaching Lisbeth to read. She felt as empty as a bird's nest in December.

The winter after the betrothal became a season of family visits, formal dinners, chaperoned walks in the courtyard, and evening games of backgammon and chess. The young couple developed a comfortable companionship, sometimes laughing, sometimes exchanging fleeting touches, like delicate brush strokes on a pastel mural. After a respectable time had passed, Master Cohen and Daniel's mother finalized the terms of the contract between the families. They exchanged gifts and settled on the bride price and dowry payments. When the buds on the cherry trees were once again ready to burst, Rebecca and Daniel took their places under the wedding canopy and exchanged simple gold rings. It was shocking how easily their lives flowed on, like a tranquil stream over smooth sand.

Esperanza helped Rebecca pack her belongings into trunks. As easily as the moon waned, their old life disappeared. She blushed as she folded the garments Rebecca would wear when her husband came to her bed to claim his conjugal rights. Rebecca would take few possessions with her other than clothing - her mother's jewelry, hair combs, and a cameo pendant Master Cohen had given her as a wedding gift. After Esperanza had gently tucked the last of Rebecca's belongings into the trunk, she stood before Rebecca and reached for her hands.

"What will become of us?" Rebecca asked. Bit by bit both of their lives were disintegrating, and no glue in the world could repair the cracks. "It seems impossible that our carefree youth could have ended so quickly."

"Dear Rebecca, you have a path laid out for you as clearly defined as a Roman road. I hope your life will be happy and fulfilled. Your husband seems nice enough. Your dowry is substantial. You have every chance at happiness, and I hope you find it."

"You're right," Rebecca replied. "But what will become of you?" Her eyes filled with tears. "I've been so busy thinking of myself, I haven't spared so much as a thought for your fate. I am ashamed."

Esperanza fixed her eyes on the wall over Rebecca's shoulder, deliberately draining her face of emotion, so she would not make Rebecca feel even sadder. It was true. None of them had spared a thought for Esperanza. She had become a ghost, drifting through the days, unseen and unappreciated.

"Don't concern yourself," she mumbled. "My future is like a great bank of fog in front of me. But just beyond it, the sun is warming the air and the fog is dissipating. Clarity will come soon enough."

When the ceremonies were over, Daniel came to collect his wife and her belongings. His servants loaded trunks of clothing and marriage gifts into a wagon, and they rolled down the road to Valladolid, a journey of eight days, through the endless plains of the meseta.

Esperanza squeezed her eyes closed, pinching the bridge of her nose. For the first time in a long time, her ears buzzed, and her eyes reddened. A vision of Rebecca's future emerged from the haze of the future. Rebecca would find happiness with Daniel, but it would be short-lived, ending with the birth of their first child. Esperanza's heart sank. In the next moment, a new vision overwhelmed her view of Rebecca's fate. She saw herself standing on a dusty road, with the scent of saltwater wafting over her. Her fate was rolling toward her, and it would not be in Burgos.

* * *

Armed with the reading and writing skills Esperanza had taught her, Lisbeth made a sure-footed step into the seat behind Rebecca's desk, directing the affairs of the household. She came to work for the Cohen family as a girl of ten, from a good Jewish family of meager means, distant relatives of Master Cohen. She understood the habits and traditions of a Jewish household. Now she was an adult, ready to take over Rebecca's responsibilities.

As Lisbeth gained confidence, Esperanza's eroded away. She felt like a marionette, jumping mechanically when Master Cohen pulled the strings. An empty place opened inside of her, and the old familiar demon of insecurity came creeping back. She knew she would be abandoned again. Though she continued to run and fetch when Master Cohen asked her, she was expendable. She had no prospects and no plans; a vague restless anxiety overtook her as she waited for the future to catch up with her. Master Cohen now treated her politely, but formally, even a bit coldly. With Rebecca married off, and Lisbeth capably in command of Johanna's desk, she no longer fit in. She was merely tolerated out of sympathy.

* * *

"They're home! They're home!" Lisbeth ran down the colonnaded hallway dodging into Esperanza's room dragging her by the arm.

"Go stand next to the reflecting pool and stay there!" she

commanded.

She flew down to the lower-level kitchen where the cook stood behind the chopping block, her apron covered with blood and chicken feathers, then to the parlor where the maid was cleaning, and dragged them out to join Esperanza in the courtyard. Then she raced to the stable to rouse the groom.

Finally, she burst into Master Cohen's office, elbowed the patients aside and bawled like an injured cow. "They're here! The twins are here!"

Master Cohen abandoned his bewildered clients and hustled to take a position squarely inside the great oak doors. A few steps behind him, Lisbeth and Esperanza took up their positions. The cook, the maid, and the stable boy lingered on the fringes. The doors creaked open, and the twins walked in, leading their road-weary horses.

Lisbeth and Esperanza caught their breath. The young men who walked through the portal barely resembled the twelve-year-old boys who left four years ago. Still tall and slim, with black ringlets cascading down to their collars, they were now broad-shouldered, straight-backed, with a regal bearing. The stable boy hurried to take the horses and led them away.

"My boys, my boys!" Aaron Cohen rushed forward to embrace each of them in turn. "Let me take a look at you." He took a step back and searched their square-jawed faces. The stork bite, the faint pink birth mark at Benjamin's hairline, had faded a bit. Ariel was a touch taller, but they were still outwardly identical. Their differences were beneath the façade. Benjamin's dark eyes surveyed the scene with the serious gaze of a scholar, while Ariel's demeanor was nonchalant. His arms swung loosely at his sides and his posture was less arrow straight. His restlessness disturbed the air around him like a breeze ripples a pool.

"My prodigals have returned." Aaron could not tear his eyes away from his boys, hidden now in the bodies of these young men. "Lisbeth has arranged a great feast for us tonight, haven't you, dear." He spoke affectionately to the young lady at his elbow.

Two pairs of dark eyes turned toward Lisbeth. Instantly she

shrank from their attention. She seldom thought about her appearance but now she cringed to think of how the handsome twins must see her. Her plain, undyed linen dress overlaid by sleeveless red tunic was as ordinary as a cooking pot. Only a brightly embroidered sash wound twice around her waist enlivened her garb. A simple white veil covered her hair.

The young men eyed her curiously trying to place her in their memory. Since they'd left, their family had been transformed. Their mother and sister were gone. Instead, here was a – what was she, a servant, a housekeeper? She appeared to be about their age. Her skin was olive, but not swarthy. Full lips and large coal-black eyes dominated her features. Wisps of frizzy black hair escaped her veil.

"You're the girl who went to the market for our mother!" Ariel exclaimed when he finally placed her. "And your name was, what? Elizabeth?"

"Yes, that's close. My name is Lisbeth. I am that girl. I am the housekeeper now." She ventured a shy smile.

"Oh, she is much more than that." Aaron interrupted. "She runs the household as efficiently as your dear mother did. I don't know what I would do without her."

"And this must be little Esperanza." Benjamin said, looking at the other girl. Her hair billowed in loose curls, barely hidden under her veil. She was small but not fragile with a forthright demeanor that was almost challenging. She looked directly at them unabashed, her grey eyes unblinking and frank.

"I remember chasing you and Rebecca through the corridors. Look at you now," Ariel exclaimed.

Esperanza refused to modestly lower her eyes as Lisbeth had. "Yes, I am that girl."

"She helps me in the apothecary." Aaron explained. "She has a remarkable gift for diagnosis. I honestly don't know how she gleans so much information from our patients." Aaron cut the re-introductions short. "Let me show you two weary travelers to your rooms. We can continue this conversation tonight at dinner."

The twins followed their father through the courtyard and down the colonnaded corridors to their rooms, their necks swiveling to absorb all that was familiar and all that had changed. Everything seemed so much smaller than it had when they left to take up their studies in Toledo. The reflecting pool seemed smaller, not sparkling with magic as it had in their childhood. There were fewer, less colorful flowers in the courtyard, and the atmosphere was drab and dusty.

When they were gone, Lisbeth and Esperanza stared at each other speechless as they tried to untangle their confusing impressions. Looking at themselves through the mirror of the twins' eyes left them feeling somehow run down, like an untended garden.

"I better get to work if we are to have a feast." Lisbeth turned and hurried to the kitchen with the cook. The maid returned to her work tidying the house to perfection. Esperanza was left stranded in the courtyard with no clear idea of what she ought to be doing. After a few aimless moments, she returned to the apothecary, and began ushering customers, one by one, into the anteroom.

Dinner was festive. Lisbeth served an impressive meal concocted impromptu from the supplies at hand. The table groaned with cooked fish in spiced vinegar alongside anchovies, a noodle kugel made with the tantalizingly clashing tastes of caramel and black pepper, and sweet and spicy spinach with raisins and pine nuts. Just that day, Lisbeth had purchased a loaf of hard-to-find white bread, a delicacy fit for aristocrats.

The conversation that evening was as lively as the menu. Aaron took his natural place at the head of the table, with Benjamin and Ariel on either hand. Lisbeth and Esperanza sat side-by-side at the foot of the table.

Ariel peppered the conversation with lively, wide-ranging stories of the hardships of their journey, their studies, their friends, and the beauty of Toledo tucked into a bend of the Tagus River.

"Now it's time to seriously consider the course your lives will take." Aaron broke in, shifting instantly to a more serious tone. "You are both at the age when you must put youthful explorations aside and settle into suitable careers. What do you intend to do,

Benjamin?"

"I had hoped, when my schooling ended, I could continue my education, but I don't think more schooling will help me. I am hungry to learn from you, father. I would love to be your apprentice and eventually succeed you in your medical practice."

Aaron swelled with pride. "Of course! I sincerely hoped one of you would follow in my footsteps. I have a fine reputation, an abundance of clients both rich and poor, and a lifetime of knowledge. I couldn't be more eager to train you." He turned his gaze at Ariel. "And you, son, what are your aspirations?"

Ariel hesitated. "I don't know how to answer. My greatest satisfaction in Toledo was browsing the market. It may sound frivolous to you, but as you know, Toledo is the hub of a thriving trade network. Merchants from Venice, Rome, and as far away as Hindustan, Persia, and Constantinople fill the stalls with all types of exotic goods. The people who trade there are as diverse as their goods - Muslims, Hindus, Assyrians, Arabs - all dressed in outlandish costumes, babbling in indecipherable tongues. It was fascinating, vibrating with possibility and the lure of the unknown. And I made some good contacts among the traders. What a diverse and extraordinary cast of characters they are!" He stopped, embarrassed by his effusive description.

"Loving the vibrancy of a bustling marketplace is not the same as making a prosperous living as a trader. It is more complex than you know, and dangerous too, both financially risky and physically arduous." Aaron stroked his chin. "Hmmmm. Let me give this some thought. I may have a plan for you. I have enjoyed the friendship of the trader, Ibrahim, for many years. Perhaps he would consent to taking you on as his apprentice, but we can worry about that tomorrow. Tonight is the time for celebration. L'chayim!" Aaron lifted his cup and gestured around the table. "Here's to the future of my beautiful young men. If only Johanna was here to celebrate your homecoming. She would be so proud." He paused, bowed his head, and sighed, then returned to a lighter tone. "May you enjoy good health, and may your futures be prosperous and satisfying." The music of clinking glasses and happy voices resonated through the room. That night they all dreamed their futures were unfurling before them like a Persian carpet down a long hallway.

7

ON THE THRESHOLD

SPRING 1264

Apale-yellow dawn lit the sky as Esperanza unlocked the door and slipped into the apothecary to prepare for the day, arranging slender vials, round-bottomed beakers, and narrow-necked amber jars. By the time Benjamin and Aaron arose, the sun had climbed well above the horizon, and all was in perfect order. She paused, closed her eyes, and breathed deeply. As happened many mornings, inspiration warmed her. This was the milieu where she thrived. Placing her delicate hand on her breastbone and closing her eyes, she felt her confidence grow; she was ready. Aside from herbal preparations for routine ailments, today she perceived she would need wild garlic, to help close a slow-healing diabetic wound. She located a tincture of calendine, anticipating she might see a bad case of psoriasis. She was pressing and straining some fennel seeds she had soaked in water and lime juice overnight for treating dyspepsia when Benjamin and Master Cohen walked in.

"Look, Benjamin. Do you remember the apothecary?" Aaron swept in, guiding his son by the elbow.

"Certainly, I do. But the assortment of ingredients and elixirs I remember was much more limited then."

"Yes, Esperanza has increased our selection of remedies four-fold in the time you have been away. She will teach you everything you see here. Soon, you will be as knowledgeable as she."

81

Benjamin nodded blandly in her direction. Esperanza's happy mood instantly evaporated, replaced with boiling stew of resentment. *"I have spent my lifetime learning these herbs and their uses. This pampered boy, despite his formal education, has never roamed the hillsides searching for rare plants, never honed the art of preparing remedies from the raw materials nature gives us. Many of these medicines are toxic if not taken correctly. How can Master Cohen possibly believe that Benjamin can learn everything that I know?"*

Her memory flashed back to her hours scouring the hills with Amika, the smell of Gabriela's soups, the simple needs of pilgrims. How would he know how to dig the deep root of burdock after the first frost when it is sweetest, and its power is at its peak? How would he know how long to chew yarrow before applying it to a wound? Her knowledge grew as deep as the roots of the burdock, and from knowledge as timeless as the flowers of the healing yarrow. A sudden pang of nostalgia pierced her heart.

With difficulty, she quelled her indignation, calmed her lurching stomach, and faced them directly. "I will do what I can. How well he learns will be up to him." Her voice was icy. Benjamin flinched, stung by Esperanza's challenge. *"How dare she assume her knowledge is superior to mine. I am the one who studied at the most esteemed schools in Toledo. We will see who is most valuable to my father."*

Sensing the friction, Master Cohen turned Benjamin back toward the house.

"Esperanza is a good teacher." Aaron turned the conversation away from the apothecary. "She taught Lisbeth to read and write. Lisbeth has stepped into your mother's role keeping the household running as smoothly as a lake at dawn. She has proven herself capable and energetic. Let's go to her office now and she will explain her responsibilities. There will be plenty of time to introduce you to the apothecary later."

Esperanza was glad to see them go, but she knew that inevitably Benjamin would become a fixture in her domain. In the first hour of her day, the gentle sun had turned as harsh and abrasive as sandpaper, scouring the joy out of her morning ritual.

The sun that spilled over the desk where Lisbeth sat hunched over her ledger was cheerful, unspoiled by unspoiled by dread. The office that had been Johanna's, and then Rebecca's, was now hers. She was so engrossed in her work she did not hear them enter. Benjamin paused at the door, not wanting to disturb her. The sun streaming in highlighted her unblemished olive skin and the tendrils of onyx curls escaping her veil. Her cheeks glowed the color of a rosy pomegranate.

"Lisbeth, Benjamin is here," Aaron called. "I told him you would explain your responsibilities to him."

She reluctantly raised her eyes from her ledger. When she raised her head and faced him directly, Benjamin emitted a soft sigh. This was not the girl who ran errands for his mother. This was not even the girl who shared dinner last evening. Seeing her here in her own domain, she seemed an entirely different creature, businesslike, capable, and forthrightly feminine. Though she was not the beauty Benjamin's mother had been, he was nevertheless smitten. The color of Lisbeth's cheeks deepened to a claret red as Benjamin's gaze bored into her.

"I am occupied now with my ledgers, Benjamin." She recovered her equanimity quickly. "Please come back tomorrow before the midday meal, and I will explain what I do."

Aaron watched attentively. Lisbeth's blush and Benjamin's speechlessness did not escape his notice. The atmosphere enveloping the two young people tingled like the air before a lightning strike. He comprehended their attraction well before they themselves recognized it. Aaron felt a smug satisfaction creep over him. If this force pulling them together persisted, they would be a perfect match. Lisbeth would reign over the household creating a calm, nurturing, stable atmosphere in which Benjamin could flourish as a Master physician. They were young; there was time for the seeds of mutual attraction to sprout. Fate would decide if it would blossom or wither and die.

Ariel, unlike his industrious brother, rose late, and left the house without bothering to eat breakfast. He walked the few blocks from the house to the market square. The outsized spires of the great, unfinished cathedral loomed over the neighborhoods, as he wandered from one stall to another. Vendors displayed white asparagus, purple eggplants, deep red beet root, dark green kale, and carrots whose colors varied as much as the pigments of a muralist. Less colorful stalls displayed basketry, pottery, sausages, animal pelts, nuts, dates, and iron ware. As varied as they were, these were all local products. This market could not match the excitement and exotic allure of the products in the Toledo market. The clothing of the prosaic local people held no fascination for him either, unlike the allure of the strange and colorful costumes worn by people from many countries that so enchanted him in Toledo. He felt as restless as a caged beast, and as out of place as a water serpent in a courtyard pool.

He made his way past fragrant barley bread, oat cakes, soft goats' milk cheeses until he reached the last building in the market, the blacksmith's blackened hovel where he sold tools, weapons, and barrel staves. Before leaving the market, he bought a loaf of bread and a skin of Rioja wine; he departed the city through the west portal in the old Roman wall, and made his way down to the river. With nothing better to do, he lounged on the bank under the warm sun, drank his wine and drifted off into dreams of exotic markets in faraway lands, envisioning strange people in their outlandish costumes, haggling in as many tongues as the tower of Babel. When the rays of late afternoon sun slanted across the riverbank, he finally roused himself and returned home.

Aaron intercepted him as soon as he entered the house. "Where have you been all day? You have weeds in your hair."

Suddenly aware of his disheveled appearance, he brushed the chaff from his hair and clothes. "Nowhere. I wandered the market, then fell asleep on the bank of the river."

Aaron scowled. Coming closer, he could smell the wine. He narrowed his eyes, sniffed Aaron's closed lips, but said nothing.

Ariel was almost a grown man now and required a longer tether, but Aaron was displeased with his son's indolence. The boy needed gainful employment, a more productive way to spend his time. He had seen cases like this before, young men with little to do falling into a dissolute life with other privileged youths, carousing, fighting in the streets, finding female companionship of the worst variety. That would simply not do. He would need to correct this situation as soon as possible.

* * *

Two weeks later, the peaceful household was jolted from its late summer torpor by the insistent hammering of the lion's head door knocker. The doors groaned as the maidservant opened them. Ibrahim strode into the courtyard.

"Where is that old scoundrel, Cohen?" he bellowed.

"I'm sorry sir," the maidservant said. "He is not here. You will find him in his consulting room caring for patients." He turned and made for the apothecary where he made another noisy entrance.

"Aaron, come out and meet your old friend." Ibrahim's voice boomed.

As he had before, Aaron abandoned his clients to Esperanza's skillful ministrations, and the two old friends retired to Aaron's private quarters adjoining courtyard's corridor. He reached for a decanter of Manzanilla wine Ibrahim had purchased for him in Cadiz.

"Things have changed since you were here in early summer," Aaron began. "Benjamin is doing well. He is learning my procedures quickly. He is intelligent and committed. Not only that, but he has taken an interest in Lisbeth."

"It sounds very promising. Just what you hoped for - one of your sons to take over your practice and a nice Jewish girl who can run the household. What more could you want?"

"Yes, yes. That is all fine and good. But Ariel is not settling down. He spends his days wandering the marketplace; but having seen so many more interesting sights inToledo, he is unsatisfied and restless. I'm afraid trouble will find him sooner or later. He needs employment."

Ibrahim crossed his arms over his chest, and imperiously looked down at Aaron. "Let me guess. You would like me to take him under my wing and teach him the intricacies of the merchant trade. Is that right?"

Aaron chuckled. "Have your years as a trader taught you how to read minds? Yes, that's exactly what I was thinking. Would you? He is bright, quick witted, and can think on his feet as the situation demands. He could sell sawdust to a lumber mill." Aaron smiled affectionately thinking of his wayward son.

"You're right in prying him out of the arms of bad companions and diverting him from the downward slope of bad habits. I have seen too many good men turn into wastrels. I would be happy to show him the complexities of my trade. I'm quite sure I could keep him occupied. But I warn you, I won't accept anyone who might foment trouble. As an apprentice of mine, he would need to be fluent in Latin and Greek. A little Arabic would be very helpful too. He must have good business skills and a facility in writing and arithmetic. I do not doubt that Ariel has these skills, except for knowing Arabic." Ibrahim was all business, rattling off the skills a trader would need.

"He has studied all those things. He was a good student when he wanted to be. His teacher, Rabbi Beneviste, was an esteemed scholar. He has a facility for languages, so he could improve his skills" Aaron swelled with pride knowing that he had provided the best education possible for his sons.

"Those are not the only requirements. He must also be of good character - faithful, loyal, obedient, and honest." Ibrahim's countenance changed. His eyebrows raised and his lips drooped as he shifted into the guise of wily, skeptical, world-weary trader. "I can't pay him, you understand. At least not until he has proven his worthiness and his ability to turn a profit for my enterprise."

Aaron clapped his hand on Ibrahim's shoulders. "Thank you,

my friend. Ariel will not disappoint you. I think he will jump at the chance to apprentice with you."

"My ship is anchored in Barcelona. From there we will stop at Mallorca, Sardinia, Palermo and finally Napoli. We ply a lively trade in woolen textiles, spices, salt, buttons, silver, tin, and amber along the way. No territory is without its specialties. We have opportunities in every location we pass through."

"Ariel haunts the markets, always seeking to catch the scent of exotic, alien lands. He will be well suited to the trade." Aaron replied.

"Well, there you have it. He will be my apprentice. I am not an easy task master, and no one takes advantage of me in a trade. The trade routes can be dangerous, riddled with pirates, and unpredictable storms are a constant threat. I cannot tolerate contradiction or dissension. I am undisputed master of my ship."

"I can readily believe that is true, old friend." Aaron smiled and extended his hand to Ibrahim. "We will speak to Ariel together. He is not the defiant sort. When he understands the rules, I'm sure he will prove himself useful."

Aaron hesitated. "There is one more puzzle I must solve." He took a deep breath. "Esperanza is no longer as useful as she once was. She is of marriageable age, but no Jewish family would have her. It would sully my reputation if I callously turned her out of my house, but she no longer belongs here. Though she is headstrong and does not demure to those above her station, she is a born healer. I don't know what to do with her. Johanna and I never looked past her usefulness as Rebecca's companion. Now I am paying for my shortsightedness."

For several minutes Ibrahim stared vaguely into the distance stroking his abundant black mustache. "I have a friend in Napoli. He is without a wife, and though he is more than twenty years Esperanza's senior, and his eyesight is failing, he craves the companionship of a woman. A young, good looking girl like Esperanza would be a good choice for him, especially since she is, as you say, a healer." He nodded his head approvingly, thinking he was clever for devising this plan. "He will need someone to be his eyes and tend to his physical needs. Won't he be pleased when I bring him a new bride as a gift!" Ibrahim chuckled with glee, like a schoolboy delighted at having raided his neighbor's apple tree.

"Esperanza would never agree to such a marriage."

"Why does she need to know?" Ibrahim gazed steely eyed at Aaron, who nervously shifted his weight from foot to foot. He really did want the best for Esperanza, and this situation could be an opportunity for her to practice her craft. Maybe a little deception would be the best thing.

In Ibrahim's mind, Esperanza was already a commodity to be traded - an ivory bauble to be exchanged for generous patronage of a trading financier. Whether she liked the plan or not was irrelevant. Women did as the men in their lives told them.

Aaron paused, weighing this dilemma. Deceiving her, betraying her unquestioning trust in him did not lay easily on his shoulders. But what else could he do with her? Perhaps she would reconcile to her new circumstances. At least she would enjoy stability, prosperity, and status. After all, many women had traded their virginity for less.

As if reading his thoughts, Ibrahim continued. "Many brides in arranged marriages are recalcitrant at first, but later learn forbearance and obedience, eventually taking satisfaction in their children. There is no place in society for an unmarried woman."

"You're right. Just the same, she could be trouble if she knew she was going to be the nursemaid and mate of an old man? She aspires to much more than that."

"What are her ambitions? What type of future would excite her?" Ibrahim's brain was already plotting his acquisition of the girl.

"She is a gifted healer." Aaron said.

"So I have heard," Ibrahim said. "I understand that there is a medical school in Salerno that accepts women students. Would she be happy if she could attend a real medical school?"

"Of course, she would be delighted." The outline of Ibrahim's scheme was beginning to take shape right before Aaron's eyes. He picked up the thread of the plan. "I will tell her I am sending her to the medical school in Salerno. That way she will comply willingly. She will be thrilled at the prospect of studying at such a renowned institution. Salerno has been training the most illustrious physicians in the world for hundreds of years. Its lineage reaches back to the ancient traditions of the Greeks, Arabs, and Romans. And they accept women!" Master Cohen paused, warming to the idea.

"That's a wonderful idea, Aaron. If she thinks she has an opportunity to study there, I'm sure she will cooperate willingly and cause no trouble." Ibrahim had no compunctions about deceiving her and didn't understand why she should be coddled, or why her wishes were even a part of the conversation. "She can travel under Ariel's protection. A woman traveling alone would be impossible. I will be engrossed with other concerns. I have a ship to captain."

"Yes, yes." Aaron gave the ploy his stamp of approval.

"First, we need to return to my ship in the harbor Barcelona. That in itself is a long journey. Will she be physically able to trek for many days to reach Barcelona?"

"Oh yes, she is strong, despite her small size, and has roamed the hills her whole life hunting for healing herbs. I'm sure she can endure such a trip."

"Well then, she can start packing her belongings. She is allowed only a single trunk. We must fill our hold with trade goods and won't be able to afford more space than that."

Aaron went to his lonely bed that night with his conscience scraping at his heart. He searched his soul. What would Johanna do? He quickly shunted that thought aside. Johanna would not have approved. But what else could he do? He assured himself that he had found a suitable situation for her, even if it meant tricking her into accepting it. He took consolation in knowing that his sons would be well positioned to make good futures for themselves. His primary responsibility was to them, not to this almost-woman who was not related, not even Jewish. Soon he convinced himself that Ibrahim's scheme was the best he could do for the girl.

8

FAR HORIZONS

SUMMER 1264

The trek from Burgos to Barcelona was arduous. Unseasonably cool wet weather made porridge of the roads. Late summer skies that should have been smiling on them, instead glowered like disapproving spinster aunts. Though the trip was a weary slog, Ibrahim provided for them well, knowing the cost of disgruntled men leaving the caravan was far greater than the cost of a well-stocked supply wagon. To keep the little caravan moving along briskly, he exchanged weary horses along the way for fresh ones; minor injuries to both men and horses received prompt attention. Day by day they made their slow, cumbersome way toward Barcelona.

Esperanza should have been delightedly looking forward to studying medicine at the prestigious Scola Medica in Salerno. It had sounded like a dream come true, but niggling doubt harried her like a swarm of gnats. Something was off; she could not name it, but she felt it in her heart. Her talent for insight did not extend to her own situation, and misgivings plagued her.

Ibrahim's party - Ariel, Esperanza, and a crew of porters - made their way to the sea, hauling bales of the finest merino wool and barrels of Rioja wine from the interior. For several days, they journeyed through a familiar landscape of placid pastures studded with fat cows, sheep, and vineyards. Eventually, the trail constricted as it descended into a menacing gorge with looming white-rock palisades. A mighty river roared and moaned in protest, throwing itself against the cliffs constraining it. Eventually, it widened and slowed, spreading out as the valley flattened, like a man loosening his waist sash after a feast. White poplars, and salt cedars lined the banks sheltering the caravan from the late summer heat.

Esperanza lost count of the number of days they walked, until one day they crested a high promontory. Below them the sight of a busy city shrouded by haze rewarded their perseverance. The sun clawed its way through a cloying fog rising from the delta below. Between the hill on which they stood and Barcelona below, was an expansive wetland. Thick stands of waterlilies, pondweed, and reeds crowded the muddy trail as marsh frogs sang in unison like choristers, providing a deep bass rhythm for the operatic reed warblers. Turtles and slithering eels dragged their bellies through the saturated muck. Egrets, ducks, and herons stalked their prey among the swamp grasses while marsh harriers circled overhead. Esperanza lifted her nose high to catch an unfamiliar scent in the air, strangely raw, rich, and salty.

"What do I smell?" Esperanza pulled Ariel aside, tugging at his tunic to bring his ear close to her mouth. She inhaled three short sniffs as if to demonstrate.

"It must be the aroma of coastal waters." He straightened and surveyed the scene before them. The boy who had chased her through Master Cohen's hallways now towered over her.

"I don't see any coastline."

"All I can surmise is that the sea must be close enough to flood this estuary." Ariel chucked Esperanza under the chin in the familiar, teasing way of a brother. As he grew into a man, he gained a greater sense of authority with every inch he added to his height. In his eyes this march to the sea was the first step in what was to be a lifelong journey of profitable adventures. Any remaining boyish self-doubt or reticence was pushed away, trampled underfoot into the sodden trail.

The familiarity of the Burgos evaporated like dew when they

left the plains and descended into the river gorge. Each new landscape they passed through enchanted Esperanza, each one was exotic, new, and teeming with alien creatures and unknown plants. She realized, to her chagrin, that her store of knowledge was painfully limited. There was so much more to learn.

With every bend of the river, her old life sank into the past like the sun setting to the west as Ibrahim's caravan plodded toward her new life. She gathered up sights and sounds and stored them away like a squirrel preparing for winter, vowing that when she reached the promised land of Salerno, she would roam new hills and learn unfamiliar plants and herbs under the tutelage of the best teachers in the world. The prospect should have elated her, but a black dread churned in the pit of her stomach. Quashing her misgivings, she threw her shoulders back and readied herself to confront her future with courage.

* * *

After weeks of travel, Ibrahim's caravan, loaded with trade goods from the interior, reached its destination. His ship, *Sultana,* lay at anchor, guarded by a few well-armed sailors. The harbor bristled with masts as thick as porcupine quills. Sand bars, seen and unseen, lurked below the water's shimmering glare creating a maze only the most skilled seamen could maneuver.

While Ibrahim was trekking to Burgos to secure financing for his enterprise, his agents were at work acquiring the best wool and wine they could find. A cadre of his brokers had remained behind in Barcelona, scouring the local markets for merchandise to trade in the lucrative markets of Sicily and Napoli. In Barcelona his agents ferreted out local products like raisins, honey, amber, and iron. After swarming over Barcelona, they had spread out, seeking specialties from other settlements bordering the Middle Sea and beyond. Barcelona stood at a maritime crossroads, where saffron from Greece, gold from Persia, ivory from Hindustan, and amber from North Africa were exchanged. Shouts and whispers of energetic haggling pervaded the markets. This would be a lucrative trip for Ibrahim. His most prized acquisition though, was the unexpected bonus of the girl, Esperanza, whose price was sure to be the dearest of all.

When the party of travelers reached the ship, Ibrahim grasped Esperanza's forearm, roughly pulling her up the gangway. He sat her down at the base of the forecastle mast. "You stay here. Do not even think about wandering from this spot. This port, these men, this ship, are all dangerous." He flung his arms wide, encompassing the entire panorama of the port. "A young girl like you would be fodder for their appetites." Not trusting her to stay where he put her, he summoned one of the crew and ordered him to stand guard over the girl.

"Abdul, make sure this girl does not stray. Do not let any of the crew near her." he ordered.

"I won't stray." Esperanza raised her voice above the ship's clamor. "I understand and I will do as you say."

Ibrahim ignored her. He locked eyes with Abdul and poked his chest with one gnarled finger. "Do you understand?"

Abdul took one look at the girl unceremoniously dumped at his feet, gritted his teeth, and growled under his breath. The lines and scars chiseled into his bronzed skin revealed a long, hard life at sea. He huffed as he crossed his arms over his ample girth, not sparing a second look at the girl sprawled on deck. Clearly, this assignment was an affront to his dignity. He was an honorable man, a devout servant of Allah. His wide experience and worldliness made him adept at dealing with all types of people, from the sly Algerians to the snake-eyed deceivers of Tunis. He thought he was irreplaceable. After all, had he not roamed the seas as far east as Constantinople, dealt with pirates and wild storms? He should not be reduced to coddling a useless waif. He grumbled but could not refuse if he wanted to get back into the good graces of the boatswain. He knew why he was demeaned in this manner. He was being punished for his haughtiness when he complained about standing the late-night watch while at anchor. The boatswain, Antonio, brooked no defiance from his men. Abdul was lucky he had not been flogged. Shipboard justice was swift, decisive, and often brutal, so he swallowed his pride and nodded his assent.

Esperanza tried to calm herself with slow, deep inhalations, prolonging each one, hoping her anxiety would be expelled with her breath. She settled herself as comfortably as she could, with her back pressed to the mast. The pungent smell of oakum permeated the air as she gazed at the huge timber pole looming above her on the raised foredeck. Amidships another huge mast reached skyward. Affixed to its highest point flew the Neapolitan pennant, a field of gold fleur-de-lis on a sapphire ground. It signaled to other ships that they were sailing under the well-respected auspices of the city of Napoli.

A long beam hung at an acute angle from the mast. On it a triangular canvas sail hung furled, ready to be released to catch breezes that would push them across pirate-infested waters. A complex system of ropes and pulleys tugged at their lashings, ready to raise, lower or pivot the great sails.

Esperanza struggled to make sense of the commotion of crewmen swarming the deck around her. The hubbub of noise and activity appeared chaotic, but after watching for a time, a pattern emerged. She realized that each man was focused on a single task. An imposing ginger-haired fellow checked every sail, rope, and knot, shouting orders to a lithe barefooted young man who scrambled spider-like over the rigging. A statuesque man with a completely bald pate and the intense gaze of a cat on the hunt checked each barrel and crate against his manifest - an incomprehensible jumble of letters and numbers pressed into a beeswax tablet. His brows furrowed in concentration, as he scrutinized every cask, trunk, and bundle, making sure they were securely bound or nailed shut, then ordered them into the hold below.

Burly stevedores laden with heavy barrels, clay jugs, and unwieldy bales of wool trundled up the gangway. The heaviest items would be stowed amid ships in the lowest level, where they would act as ballast. The ship creaked and groaned as its hull sank deeper into the water until the waterline reached within a few arms' lengths of the railings.

During the weeks Ibrahim had been away from the ship, skilled divers had been at work scraping barnacles from below the waterline while swabbies scoured the brine from the decks. The smell of oakum, a preparation of tarred fiber used to seal every seam and sail, permeated the ship.

Ibrahim summoned the men who were overseeing the ship's operations and introduced them to Ariel. Esperanza strained to hear their conversation. She need not have worried; captain Ibrahim's booming voice carried in the salt air. The ship's boatswain, Antonio, the imposing bald man Esperanza had already noticed, had been in charge during the captain's absence and was called to account for the overall readiness of the ship, its supplies, rigging, and sails. The ginger-haired hulk was Aiden, the ship's carpenter, a Scot from the wild highlands in the northland of Britannia. He reported on the repairs made in the captain's absence, and the general seaworthiness of the ship.

When Ibrahim was satisfied the *Sultana* was seaworthy and prepared for her voyage, he interrogated the sailing master, Ibn Shadhan Aban, a majestic third generation Arab navigator, as dignified as his regal-sounding name would suggest.

"What is the forecast? Will we have fair winds for our voyage to Napoli?"

Aban flung back a corner of his bisht, a long cloak made from fine, light linen, trimmed with gold thread, revealing a mysterious instrument - a square board with holes in the side a small stake directly in its center. He held it horizontally and proceeded to closely examine the shadows cast by the central stake.

"With this instrument I can discern our direction of travel and keep the ship on course. I have also checked the sea currents, the winds, the color of the skies at dawn and dusk, the flights of birds, and the astrological charts. We are leaving very late in the season.

There will likely be storms. May Allah shelter us."

"And what do you suggest we do? Wait in port until spring? The lateness of the season cannot be helped. I have responsibilities to my investors." Ibrahim barked at the dignified man.

Aban bowed his head and stepped backward distancing himself from the irascible captain. "As you wish, Captain." With that, he returned to his post.

Ibrahim returned to managing the preparations. He seemed to be everywhere, circulating among the men shouting instructions. Ariel scuttled along beside him.

Esperanza watched as her trunk, embellished with the finest hand-tooled Valencian leather, was toted up the gangway.

Master Cohen's words when he had presented it to her as a farewell gift echoed in her memory. "I will miss you, Esperanza, I have grown fond of you." Master Cohen had said.

"Thank you. You have been more than generous to me, allowing me to share life within your family, a life I would never have known were it not for you. I will write to you as often I can and tell you of my progress in school. You will be proud of me."

"I know you will make the best of it, whatever your future brings. Life can be unpredictable." It sounded to Esperanza more like a warning than encouragement. She sensed a touch of guilt or apology in the way he avoided looking directly at her.

Esperanza had packed her personal belongings in the trunk - a tunic embroidered at the neck with delicate purple and blue flax flowers, the one she had worn the night she and Rebecca had dressed as twins, as well as her every-day, undyed linen smock, with its simple green scapular. Now that she was of marriageable age, she would need to cover her hair. She brought a wimple, coif, and veil indicating that she was, if not a high-born lady, at least a girl from a respectable family. Lastly, she packed a cowled cape sturdy enough to withstand wind, rain, and cold, and a woolen blanket to sleep upon.

The trunk had smelled of the herbs she sprinkled on the clothes to deter tiny worms that hatched into hungry moths. She had painstakingly considered which herbs she should bring from the apothecary. It had been a difficult choice, not knowing which herbs and oils she would find in Salerno. Would there be hills to climb, open fields to scour for herbs and seeds? The items she brought would need to fit into small containers, last long enough to not deteriorate during a long voyage and be useful aboard a ship. Seeds, roots, and dried herbs seemed the best choices. She settled on licorice root for cough, ginger for sea sickness, sweet-smelling herbs - rose, lavender, sage - for headache, bee balm to counter feverishness. She chose flaxseed oil tightly sealed in glass vials, and seeds with many uses - clove, fennel, rosemary, oregano, dried rosehips, and aromatic dill. After she had carefully packed them in her trunk, there was barely enough room for her clothing, but she hated to leave any of her precious stock behind.

She inhaled the dill scent deeply. It would always remind her of Gabriela's soup. She would bring the entire apothecary if she could, but eventually she ran out of room. As an afterthought, she brought a special salve she had concocted from beeswax, infused with oils of lavender, yarrow, and chamomile. Sitting where she was, backed up to the main mast, she watched as her precious trunk was hauled below deck.

The frantic bustle of loading eventually calmed, and Esperanza caught sight of an elegant passenger boarding the ship with a confident stride. She was in her middle years, no longer young, but still tall and erect. A red woolen cloak lined with golden fox fur shrouded her. Beneath the cloak, Esperanza glimpsed a sumptuous, high-waisted dress made of precious damask decorated with gold embroidery. The woman traveled alone, something Esperanza was told women never did. She supposed the woman must be very important. As soon as Ibrahim saw her emerging from her elegant palanquin, he hustled down the gangway to meet her. He bowed slightly and offered her his arm. She boarded gracefully, her hand resting on his outstretched arm, concentrating on each step as she boarded the ship.

Esperanza's anger at her own ill treatment drained into the tarred deck boards, and curiosity replaced irritation as she watched this dignified woman. Who was she? Where was she bound? Why did she travel on a humble merchant ship? Her speculations ended abruptly when Ariel returned.

"I see you've stayed where Ibrahim put you."

"He treated me like a child." She protested; chin held high.

"No, you misunderstood. He treated you as would a busy man who did not have the time to worry about the welfare of an errant girl."

"Errant girl!?"

"Women are not welcome on ships. The sailors are superstitious and consider the presence of a woman bad luck. In that sense you erred simply by being aboard."

"I see. I erred in being born a woman." She flung his words back at him like a dirty rag. "I am not the only woman, and she is not enduring the humiliating treatment I am receiving." She pointed her chin toward the refined lady. "So, Ibrahim must be open to making exceptions."

"Ah yes. You must have noticed the Contessa Amelina Russo. She is from Neapolitan nobility, bound for her estates in Italia. She is a special exception. Ibrahim is indebted to her family for its financial support in the same way he is indebted to my father."

"If he is indebted to Master Cohen, then why am I suffering such rude treatment?"

Ariel looked at her, puzzled by the question. "But you are not part of my father's family, and you are not related to me."

Esperanza was shocked into silence. Her heart turned to stone. She was not and never was a part of the Cohen family. *I was nobody to them, only a companion to Rebecca, nothing more. They educated me only because Rebecca was happier having a friend. I wrongly assumed they accepted me as one of them. Only in my imagination was I part of their clan.*

"Don't look so shocked," Ariel blithely dismissed her feelings. "I am here to learn Ibrahim's business. There is so much more to know. His financing and trading networks are like a fisherman's nets, and he casts them wide to ensnare as many connections as he can. He is a shrewd man."

"Well, I hope he will treat me better than he did today, despite my insignificance."

"You would do well to not draw attention to yourself." Ariel's words grated like sandpaper. "Stay out of his way. He seems to have conflicting thoughts about your presence."

"Well, he need not worry. I am here now. He is merely transporting me to the college in Salerno. Do I need to earn my passage in some way?"

"I am not saying that. Just stay out of his way."

The puzzling conversation left Esperanza with a sour feeling in the pit of her stomach. Again, she sensed that something was off. What did it mean that Ibrahim had 'conflicting thoughts?'

Ariel hurried away to re-join Ibrahim. Esperanza's eyes trailed him as he made his way to Contessa Russo boarding the ship. She pushed her cowl back to lie against the rich, red woolen cloak. Ariel swiveled his head toward Esperanza and gestured casually in her direction. Esperanza's eyes met the Contessa's for the briefest moment as they silently acknowledged each other's presence.

Esperanza was suddenly acutely aware of her appearance. She hadn't bathed or washed her hair in many weeks. Her mousy brown hair, always thick and unmanageable, was now springing out from under her veil as if trying to escape her head. She must be a sorry sight. The dust and grime of travel covered her well-worn linen tunic, and it was nearly impossible to perceive that her scapular was once a delicate pale blue. She put her embarrassment aside. She couldn't help her appearance after having endured a weeks-long trek over rugged terrain. She dismissed her vanity and sat up straighter.

After leading the lady up the gangway, Ibrahim cupped her elbow in his palm and guided her to a short ladder that led to a door below the quarterdeck. Ariel left Ibrahim's side and returned to Esperanza. Gripping her wrist, he pulled her toward a ladder protruding from the hatch.

"The ladder leads to a deck between the main deck and the

hold. This is where the sleeping quarters are."

Esperanza did not resist; she gingerly climbed down the ladder to the deck below. Darkness enveloped her. As her eyes adjusted, she saw pallets scattered among coiled ropes, barrels of ale, and oakum. Untidy swaths of straw spread over the floor like flour in a baker's kitchen. The place smelled rank - a fusty stew of musk, unwashed men, and damp straw bedding in a state of imminent decay.

"This is where you will sleep during the voyage." He gestured toward a litter of fresh rushes loosely mounded on the floor next to a mildewed woolen blanket.

"I know it doesn't look like much, but I will hang a canvas around your pallet to give you some privacy." Esperanza remained stoic, trying not to let her face betray her acute dismay. She was, after all, on her way to fulfilling her dream, and she did not want to whine or seem ungrateful. A drape around her pile of rushes would do little to separate her from sounds and smells of the crewmen, but at least it would shield her from prying eyes.

"Thank you, Ariel. Could I ask one favor? Would you bring my trunk up from the hold? I will need some of my things." She paused, looking around the room. "Where will you sleep?"

"I will sleep on the floor too. But at the foot of the captain's bed. His cabin is tucked beneath the quarterdeck."

"And the lady? Where will she sleep? Surely she will not sleep on a bed of rushes."

"There is one more sleeping compartment next to the captain's. It is much like his quarter, though a little smaller. It is cramped, but there is a small writing desk, a raised bedframe with feather-filled pallet, a basin and ewer, and a candlestick. She will be comfortable there. I need to return to my duties now." He turned and hurried back up the ladder to the main deck.

Esperanza followed him to the upper deck and took her place against the mast. Abdul was gone. She settled, more comfortable now, and took a long look around. The smells of pine tar, decomposing waste pumped from bilges, and the harbor's stagnant, mucky bottom blended into an unhealthy miasma. The ship rocked gently at its mooring. As the gangplank was hauled up, Contessa emerged from her compartment below and stood leaning into the rail, head thrown back, eyes closed, elbows locked to steady her.

What is she was thinking about? Why is she here? What kind of a life is she returning to?" Esperanza could not pry her eyes away from Contessa Russo. Overcome with curiosity, Esperanza descended the short ladder from the quarter deck to the main deck. She sidled up to the rail not daring to approach too closely. She was dirty, disheveled, and probably smelled almost as bad as the fetid air. That suspicion was confirmed when the lady sniffed, took a quick look at Esperanza, and stepped sideways.

"You are the only other woman on board, my lady. I was overcome with the need to talk to another woman. I apologize for startling you," Esperanza began.

"Who are you?" The Contessa spoke into air, not turning her head toward the shabby, ill-smelling girl intruding on her privacy.

"I am Esperanza. Most recently I lived with Aaron Cohen's family in Burgos. He is the father of Ariel, the captain's assistant. I am going to Salerno to study at the medical school there."

The lady slowly turned and looked straight at her, eyebrows raised, lips pursed with skepticism. "You are going to study at the famous school in Salerno? Is this true?" The Contessa inspected her, from her battered leather shoes, like those worn by peasant women in the fields, to her rumpled, stained clothing, to her untamed hair peeking out from her under her veil. The girl's claim was obviously beyond reason.

Esperanza looked down, her shoulders slumping, momentarily embarrassed by the weight of the lady's obvious disdain. In the next moment she recovered her dignity, stood erect and addressed the lady frankly.

"I know I must be a sight to behold!" She couldn't suppress a chuckle. "I've had a long journey. I walked with the captain's company all the way from Burgos to Barcelona."

"Well, you must have quite a story to tell." Contessa's face relaxed into bemused perplexity.

"And I suspect you also have had a fascinating life," Esperanza replied. "I hope in time we will share our stories."

Contessa turned away tilting her head back to scan the cobalt sky. "We shall see."

Esperanza sensed she had been dismissed. But she did not leave the rail.

"Ah, here you are." Ibrahim found them. "I see you have made the acquaintance of Esperanza." He threw her a pitchfork-sharp look. "It's time to return to your quarters, my lady. We are about to embark. It can be a complicated maneuver for a big ship like the *Sultana* to exit a busy harbor under sail with only the side rudders to steer us." Again, he cupped her elbow in his palm and guided her down the ladder to her quarters. With a backward glance over his shoulder, he ordered Esperanza below.

"You too, Esperanza. Return to your sleeping quarters right now. And this time don't come back topside unless you are told to do so."

Esperanza descended the ladder to the lower deck, sat on her pallet and leaned against her trunk. Waves of conflicting emotions broke over her - confusion, excitement, humiliation, anticipation. This was not what she expected.

In the darkness of her sleeping quarters, she felt the ship move, rocking, tipping sideways, righting itself, then picking up speed. She could hardly contain the urge to rush back up to the open deck, but she dared not do so. She was content knowing she was on her way.

9

THE REVEAL

LATE SUMMER 1264

After the frenetic activity of loading the ship and maneuvering out of the busy harbor, the sailing was uneventful. The sailors no longer shouted instructions and commands as each man settled into his well-practiced routine. Despite Ibrahim's warning, Esperanza once again ventured back to the open deck. A gentle wind billowed the sails and cleansed the air of the fetid odors of unwashed men and old hay. The water danced as sunlight caught the top of each tiny wavelet making it sparkle as if it was sprinkled with fireflies. Esperanza grew accustomed to the rhythm of the ship. She practiced walking as the crewmen did - knees bent, feet wide apart to keep from tipping over or needing to grip the rail. She imagined she looked like a barrel with legs with her strange gait, but at least she wouldn't be pitched into the sea. They sailed east until the land sank below the horizon, and the world transformed into a limitless expanse of blue water mirroring the azure sky.

A flurry of activity caught Esperanza's attention as a great flock of gray-backed, white-bellied birds swooped low over the water on elegant long wings. With the delicate choreography of palace dancers, they splashed into the water then quickly lifted off again grasping small fishes in their talons. High above, she recognized the silhouette of a bustard buoyed aloft by air currents rising from the warming waters. With a renewed sense of wonder, she tracked the sun across the unobstructed dome of sky from one horizon to the other.

As the sun kissed the soft pink horizon that first evening, Esperanza once again stood wordlessly at the rail next to Contessa Russo. Their vessel seemed to shrink to the size of a pinecone in a mountain forest, minuscule under an immense sky upon a borderless sea. The night watchmen took their posts, lanterns swaying, ready to pass an uneventful evening spinning yarns about their adventures. They tried to outdo each other, concocting tales that grew ever more dangerous and suspenseful until every man became the hero of his own epic adventure.

The sky deepened to purple, then ebony, and uncountable stars blinked down at them as the wind picked up and turned colder. Esperanza reluctantly left the open deck and climbed down to the sleeping quarters. She drew Ariel's canvas curtain around her. Though it provided a visual barrier, it did nothing to mask the sounds of snoring, grunting men so close to her that she could hear the straw in their pallets crackle. She rummaged through her trunk, found her blanket, and wrapped herself up like a moth in a cocoon. To soothe her disquiet, she conjured scenes of past happiness and security. In her imagination she was once again sitting between Gabriela and Amika before the open fireplace sipping soup, enveloped by its rich aroma. The reverie sent a spear of nostalgia shooting through her, so painful she had to squeeze her eyes shut to hold back tears. Only one day had passed since they set sail, but it seemed a whole world lay between herself and her homeland. She clung to her memories; it was a balm to assuage the anxiety of facing a future as hazy as a fog-filled valley.

Next morning the sun broke over a red-tinged horizon, a harbinger of rough weather for superstitious sailors. The undersides of clouds bulged like softly rounded pillows marching in rows across a steely sky. Overnight the temperature had dropped, the wind picked up, and rain threatened. The bow of the ship rose and fell forcefully as it faced the waves head on, no longer rocking gently, but pounding up and down like a butter churn. The triangular sails, bellied out by the wind, pulled the ship along faster than seemed possible, focusing the crew's attention more fervently on their tasks. All that day, the wind and waves neither abated nor intensified but continued to demand the sailors' concentration.

On the second day after departure, though Esperanza was growing accustomed to being out of sight of land, the weather never settled down enough to abate her anxiety. Mares' tails, whipped by brisk winds into feathery filaments, grew into bulging cumulus clouds scudding across the skies. Salmon sunrises gave way to angry, crimson sunsets both signs of angry seas ahead.

Despite the wind and chill, each day Contessa took up her position at the rail resolutely facing the unsettled weather, and each day Esperanza joined her, keeping a respectful distance. Slowly short exchanges between them grew into tentative conversations. Contessa's knowledge of the Middle Sea was impressive. Esperanza absorbed each fascinating detail Contessa Russo shared.

"The Romans called it 'Our Sea' while the Turks called it the White Sea, and to the Jews it was the Great Sea," she explained, never looking at Esperanza as she watched the waves.

It was evident that the elegant older lady was well-educated and wise. She maintained an aura of mystery, not unfriendly, but aloof. The strength, composure, and the self-assurance she exuded comforted Esperanza.

After ten days of watching squalls race across rolling seas, rugged white cliffs reared up out of the turquoise water. The waves plunged and surged from every direction, lashing out at chaotic rock escarpments.

"What is this place called?" Esperanza asked.

"The ancient inhabitants of the island called it the 'Meeting Point of the Winds.' But now it is known as Majorca. The cliffs are made of limestone," the Contessa explained. "Quite impressive, aren't they?"

"Limestone?" Esperanza wondered aloud.

"Yes, the stone is porous, water can seep through its many gaps. Sometimes the water melts the stones and miraculous caverns form with long tapered spears of slick rocks growing both down from the roof and up from the cave's floor."

"Have you have seen this miracle?" The girl stared at the cliffs in wide-eyed wonder.

Contessa Russo paused, to look at Esperanza. She stood rapt, trying to imagine stones melting beneath the earth. Her face glowed with an incandescent wonder, childlike and eager. *What a tangled mass of contrary natures she has!* Contessa thought. *She is defiant and bold, but she knows almost nothing of the world. She is innocent, even naïve, yet she is intelligent and eager for knowledge. She is as vulnerable as a baby chick, yet she is unafraid; she will need protection.*

"The ship will pause for a short stop at Majorca and then we'll sail onward to the island of Palma. It has better harborage and a busy market where the captain and your brother can trade the freight, they brought from Iberia for goods that will be sought after at the next stop. By knowing what goods are valued at each port along the way, they will increase their profit at every anchorage."

"Majorca is beautiful. Look at the white cliffs, turquoise water, lush vegetation. I can't wait to explore." Esperanza's eyes wandered over the island.

"No, dear girl, the captain will not let us disembark here nor at any of our other ports, until we reach our destination."

Esperanza's shoulders slumped, but within a few moments she had shaken off her disappointment and was again engrossed in the wondrous new sights.

That evening, the ship rounded a rocky cape and *Sultana's* seamen maneuvered the ship into the gentle waters of a sheltered aquamarine harbor. Under the supervision of Abdul, now back in the captain's good graces, the crew performed the entire operation of anchoring in the small harbor faultlessly. They nudged the ship into the bay as delicately as a dancer tip-toeing across a stage. Once in position, Antonio, the bald boatswain, took over, directing the deck hands to reef the sails and drop anchor. When it was securely tethered, the ship rocked like a baby's cradle.

This time Ariel allowed the two women to remain on deck, tucked out of the way alongside the hatch where they could observe the activity but would not be in the way. They stood side-by-side at the rail watching burly sailors unload trade goods destined for the market, returning with new barrels and bushels of cargo to replace them. When the stars began to peak out from behind the black veil of the sky, the Contessa retired to her quarters. Esperanza remained on deck, listening to the ship's creaking voice and the now-familiar accents of the crew members until Ariel found her and ordered her below decks to her curtained pallet.

Esperanza tried to doze off, but her ears began to ring, and her eyelids tingled. She hadn't felt this sensation for months. She inhaled deeply then slowly exhaled. Someone near her was ill. The grating rasp of a persistent cough stood out from the snorting and hacking of the other men. Tomorrow she would try to find the ailing sailor and help him. Vague anxiety simmered below her calm facade like tiny bubbles erupting suddenly into a full boil. She spent a fitful night, never relaxing enough to descend into deep sleep.

The following morning as the night watch sailors returned below decks, retiring to the still-warm beds the day watch sailors had just abandoned, cook was already busy in his galley preparing the porridge as he did every day. Esperanza brought her cup to him early before the day shift crew made their way to the cook pot. Ariel sought her out sitting in her unobtrusive spot next to the hatch spooning the gruel into her mouth.

"There you are!" he hailed her. "Did you have a restful night? Have the men been leaving you alone?"

Esperanza lit up at the sight of Ariel. "I slept fitfully but was comfortable enough."

"Good." Ariel breezed past her remarks. "The ship will spend today and tonight at anchor so Ibrahim and I can trade our Rioja wine for cotton fabric. He tells me Majorcans produce marvelous textiles, painstakingly patterned on both sides and we hope to acquire some in the market along with Palma's distinctive blown glass. If we are lucky, we might find a few of the delicate embroidery pieces this island is known for. He tells me they are so perfectly crafted the individual stitches are almost too small to see. Ibrahim says these goods will bring high prices in Corsica or Napoli. Don't be surprised if I don't return tonight. Some of the crew and I have been granted shore leave." He grinned. He didn't mention that they also hoped to find the willing young ladies that frequented busy ports.

"Can I come too?"

Ariel guffawed. "No, I'm sure Ibrahim will confine you to the ship. It's not safe for an innocent girl like you to walk the streets without a guardian."

"Are you so devoid of innocence that you can wander at will?" Esperanza tossed her words at him indignantly.

"Remember," he smirked. "I spent four years in Toledo without parental supervision." A sly grin lifted one corner of his mouth. "We had curfews and chaperons of course, when we explored the town, but the chaperons were as intent on amusing themselves as we were." Ariel winked at her. "I am not an innocent boy. I will see you tomorrow. Have a peaceful day on the ship."

Esperanza resigned herself to another day on board watching, waiting, dreaming of all she would learn in Salerno. That day a stiff, salty breeze riffled the water into small white-capped waves that danced chaotically around the ship. Esperanza hunkered down in an out-of-the-way corner on the quarter deck watching the men, whose wheezing and snoring had grown familiar to her, go about unloading their wares for trade.

She recognized the raspy cough she heard the night before. It was the bald boatswain, Antonio. He was slim, swarthy with an erect posture and regal bearing. She surprised herself with the realization that she found him attractive. This was new emotional territory for her. She knew what it meant. These feelings came with the rest of the changes her body was undergoing. *I will not let myself be distracted by him or any other man. I have much more important work to do, and an attachment to any man would mean the end of my dreams. Life is long. Perhaps I will have time for a man later, but certainly not now.*

A violent coughing fit overtook him, rounding his shoulders as if he had been punched in the chest; he struggled to breathe. He could inhale only short, rasping gulps of air punctuated by uncontrolled hacking. After the spasm abated, he regained his prideful bearing, surreptitiously looking around to see if anyone had noticed his weakness.

Esperanza descended the ladder to the sleeping deck and dug through her trunk until she found some dried licorice root. She snipped off a small piece and ground it in the mortar she had tucked in her trunk at the last minute, then went to the cook and begged him to fill her cup with hot water. If she were in Master Cohen's apothecary in Burgos, she would have topped off the elixir with warm wine and a little honey, but for now, steeping it in hot water would have to suffice.

Esperanza waited until Antonio stopped for a short rest from his duties before she approached him proffering the cup in her outstretched hand. "Here, this will help relieve your cough."

He glared at her from beneath his brow and growled a guttural, vaguely hostile sound, but he took the cup and drank.

"I am Esperanza. I came from Burgos where I worked in the apothecary of Ariel's father, Aaron Cohen, a well-respected physician. I was his assistant."

"I hear you are on this ship being transported to Napoli."

"Yes, I am going from there to the school in Salerno to study medicine."

He harrumphed, "Interesting." She sensed that he had more to say but he simply drank his cup, handed it back to her, and turned back to his work.

The blustery sea air was bracing, as the lingering fog of her sleepless night dropped away. Once again Esperanza found herself drawn to Contessa Russo's side. The water's surface suddenly roiled as if Neptune had decided to stir it like soup. A long, smooth-skinned fish with a protruding nose leaped out of the water next to the boat. It arced gracefully through the air before plunging back into the sea, racing through the water a few inches below the surface, ruffling the water like a puppy wiggling beneath a blanket. Several more of these strange fishes joined the group. They streaked through the water accompanied by smaller copies of themselves. A subtle, enigmatic smile turned up at the corners of their snouts. They sped through the harbor, leaping and diving, like children at play until they suddenly left, and disappeared into the sea.

"God's mercy!" Esperanza yelped. "What are those creatures?"

"Those, young lady, are dolphins." Contessa could scarcely suppress a smile amused by the girl's utter astonishment. "They are like no other fish; you can see how playful they are. The swiftest, most exuberant creatures in the sea, they can leap high out of the water. Sometimes they gather in crowds and sing in pure, high-pitched staccato tones. Sailors consider them good luck."

Esperanza beamed and clapped her hands gleefully. "I can certainly believe that they sprinkle good luck like water fairies. I hope they will bring me good luck too."

Contessa took a long look at the girl. "How old are you, girl?"

"I think I have sixteen years."

"You don't know?"

"No, I was orphaned at an early age. Ariel's family took me in to be a companion to his sister, Rebecca. A year ago, Rebecca married and moved into her mother-in-law's home. I worked with Master Cohen in the apothecary, as I mentioned, but when Ariel and his brother returned to Burgos from their studies in Toledo, Ariel's brother, Benjamin, replaced me, so I had no role in the household. That is why Master Cohen is sending me to the school in Salerno."

"Interesting."

"That's the second time I have heard that response." Esperanza looked at her quizzically. "The boatswain had the same reaction. I almost feel like there is a secret everyone else knows but me."

Contessa made no response. Esperanza felt queasy, as if struck by sea sickness. She shook off her uneasiness and focused her attention on the Contessa.

"If I may ask, what brings you from Barcelona on a merchant vessel?"

Again, there was a long pause. Esperanza's large, sea-gray eyes fixed on the regal lady. The Contessa hesitated, appraising her as she pondered whether she should respond. The girl didn't look like the ragamuffin anymore, as she did when she first boarded the ship. Somehow, she had persuaded the cook to give her some hot water so she could bathe. Now she was properly dressed, befitting a young lady from a good family, but there was something wild about her. Just below the façade of respectable maidenhood, an internal force was boiling like the lava beneath the volcano's surface. She was drawn to the girl in a way she did not understand. It was not maternal affection, nor friendship, but a kind of unfamiliar tenderness. This girl had something special. She was certain of it. She was an enigma of contradictory qualities, seemingly as knowing as an ancient sage, but innocent and childlike as well. She was defiant and strong-willed, but vulnerable and fragile. Contessa's fondness was visceral. The girl attracted her as a lodestone attracts metal shavings. Despite her mixed feelings toward the girl, she knew she must keep her distance. It would not behoove her to develop an attachment.

"Dear girl, it is impudent of you to ask, but I am inclined to be indulgent today, so I will answer. I am returning to Napoli to inspect my estate. I have not been there for a long time, and I can't foresee what I will find. A bailiff has lived in the manor house for many years, overseeing the operation of the olive groves and lemon orchards and maintaining order in the surrounding hamlets owned by the estate. One can only guess what has changed in the years since I left."

Contessa Russo became quiet, and gazed intently into the water, letting her anticipation and anxiety drown in its inky depths. She would know soon enough what awaited her at her Neapolitan estate.

"I hope returning to your estates will be a happy homecoming, and you will find all your affairs in order." Esperanza touched her arm lightly. A warmth coursed through Esperanza's body. Contessa felt it too; she straightened abruptly, pulled her arm away, and resumed her aristocratic aloofness.

"I am going to retire to my cabin. Sleep well, child." Contessa Russo descended the short ladder to her cabin leaving Esperanza alone on the deck.

For a long time, Esperanza gazed into the dark waters as Contessa often did, searching for peace of mind. The sea offered her nothing but her shattered reflection. The sky faded into purple, then black, and the stars shimmered, reflecting off the water, until she could no longer distinguish sea from sky. She climbed down to her sleeping quarters, delaying the inevitable discomfort of sleeping among men as long as she could.

Esperanza again wrapped herself in her blanket, pulled the curtain closed around her, and mercifully drifted into a sound sleep. The snores and snorts of the sailors were fewer this night as many of the men were carousing on shore with Ariel. The noises that drifted through the dank air troubled her less than they had on previous nights. She no longer feared the men, knowing that to them, she was invisible, of no more importance than the rats that nibbled at their beds of hay.

In the small hours of the night, heavy footfalls awoke her. She listened closely as they grew louder and closer until her curtain scraped against its rope as it was ripped open. She sat bolt upright, clutching the edge of the blanket to her chin. Shock coursed through her body blinding her so completely that she didn't recognize the figure looming over her until he was upon her. His calloused hand pressed against her mouth and nose so she could hardly breathe.

"Don't make a sound or I'll throw you overboard." She recognized Ibrahim's voice, but it was strangely garbled and muddy, and his breath reeked of wine.

Instinctively, she kicked and writhed, reaching for his hair, dislodging his head cover. Free of its turban, his hair hung in grey, spidery hanks over his cheeks. He clenched both of her wrists with one hand, and pinned them to the floor over her head, then pressed a strong forearm against her neck hard enough, that, with only a little more pressure he could easily choke her.

"I am here to help you." His words rumbled from deep in his throat, as garbled as far off thunder. "I am going to show you what you can expect on your wedding night. Your new husband is an old man, used to the ministrations of women. He will appreciate a wife who understands how to please him."

Outrage and disgust overwhelmed her. She fought back, struggling and kicking with all her strength. He released the arm pressed against her neck but continued pinning her hands to the ground. With his free hand he clutched her shift, pushing it up. For a mere second or two, he shifted his weight as he adjusted his position. In the tussle, the hand that fumbled for his clothes slipped just enough for her to bite it. She bit hard until the metallic taste of blood oozed onto her tongue.

"Damn you, you little bitch!" He howled as he shook his injured hand.

Just enough space opened between them for her to jerk her knee upward into his groin. He curled onto his side, immobilized by pain, blood dripping from his hand. The sliver of time before he lunged at her again was just long enough for her to spring to her feet and race up the ladder.

"Wake up! Let me in!" Esperanza pounded frantically against Contessa's door. The girl's shrill, hysterical voice alarmed the lady. In two steps she reached the door and flung it open. She grabbed Esperanza's arm and yanked her inside, slammed, and barred the door.

"What has happened to you?" Esperanza wore only the linen shift she slept in. She was a disheveled mess; her hair sprang wildly from her head; red abrasions scored her arms, neck, and wrists. Blood smeared across her mouth. Her wide eyes brimmed with tears.

"Can I stay with you? It's not safe for me down there."

"Esperanza, what happened? Who did this to you?"

"Captain Ibrahim attacked me. He gave Ariel and some of the others shore leave, so the men who slept near me were gone. If anyone else overheard the commotion, they made no move to intervene."

"Of course, dear girl, you can stay here with me. I will bar the door from the inside. You will be safe."

"There's more!" Esperanza's voice became shrill. "He said he was going to show me how to do my wifely duty to my husband on my wedding night! What wedding? What husband? What does he mean?"

Contessa shook her head. "Sit here." She patted the edge of the bed next to her. "I have heard rumors. Some of the crewmen were chuckling about how you were suffering delusions, thinking you were being transported to Salerno to go to school. They all seemed to understand you had been sold to an older man, a widower, the captain's friend, and patron.

"But Master Cohen never told me!" She stopped abruptly. His words echoed in her brain. *"I know you will make the best of it, whatever your future brings. Life can be unpredictable."* The odd reactions of the crew calling her plans "interesting" made sense to her now.

"Did Ariel know?"

"I'm sure he must have known if the rest of the crew knew."

Esperanza's heart turned to ice, and a tempest raged in her stomach. She grew hot and sweaty, then cold and dizzy, as if the floor had just dropped out from under her. She reeled, fearing she would lose consciousness.

Contessa slid closer and wrapped an arm around the shaking girl.

"It will all be set straight. I will help you." She tried to comfort the girl.

Esperanza bolted to her feet. "How could they! They lied to me! Even Master Cohen and Ariel betrayed me. I can't even bear to think about them. It makes my stomach hurt. What will become of me now? What about Salerno?"

That thought broke her; and she sobbed uncontrollably. Her wails transformed into a low, keening howl like the unearthly scream of a fox, eerie enough to frighten the night itself. Contessa did not speak, just rocked her until, exhausted by shock, she fell asleep. The Contessa gently lowered her to the pillow, laid down behind her on the bed spooning her body against the girl's. The feral smells of fear and rotten rushes filled her nostrils, but she ignored them. She draped her arm across the sleeping girl and fell asleep.

The following morning, the captain and crew acted as if nothing had happened. Ariel and his mates returned to the ship with red eyes and aching heads as they took up their duties. The captain laughed and joked with his men about their previous night's adventures. The cook made porridge as usual, and the crew set about their appointed tasks, checking the rigging, sealing the cracks, and waterproofing the sails. The boatswain gave the command to lift anchor, unfurl the sails and they carefully maneuvered their way out of the harbor, heading to their next port of call.

Contessa Russo brought two cups to the cook to fill with porridge and returned to her cabin. Esperanza was sitting up in bed, the blanket rumpled in her lap.

"What will I do now?" Esperanza muttered. "I can't leave your quarters dressed like this." She looked down at her wrinkled, soiled shift. By now the men must have heard the gossip and I will be a target, easy to overpower. It won't be safe to sleep below deck."

"I will speak to Ibrahim," the Contessa murmured. He is usually a faithful Muslim and unaccustomed to drunkenness. He must have lost control last night. His conscience is no doubt needling him today."

Esperanza's eyes widened, indignation building in her like a wave gathering its strength before exploding on the shore. She swallowed hard, quelling her desire to lash out. After all, she could hardly castigate her rescuer. They ate in silence; then Esperanza fell back curling around the pillows and rocking back and forth. Long minutes ticked by before Contessa finally spoke.

"I grew up in a noble family on a manorial estate in the hills above Napoli. My father wanted the best for me, which meant finding a husband who would improve my family's standing among the powerful aristocracy. I was about your age when he married me off to a man in Barcelona twenty years my senior. My family was indebted to his, and though my father had high social standing, he owed money to my suitor. It was a debt he had no way of settling. I was the payment that balanced the scales. My husband was not a bad man, but even after twenty years of marriage I had not grown to love him. I did not bear him the son he desired, so he put me aside. We lived harmoniously enough, and I was relieved when he found respite with other women and left me in peace. None of them ever produced an heir. When my husband died, I was his sole inheritor."

Esperanza did not respond, but she stopped rocking and listened intently.

"I never knew married love as some women do." She waved her hand in front of her face as if shooing away a fly. "Such thoughts are foolish. I am a woman of nearly forty years now, too old to indulge in such frivolous nonsense. To be honest, I have come to believe very few women experience mutual love in marriage." She drew a weary breath as though the weight of her memories had grown too heavy to bear. "Now I am returning to Napoli to inspect my ancestral estates. I can't foresee what I will find. It has been so long."

Esperanza could no longer restrain herself. She sprang from the bed and howled. "Are you telling me I should accept my lot and suffer through a loveless marriage so I can inherit whatever wealth my husband has?"

"What else can you do?"

"You don't understand. I am a healer. Ever since my mother died, I have been able to sense people's maladies, sometimes even before they themselves realize their affliction. I spent my entire life learning about herbal medicines and treatments of all sorts. I have a gift, and valuable knowledge. Master Cohen blessed me with an excellent education; I am conversant in Latin, Greek, and Hebrew, even a smattering of Arabic. I have a purpose in life. I am not like you. I will be a physician."

Contessa Russo listened to the girl vent her rage. She was right, Esperanza was not like her. A firm, purposeful ambition filled her sails, and propelled her relentlessly toward her goal. The Contessa would hate to see a young woman like her weighed down by the chains of marriage like those that had restrained her own life. But, like it or not, Esperanza's fate was sealed. All Contessa Russo could do was help her endure the transition to married life.

10

THE PLAN

AUTUMN 1264

Contessa's quarters became both Esperanza's refuge and her prison. She escaped its confines only to scrounge food from the galley. Wafting ghostlike into the dank kitchen twice each day she presented her pewter cup to Aiden, the fiery Norseman, who served as both the ship's carpenter and cook. If anyone complained to the cook about the meager offerings - dried pork or fish, hard bread made with flour, water, and a pinch of salt, or a thin stew of fava beans – they were met with an icy blue-eyed glare and threats of short rations the following day. He dished up Esperanza's rations in silence, never so much as looking at her. As far as he was concerned, she had no business being on the ship, attracting the malevolence of Neptune and distracting the men. If she disappeared into the inky depths, he would be quite satisfied. She looked forward to the days when the hard-bitten cook made pea soup. Though not the thick, rich pasticcio Gabriela prepared, the smell was tempting.

Contessa Russo exercised her privileged position, abandoning Esperanza at mealtime to take her meals in the captain's quarters where they dined on epicurean delights compared to the repetitive diet of the crew. The first few days after leaving port, there was fresh food, and farther away from port they got, the more they ate dried or preserved foods. Ibrahim did not stint on his rare delicacies and was delighted to share them with the Contessa.

Often the first mate and the navigator joined the captain and Contessa Russo for meals of rich, aromatic semolina bread dipped in olive oil with garlic, tomato and cheese, or pastries stuffed with cabbage, chard, pine nuts and raisins. When the seas were calm and the navigator and first mate returned to their duties, the Contessa remained in the captain's cabin for hours, occasionally not returning to her room until after midnight.

Their routine changed when they reached the port cities along the route. At each harbor Ariel and captain Ibrahim disembarked to scour the markets for bargains on valuable trade goods. Their local agents, the dragomans, who were as diverse and colorful as the towns at which they moored, worked as independent agents facilitating complex transactions. Their livelihood depended on having an impeccable reputation for honest dealings among all parties. They negotiated contracts that benefited all parties and made sure local officials did not overcharge taxes and tariffs. Respected equally by Arab, Jewish, and Christian clients alike, they knew the special preferences of each group. Their Arab contacts traded in spices, including the very rare and extremely expensive "sweet salt" from Cyprus, called al-sukkar. A few grains on Ariel's tongue produced an effect so pleasurable that his eyes rolled back in bliss. Ibrahim cared little about the origins of these rarities, only their market values, though some of them came by circuitous routes from distant lands. Mysterious aromatic cinnamon sailed up through the Red Sea to Egypt, but no one seemed to be able to tell him where it originated. North Africa produced an abundance of valuable spices like ginger, pepper, nutmeg, clove, and turmeric. Besides adding flavor to food, many spices had other practical uses. Cinnamon for instance, was useful as a treatment for colds, coughing, and congestion. Thin strips of the bark, rolled into cylinders, could preserve meat, season food, and freshen the breath. Egyptians even used it to embalm the dead. More importantly to Ibrahim and Ariel, was the fact that it was worth more than gold, was easy to transport, and attracted the wealthiest clients. Spices like pepper, ginger, clove, and saffron, if they could be found, always turned a nice profit.

Ariel enjoyed the hunt for rare goods as much as a wolf enjoys stalking its prey. The excitement of the hunt, and the fine art of matching the goods with the right markets provided great satisfaction and solid profits. Many years of experience taught Ibrahim the subtle nuances of the trade and he had developed a reputation as a canny old fox who could not be fooled. There was profit in trading glass, hides, damask, and the works of local artisans. He made sure his treasures would not go to waste because of careless handling; every bin, bundle and crate was securely stored in the hold, its weight distributed to increase the ship's stability. He kept a large chest of his rarest and most valuable treasures locked in his own quarters. He relished boasting of his cache.

"Look at this," Ibrahim proudly displayed a rock crystal ewer from his treasure chest to the Contessa when she came to visit him. "See? It is hollowed out so thin and clear it reputedly wields magical powers. I will sell this to the Bishop of Napoli." He wrapped the translucent vessel in an exquisite silk scarf shot through with gold threads, and delicately replaced it back into the chest.

"And this!" He revealed a polished brass basin inscribed with Arabic characters. "This basin is used by priests for their ablutions." He held it up before her eyes so she could properly admire its craftsmanship. "I will tell the Bishop I found this exquisite bowl in Cadiz where it was sold to ransom a knight templar during the last crusade. The bishop will covet it as if it were a nail from the true cross."

"Is it true you found this in Cadiz?" Contessa ran a forefinger around the rim of the basin.

"Does it matter? He will believe the story and pay extra because it belonged to a crusader."

"You are truly a gifted trader." Contessa's compliment swelled his pride, and Ibrahim beamed. "I can see why my husband decided to become your patron." She lowered her chin and turned one shoulder toward him as coquettishly as an ingénue.

"Yes, your husband and I had a very profitable association for many years." He peered into her eyes, his eyelids seductively lowered to half-mast, his breath quickening. "He was lucky to have you as a wife, though it was a shame he didn't properly appreciate your charms." He took a long step forward. She took a small step back. She was navigating dangerous waters now, teetering on the narrow edge between allure and invitation.

She brought her fingers to his chest, touching him so lightly he barely felt it. "I'm sure you will need all your energy for your duties in the morning. I should retire to my quarters." She took another step back, then turned to leave. As she headed for the door, she turned her head and once more smiled at him over her shoulder.

In the following weeks, her evenings with the captain became routine as *Sultana* plied the waters between Majorca, Sardinia, and Sicily. Each island offered the captain its best trade goods - embroidery, pottery, blown glass in Majorca; Mitra liqueur, Cagnulari wine, and wheat in Sardinia; and sulfur, cinnabar and vermillion dye in Sicily. Ibrahim took pride in the quality of his goods, knowing he was amassing wealth unattainable for most men, especially those of humble origins like himself, the son of a humble bodega owners.

As the season progressed, the weather burned and the ship creaked and groaned as late-season storms buffeted it about like the ball in a game of pelota, just as the navigator warned him. Sailing master Aban, and first mate Antonio remained on the main deck for interminable hours each day charting a course over the restless waves to the next port. Deck hands worked through the nights sealing and re-sealing the cog's joints, mending tears in the sails, and repairing the rigging. For two grueling months the ship made its precarious way to Napoli. When they arrived at their destination, the captain and crew were spent and exhausted, but *Sultana* was intact. When they arrived in Napoli, the crew's celebration was fit for conquering heroes, as they surely were.

Those months were harrowing for Esperanza as well. She felt

unsafe, and was trapped in the Contessa's quarters, only able to venture out on deck at night when the Contessa kept Ibrahim occupied with her flirtations and flattery. The anxiety of the voyage vied with the uncertainty about her future, sapping her youthful confidence. Contessa's physical presence comforted her, but it did not shed light on what would happen when they reached Napoli. She gleaned from her conversations with the Contessa that the journey to Salerno would take another ten- or twelve-days hiking along the Amalfi coast on a path so narrow that two carts traveling in opposite directions could barely pass each other. After weeks of uncertainty, Esperanza broached the paramount question that hung in the air between herself and Contessa.

"We will arrive in Napoli soon, and no one has explained how I will make my way to Salerno. I will need an escort, a donkey to transport my chest, and letters of introduction to the Dons at the Schola Medica. I thought Ariel would do this, but he won't look at me now, much less speak to me. He is entirely focused on Ibrahim and the merchant trade. What will I do? This prospective marriage is simply not an option. I must have a plan to escape and reach Salerno."

Fond as she was of Esperanza, Contessa Russo grew weary of her single-minded fixation on medical school. "You might have noticed that I have been cultivating a relationship with the captain," she said. "Did you think I did this for my pleasure?" She turned her head to the side and mimicked spitting on the ground. "The man is a boor; crass, lacking culture, and with minimal education." She patted Esperanza's hand. "He is supposed to deliver you to your husband in Napoli." Esperanza gritted her teeth and held her breath.

"Never! I will not marry that man. I don't even know his name. All I know is that he is old and ill, and I am meant to nurse him and service his carnal needs. Never!" The heightened color of her anger spread from her cheeks to her neck and ears.

"Calm yourself, girl. I have devised a plan. I will talk the captain into allowing me to deliver you to your future husband myself. You will belong to him. Those are the terms of the agreement Ibrahim arranged between Aaron Cohen and Adolfo Marino. That is his name. At least I may be able to negotiate an early release from your servitude."

"What do you mean? You make it sound like I have been sold? I am a slave?!"

"No, it is not exactly slavery. It is called indentured servitude. If you can repay Signore Marino the price he paid for your service, he is required to give you your freedom."

"I will not agree to this! No one can make me do it." Esperanza flung herself against the door, flailing ineffectually, increasingly desperate as the realization her helplessness descended upon her like an anchor pulling her into an ocean of despair.

"Stop this instant!" The Contessa ordered. "Your tantrum is worthy of a two-year-old, not a young lady of sixteen. You are already past the age most men would prefer for a wife. Think this through. How would you survive alone in a strange land, not knowing the language, with no money, no connections, nothing but a few clothes in your chest?" Contessa Russo snaked an arm around the girl's shoulders. "It will be alright. Signore Marino is a wealthy man. You will live in his beautiful villa, enjoy food prepared by his talented chef, dress in silks from Byzantium, and velvets from Cairo. All you need to do is care for an old man. You are ideally suited to tending to the needs of an ailing man. This is the profession you chose for yourself, after all. Despite yourself, you may develop a fondness for him over time."

Pale and silent Esperanza fumed. She could not force herself to face Contessa. "You deceived and betrayed me like all the others."

"You are behaving like a spoiled child. Even your friend, Rebecca, had to leave her father's house and face an uncharted future under the governance of an unknown mother-in-law. Did you expect Master Cohen would support you forever? He has done the best he could. You should be grateful." Her voice was sharp and judgmental. She had exhausted her store of patience and sympathy for Esperanza. "Now stop this display. You are humiliating yourself."

That night, Contessa turned her back to Esperanza. She no longer draped her comforting arm across the girl's shoulder and warmed her with her body. Desperation and humiliation had finally silenced Esperanza's defiance. *Is she right? Am I allowing myself to be consumed by a self-centered rage? Should I be grateful, as she suggested? No, I may be childish, selfish, and ungrateful, but so be it. I will not give up my dream of becoming a true Master of Medicine. The path to my dream will reveal itself. I will be vigilant looking for an opportunity to free myself, but I will not give up.*

11

NAPOLI

AUTUMN 1264

The city shimmered in the late season sunshine. The desperate, cloying heat of summer had abated from a full boil to a subtle simmer. Ships and vessels of all sorts crowded the harbor, bobbing on the sun-drenched sea. Hulking cogs, like Ibrahim's ship, rested their flat bottoms on the harbor's soft seabed, their square sales furled tightly against their masts. Sweating men groaned under heavy loads as they descended the gangway. The sounds of shouting in many languages were like lyrics of a song in which the creaking boards of ships provided the bass notes, and seagulls shrieking above sang soprano. The triangular sails of dhows hung limp after their voyage from the Red Sea and eastern Arabia to Napoli's bustling port. Their cargoes of fruit, wines, and Asian spices, from as far away as the mysterious eastern empires, would soon be snatched up by aristocrats eager for exotic goods. Menacing galleys, used for war and piracy since the time of ancient Rome, lurked around the outer edges of the harbor. Their striking red sails and the banks of oars for one hundred rowers lay still. Dozens of fishing boats, some made from hollowed out logs, some cobbled together from driftwood recovered from shipwrecks, threaded their way among the great masted ships, expertly piloted by fishermen bringing nets full of longfin tuna, bream, mullet, and sea bass to the quayside fish market. Esperanza drank in the novel scene, storing it away in her mind along with the growing collection of wonders she'd gleaned from her journey since leaving Ponferrada.

Esperanza thought Barcelona had been a huge city when she first saw it, but Napoli dwarfed it in size. Thick walls ringed the entire city and an impenetrable fortress castle, sitting on a spit of land jutting into the harbor, loomed over the shore. Anyone seeking entry had to pass through well-guarded entry portals that pierced the city walls at regular intervals. Church steeples, three- and four-story tall buildings, and towering, square defensive towers tickled the sky. A congested, disorderly patchwork of attached dwellings crowded every available plot of land. Above the city two huge summits dominated the landscape.

"Those mountains," Contessa Russo explained, gesturing toward two peaks east of the city, "are the twin peaks of Mount Vesuvius. Vesuvius was an enormous volcano that decimated Pompeii and Herculaneum when it erupted hundreds of years ago. At that time, the volcano was a single peak. The Bay of Napoli came right up to the foot of the mountain. When it exploded, it spewed so much ash upon the land that the water is now ten miles from the mountain, and Vesuvius's enormous peak was split into the two much lower peaks you see today. Pompeii and Herculaneum are now buried in ash.

"I cannot imagine such an enormous calamity." The irascibility of the previous night's outburst gave way to the excitement of reaching their destination.

Esperanza's heart opened with relief and gratitude. "I'm sorry I behaved so badly last night. I understand that others are trying to do their best for me. I will not resist. But neither will I relinquish my dream."

Contessa made no response, but inwardly breathed a sigh of relief.

"Do you live here? Where is your home?" Despite their falling out, Esperanza was bursting with questions for Contessa Russo.

"Do you see those villas high up on the hills behind town? The one on the right is mine." She pointed to a moderately sized castle surrounded by thick parapets bristling with toothy battlements and a scattering of smaller buildings. "Those are olive groves." She waved a hand toward well-tended trees with thick trunks and silvery green leaves. Below them on the slopes grew more delicate trees with bright green leaves and their branches bent low with the weight of bulbous yellow fruit. "And those are our famous lemons." Pointing up the slope and to the right she said, "And *that* estate belongs to your future husband."

Esperanza flinched at the thought but followed her pointing finger to a villa whose orchards, fields, and adjoining village sprawled over the hillside. It was as large as a nobleman's palace. She could not imagine anyone living in such a place.

"That is Villa Marino." She watched Esperanza's expression change to stunned awe. "As I said, your Adolfo Marino is a very wealthy man."

Esperanza's stomach clenched and her heart beat faster, until she was distracted by the sight of the dockhands unloading her chest. "My trunk!" she yelped. "I need to . . ."

"Don't concern yourself. They have their orders, and know exactly where to send your belongings."

As they watched, strong-backed workers unloaded the abundant goods Ibrahim and Ariel amassed along the way. The two of them worked as a team; on board, Ariel directed the unloading operation, while on shore Ibrahim kept an eagle eye on the accumulating cargo, watching closely for anyone pilfering or "misplacing" the goods.

"There they are," Contessa Russo said as two horse-drawn carriages clattered up to the dock. "That one is yours." She tilted her head toward the larger one. It resembled the highly decorated palanquin the Conte's paramour had used years ago in Ponferrada, except this one had four large wheels and a team of four caparisoned horses rather than litter bearers.

Esperanza and Contessa Russo faced each other. Esperanza suddenly realized that she might not see Contessa again. Her heart skipped a beat. The security of having a maternal figure in her life evaporated and she realized she would once again be alone without anyone to guide her. Crippled by her confusion, she stood there wondering how to say goodbye. Contessa Russo leaned forward, placing her hands on Esperanza's thin shoulders, leaned in, and lightly planted a kiss on both cheeks. Her lips were warm and soft, and Esperanza regretted that she had not gotten to know the Contessa better, drowning as she was in self-pity.

"Thank you for . . . ." Esperanza floundered. "Thank you for, well, everything." She felt like the abandoned child she was - another brief encounter with someone who made her feel secure, torn away and replaced by deep apprehension and an unknown future.

Contessa smiled. "All will be well, dear girl. Your strength does not lie with me or any other person. You are the strongest young lady I have ever known. You will make your own way. Keep your heart open." She gently laid her palm against Esperanza's wildly beating heart. Esperanza stood motionless, as if glued to the cobblestones, as the Contessa turned to board her own carriage.

A hand on Esperanza's shoulder startled her back into reality. A robust man in a short, royal blue tunic and finely woven wool hose loomed over her. Around his neck hung a thick gold chain with gold fleur-de-lis pendant. The footman's firm hand gently steered her toward an ornate carriage. *This can't be happening,* she thought as it jerked forward, propelled by four strong horses.

Curiosity overcame anxiety as they climbed higher up the slopes of the sleeping volcano. Deep green olive groves gave way to aromatic lemon trees and fields of rye and barley. The peasant cottages, though simple, were not hovels, and many of their occupants paused, leaning on their hoes, to watch them pass by. They looked healthy, with ruddy complexions and leathery skin from laboring under the powerful Neapolitan sun.

She did not stop gaping at the scenery until they slowed to a halt at an imposing stone tower that marked the entrance to the small village adjoining the villa. A lone guard swung open a wrought iron gate and Esperanza's carriage rolled into the village.

Inside, a bustling town square, a church, and a scattering of shops, and residences huddled in the midday sun.

"Who lives in these buildings?" Esperanza craned her neck around trying to see everything at once.

The footman swiveled in his seat taking another look at the young woman. "It's just a simple village, mistress. There is a communal oven, a baker, a blacksmith, craftsmen's shops, a few laundresses, two or three bodegas, a church, and a convent. Those attached dwellings over there are for the field workers."

"Is the convent Benedictine or Franciscan?" Esperanza asked.

"The convent is called the Casa dell'Annunziata. The sisters are Benedictines, and they take in abandoned babies. If a mother cannot care for her child, she brings it to the Casa. There is a round turntable built into an opening the wall. The mothers place their babies on the circular platform, often in the dark of night to hide their shame. They rotate it until the baby is inside the building. The sister stationed on the inside of the wall welcomes the infant to the Casa where each one is lovingly cared for. They do not ask questions about who the mothers are.

They slowed as he guided the carriage through the crowded streets. "This is the village square. The well is the main gathering place. "There," he pointed to a modest two-story house with a red-tiled roof tucked up against the wall? "That is my home." He beamed proudly. "Because we are inside the wall our lives are relatively safe and pleasant. The crusaders who overran our town and created untold havoc are long since gone, but our walls will protect us if they return."

The carriage jostled its way over the cobblestones, through the village square, and down a narrow street to a stone tower, identical to the one through which they just passed, to the far side of town. As they rumbled along, townspeople called to the driver.

"Hey, Paolino! What are you delivering to the Signore today? Is she as beautiful as the last one?"

"Ciao, Paolino, your family will expect you at eight bells. Don't be late like you were the last time."

"Paolino, you devil," A saucy black-eyed beauty tossed her abundant wavy tresses over her shoulder as she cast him a provocative sidelong glance. "Later, si?"

Paolino didn't respond to any of them, just kept his eyes focused on the tower gate. Once outside the walls of the village Esperanza caught sight of the villa, perched on the volcano's flanks, a short distance above town on a well-traveled trail.

"And this," he said, gesturing to the elegant edifice, "is where you will live."

The Villa Marino glowed peachy in the late afternoon sun. Unlike Contessa Russo's walled compound, this building was not a defensive fortress. An elegant, open-air loggia with three tall arches topped a simpler first story gallery. Two square wings flanked the two-story loggia. The open-air loggia, positioned to catch cool evening breezes, hinted of warm, leisurely, afternoons lounging in the shade of frescoed arches. The first-floor loggia was a modest structure that served as an entry hall. The villa was elegant but not imposing. It seemed almost homey and welcoming.

A broad swathe of flowers, and decorative shrubs graced the formal gardens spread out before the villa. Orderly plots of various shapes and sizes created an artistic pattern of interconnected beds through which a maze of narrow gravel walkways meandered. The coachman set the brake, dismounted, placed a stool next to the carriage, opened the door, and offered Esperanza his hand. He accompanied her up a sweeping stairway to the front door and pulled the bell chord. A butler, another powerful-looking man, emerged and escorted Esperanza into the comfortable entry parlor furnished with embroidered chairs, each one flanked by a table. The steward briefly disappeared, but soon reappeared with a tray holding a glass of white wine and a few dates.

"The master of the house will be with you shortly." He said curtly and then turned and disappeared, leaving Esperanza alone. She felt like a pawn on a chess board, moved from place to place, waiting for the hand of the chess master to determine her fate. Her helplessness was suffocating and uncomfortable, like tight-fitting clothing, and made her stomach churn. Unable to sit passively, she rose from her chair and wandered around the reception room, inspecting everything from the carved legs of the side tables to the gilt frames of the gauzy, indistinct landscape paintings on the walls. She was just reaching out to examine a delicate crystal decanter when the door opened behind her. She jolted upright. The butler entered followed by a rotund man who, despite his luxurious attire, presented a somewhat slovenly appearance. His battered seaman's cap sat crookedly on his head, contrasting incongruently with the fur-bordered opulence of his purple woolen cloak and knitted silk hose. Before he had uttered a word, Esperanza's eyes tingled, and her ears buzzed. *This man is ill, very ill.*

She did not bow or curtsy, or even give him a nod of the head, just stared frankly into his blotchy face, her chin jutting defiantly. "I will not be enslaved," she declared. "Despite what you and Ibrahim have arranged, I have other plans. I was duped into coming here."

A chuckle emerged from deep within his barrel chest and he managed an indulgent smile. "Just as Ibrahim described you. Uncivilized, without manners, defiant, self-important." He looked her up and down, like a merchant inspecting the goods. "Let's take a step back and introduce ourselves properly."

"I am Adolfo Marino, mariner, trader, well-known and respected merchant." He bowed, slightly revealing a bright ruby ring. "You haven't sampled the delicious wine my groves have provided for you. You really must try it, a light, white - lacrime del vesuvio, 'the tears of Vesuvius.'" Adolfo shifted his gaze from the wine toward Esperanza. "And how would you introduce yourself to me?"

Taken aback by his gracious introduction, Esperanza blushed despite herself. "I apologize for my outburst. All I know is what Ibrahim and Contessa Russo have told me. They said you purchased me to be your wife." She took a deep breath, trying to slow her pounding heart and continued. "I am an orphan and a healer. In my early childhood, I was educated by the nuns at the monastery in Santiago de Compostella. Since then, I have been dedicated to perceiving people's maladies and relieving their suffering. Since I first heard of it, I have dreamed of studying at the Scola Medica in Salerno, to become a real doctor. My understanding was that they accepted women students." Again, she eyed him defiantly. "And I won't be deterred. That is what I will do."

Signore Marino regarded her more seriously. "Despite what you may have been told, I did not bring you here to be my slave or to ply your feminine wiles. I have known plenty of women, most of whom never aspired to anything beyond being paid for their services; being a doctor would have been beyond their comprehension." Signore Marino gestured toward the chair next to the wine tray. "If you'll excuse me, I must sit down." He lowered his corpulent frame into a small chair, breathing heavily. "You are here because of your learning and your reputation as a competent healer."

"But you paid for me. I was told I was indentured to you."

Again, the deep-chested chuckle. "Who do you suppose paid for your voyage? Yes, I brought you here intending that you would repay my generosity with your service, but that's far from indenturing or enslaving you."

"You mean I am free to go?"

"This is no way to start what I had hoped would be a mutually beneficial relationship." He clapped his hands, and an older woman dressed in a simple linen tunic and dark grey scapular entered the room. "Take this girl to her quarters. And make sure you scrub her well. She smells like a fishmonger rather than the scholar and the healer she purports to be. Feel free to scrub off some of her rough edges while you're at it." Then, turning back to Esperanza, "I will see you at dinner." He plodded away, shoulders drooping, clearly disappointed with their introduction.

"Follow me," the austere woman ordered Esperanza curtly. "I will burn these things. They are likely full of pests. I do not want them brought into this house." She marched off down the hallway expecting Esperanza to follow her. *This is nothing like the warm, friendly welcome I received when I first met the Cohens,* she thought.

"Disrobe." The bluntness of the statement shocked Esperanza. The hawk-nosed woman watched dispassionately as Esperanza stepped out of her clothes and into the bath. The water was pleasantly warm and fragrant, with lilies scattered on the water. Esperanza's discomfort at being watched dissolved the moment the woman's luffa sponge sluiced the fragrant warmth over her back. She closed her eyes and let go of the anxiety and fear that had plagued her since she left Ponferrada. She could not as easily dismiss the anger and defiance that still gripped her soul. *It might be a long battle, but I will leave this place. I know it. I will make my dream happen, one way or another. In the meantime, this bath is delightful.* She laid back and submerged her entire body.

"Get up. You are done." The woman interrupted her reverie. Though the towel the woman wrapped around her dripping body was soft, the woman was not.

"May I ask your name?" Esperanza asked.

"I am called Dolores." She did not volunteer any further information.

"Dolores, Lady of Sorrows," Esperanza mumbled. "I am pleased to meet you. I hope you will forgive my intrusion into your life. It was not my choice."

Dolores eyed her with suspicion. "You will be like all the others, used up and cast away within months." Everything about Dolores was angular, her pointed chin, her elbows protruding from under her thin, crepe-like skin, her shoulder blades cutting across her chest like a clothesline, and her sharp tongue.

Despite herself, Esperanza shivered, not from a chill, but from dread that this severe woman might be right. Had Adolfo lied to her like all the others? Did he intend to keep her here in some kind of bondage. If she meant to flee, she would need to plan her escape soon. She didn't even know in which direction to go, how far it was, or whether the faculty at the Scola Medica would accept her.

Her icy sense of resolve melted just a little, as the droplets rolled off her nose.

"These are your chambers," Dolores said, directing Esperanza into an adjoining bed chamber and its attached ante chamber. "These are the clothes you will wear for dinner," she said, pointing toward a simple but elegant silk dress laying across a large bed. "The last girl was about your size. It will do. I will come to get you when dinner is ready. If you need anything, pull this bell cord," she said touching a long velvet ribbon exiting through a circular opening in the wall to a bell in the hallway. Esperanza pulled it once to try it out, and a resonant peal sounded outside the door.

"Stop!" Dolores barked like an angry dog. "I am the only one here allowed to respond to the bell, and I am right here." She turned abruptly and left. Esperanza could hear her steps receding into the distance.

The Signore's warm welcome, followed by the cold, almost hostile treatment from Dolores baffled her. Relaxed from the bath, she collapsed on the bed, exhausted. It seemed like only moments had passed when Dolores knocked loudly on her door, then marched in.

"You're in bed?" she glowered at Esperanza. "I will return in a few minutes, and you'd better be dressed for dinner." She stalked off.

The blue silk dress was sumptuous. The scooped neckline, outlined in gold embroidery, exposed the white skin of her neck and upper chest, without dipping down far enough to reveal any cleavage. Gold lacing crisscrossed the bodice down to her waist. The long, flared sleeves had gold edging, as did the waistline. She ran her hands over the smooth, creamy fabric clinging to her body. Her hair, still slightly damp from the bath, coiled into loose ringlets cascading to her shoulders. The dress changed her perception of who she was. She was no longer a girl, but a young woman, with womanly curves, and the dress of a princess.

The next time Dolores banged on her door Esperanza was ready. She straightened, raised her chin, and marched out of the room, following Dolores to the dining room. *I will not be bought off for the price of a dress, no matter how elegant.*

Adolfo rose unsteadily from his chair at the head of the table as Esperanza entered. His expression did not change, though it was a struggle to suppress a gasp at her transformation. When she arrived this afternoon, he saw a graceless but comely girl. Now a vision of elegance filled his senses as the lavish silks swayed around her body, accentuating the form of a grown woman. He pulled out the chair to his right and beckoned her to sit.

"You look lovely. The dress suits you," he began.

Esperanza fixed her eyes on the table-setting in front of her and did not reply. As hard as she tried to ignore him, her eyes tingled, and her ears buzzed.

Dolores entered with a plate of walnuts, peaches and plums soaked in honey, silently placing the tray in front of them.

"Try these, my young guest, they are from my own orchards and beehives." He leaned toward her plate but his protruding belly pushing into the table's edge shortened his reach and he dropped a glistening peach onto the tablecloth. "I am sorry. I've grown clumsy in my old age."

Esperanza caught a metallic smell on his breath and a repellent body odor, quite incongruous in a well-groomed, prosperous gentleman. She wasn't sure what malady troubled him, but she was quite sure he suffered from a complex mix of ailments. *He is an old, lonely man and he is ill,* she thought. She did not know the nature of his problems but perhaps she could find out. Another drop slid off her icy heart.

Adolfo began the conversation. "My eyesight is failing. Over the course of my career, I have accumulated some important parchments and manuscripts. I would appreciate you reading them to me."

"Fine," she said not rewarding him with more words.

"Perhaps tomorrow, you will come to my library, and I can show you."

He proceeded to eat a prodigious helping of cabbage chowder

and creamed fish. Esperanza nibbled on the fine white bread indulgently spread with butter and washed it down with a swallow of Napoli's finest Fiano wine.

"I will ask Dolores to show you to the library tomorrow morning." He looked at her somberly. "I understand you resent me. But since you are here, you might try to behave in a more charitable manner." Signore Marino heaved himself up out of his chair and lumbered away without saying good evening.

Esperanza fought off a sense of shame. He was right. At least she could be civil. After he left, Esperanza devoured the honey-soaked fruit and nuts and ladled cabbage chowder into her bowl. They were delicious. She really should thank Dolores and send words of appreciation to the cook. Maybe she would do that tomorrow.

When she returned to her rooms, her trunk sat in a corner of her dressing area. Her heart sang. It was like being reunited with an old friend. Before she slipped into the muslin shift laid out for her to sleep in, she rifled through her store of medicinals, searching for something that might help Adolfo. *I brought these all the way from Burgos, surely there must be something here that will help him.* Tomorrow she would begin her work as a healer, even if it meant healing a man she was determined to detest.

12

THE PIRATE'S TALE

AUTUMN 1264

The bells chiming terce from the Church of Santa Maria below drifted up to the loggia where Esperanza stood. She had slept fitfully, besieged by a series of dreams - Amika and Gabriela setting up their table of herbs and medicines for weary pilgrims along the Camino de Santiago, Contessa's wave as she pulled away in her carriage, her mother's leprosy-riddled body lying in her lap. But the vision of Ibrahim's attack jerked her awake, bolting upright in her bed. After that, she lay awake until the sun rose.

She slipped into the dress Dolores had laid out for her, less sumptuous than the silk confection she had worn for dinner the night before, but still attractive in its simplicity. She then she made her way to the dining room. Adolfo did not appear, but Dolores laid a simple morning meal before her - watered wine, millet bread, and a pasta tossed with a creamy sauce of raw beaten eggs, accentuated with crisp bits of pork, and finished with a shower of grated aged Pecorino. By the time she had finished, Dolores reappeared.

"Follow me," she said, terse as ever.

Esperanza rose and followed her quick steps to Adolfo's quarters, where she found him sitting amid a scattering of manuscripts, scrolls, and old books with gold lettering flaking from their stiff spines. He looked pale, sitting uncomfortably in an overstuffed chair. Distracted by the books and manuscripts,

138

Esperanza hardly glanced in his direction until he beckoned her to sit in the chair next to him.

"I have accumulated these books over the years, but I cannot read them. Choose one," he said.

Esperanza was stunned. Master Cohen owned a small collection of medical books, but this was different. This collection was as varied as the weather in winter, containing a variety of writings like nothing she had ever seen before.

"Where did you get these?" she asked as she started to rifle through the collection, carefully running her fingers across weathered leather bindings and soft vellum scrolls as she read the titles. There were books and manuscripts from every tradition - from the Northern Isles to the Middle Kingdoms of Hindustan, spanning every age from the flowering of Grecian culture to current Salterian texts. There were books suitable for use as medical texts, describing simple herbals and elaborate mixtures, literary works, scientific treatises, a Latin translation of Rumi's Arabic poetry, and a four-part chronical of the history of the world, *Chronicum Mundi*, and an old parchment of Aristotle's *Metaphysics*. Then her eye fell on a book that made her heart jump to her throat - a translation of Galen's *On Diseases and Symptoms* translated by Gerard of Cremona.

"These are priceless," Esperanza gushed, lighting up with pleasure and curiosity. "Where did you get them?" she asked.

"I acquired them over my years as a merchant plying the Middle Sea." Many more words were aching to spill out, but he did not go on. He decided she did not need to know the details of how he acquired his collection.

"Did you trade for these over your years as a merchant? Were you born to the trade?"

"You might say that" he began. "My father was a pirate."

Esperanza flinched. "You mean you stole these?" She could not disguise her repulsion at the revelation.

"It's not so simple. My father started out as a pirate. He pulled me away from my blessed mother, God rest her soul, when I was six. I was as attached to her as any little boy alive. I cried for days. But my father did not want me to become a 'mama's boy,' who lacked the toughness and fearlessness of a man, so he made me join him aboard his ship. He shielded me from the worst of the sins common among the seamen but, nonetheless, I was confused and horrified by their crude language, sinful behavior, and careless disregard for life. When our ship, *Neptune's Daughter,* a mighty cog of 200 tons, pulled abreast a merchant ship, and threw the grappling hooks over the rails, my father turned into another man, a savage beast I did not recognize, slashing and stabbing any foe within reach. Naturally, I was horrified and cowered in the farthest corner I could find. During one of these battles my father was impaled on the sword of a sailor defending his ship.

"Without his protection, I soon learned the toughness he tried to teach me. I learned to fend for myself, pulling a well-honed dagger on any of the crew who threatened me, there were those among them who slavered like dogs at the possibility of ravishing a young boy. Any of them could easily have overpowered me, but they found my combative behavior amusing. Sailors are a superstitious lot and eventually I became a kind of talisman, a bringer of good luck, like a charm. They softened toward me, but they were far from kind.

"Everyone on a pirate ship has a job. No one has higher status than the others. Everyone on the ship worked, and the leader was chosen by the entire crew. If he lost the favor of his crew, he was simply set aside for a new leader. I became a sort of cabin boy, if you could call it that. I performed small tasks for anyone who asked. If I spoke up or dawdled, I got smacked. Over time, I found a place as the cook's helper, carrying buckets of food from the galley to the forecastle hauling precious potable water from the barrels in the hold, sharpening weapons, and doing whatever odd jobs were asked of me.

"As I grew, I learned every function involved in running a ship. I learned by doing, receiving a cuff to the side of the head, or a hard slap if I didn't perform them correctly. Violence is a compelling teacher, and I was a quick learner. As a youth, I was slim and fit, very unlike the man I have since become, and I began participating in the raids myself, thereby reaping my share of the spoils. Pirates practice a system of equality unheard of on a so-called legitimate trading vessel. I hoarded my booty in a locked trunk, not unlike the trunk you brought with you, but much larger. A pirate caught pilfering his mate's goods is subjected to pirate justice. Some do not survive the harsh lesson. I used my experience to maximize my booty's worth by trading my goods for more costly items. I was not above misleading merchants in the local markets by overstating the value of my goods, or generally taking advantage of dimwitted blockheads or inexperienced simpletons I met.

"While still a young man, I had accumulated enough booty to acquire my own ship, a sleek beauty, smaller but faster than *Neptune's Daughter*. I named her *Angelo Oscuro*. She was indeed my 'dark angel,' flying over the seas on her wide black sails. She was swift and maneuverable, able to descend on a victim like a diabolical archangel. I came to know the most lucrative trade routes. I learned from inebriated seamen and quayside gossips the reputations of sea captains – which were drunkards, which were brutal or cruel, which were inexperienced, and which were derided by their crews for making poor decisions that endangered them all. I learned the value of buying some besotted sailor his fill of 'al kohl' as the Arabs call it, a particularly strong drink distilled from fermented grains. It was a quick path to oblivion and sailors loved it.

"After many years, I tired of the rough life of a pirate captain, and the unsavory company of ill-begotten pirate sailors. It was time to become a legitimate trader. My years of experience on the other side of rectitude gave me a unique insight into the tricks of plying the waters as an honest merchantman. I learned from my Arab crew members the art of the abacus, and from the Iberians basic letters used to name trade goods, but I never properly learned how to read anything more difficult than a ship's manifest. I found a trustworthy Greek dragoman, fluent in Arabic, Persian, and Turkish, all the languages spoken along the trade routes from the

Ottoman empire to Europe. He skillfully bargained for the best prices at which to buy and sell our goods. I found Hebrew bankers and wealthy investors, like your Master Cohen, to sponsor my voyages in return for a portion of the profit.

"Wealth begets wealth, and despite raging storms, lost cargo, and ships run aground on deserted shores, I prospered. When I got too old to carry on, I used my profits to buy this villa and took up the peaceable life of an orchardist, raising crops of olives, lemons, and grapes.

"Perhaps because of my dependence on literate associates, or because I regretted not having received an education, I never traded the books and manuscripts that fell into my hands. To me, they were irreplaceable, and far too valuable to sell. Now, I am old and nearly blind. I only hope there is still time for me to benefit from these treasures." He gestured toward the haphazard assortment before him.

"That is why I assigned Ibrahim the task of finding me an educated helper. And here you are."

Esperanza pulled her hand away from the Roman scroll she was holding as if it bit her and peered into Adolfo's bloated face. Again, her eyes tingled, and her ears buzzed. Words to express her conflicted emotions stuck in her throat; her resentment dribbled away drop by drop, but she was not yet willing to forgive.

"Why should I believe your fantastic tale? Your henchman, Ibrahim, has done nothing but lie to me, kidnapping me, selling me to bondage, and robbing me of my dream of going to Salerno." She watched Adolfo's face crumble. He had hoped for sympathy, something he had experienced very little of in his life. As much as she wanted to cling to her resentment, she couldn't quell compassion for this sad old man. Softened by his story, her voice grew calmer, her defiance less sharp-edged.

"See these?" Adolfo touched the book of poetry. "These are the treasurers of an educated man, the man I'd always hoped to become someday," he said lifting his eyes to meet hers. "Did you expect to learn more from these works because they resided in the libraries of Salerno? Aren't their secrets and revelations worth as much to you here as there?"

"They are stolen." Esperanza squawked, more shrilly than she intended.

"I suppose they are, but their previous owners are likely dead and gone, and who knows if they acquired them any more honorably than I did. I couldn't return them even if I wanted to. If you intended to use your learning for healing, here I am before you. Look at me. I need healing too."

Esperanza calmed herself and studied his face. His brows were furrowed and heavy. His fleshy eye lids overhung his onyx eyes. Looking almost desperate, he pressed his lips firmly together creating a straight line across his puffy face.

Esperanza relented. "I will do what I can. I will study your collection. Many of these were written by the greatest scholars of their times. You are right, I would have given anything to study these works in Salerno. Will you give me unfettered access to your library?"

Alfonso nodded, almost as demurely as a matron before the parish priest. "Yes, certainly, and you may move them to your ante chamber if it is more convenient."

"I will study these and help you as best I can. I can sense that your health is deteriorating rapidly. I can feel it."

"You can feel it? You haven't even touched me."

"Since I was very young, I have been blessed with a certain intuition about people's illnesses."

Adolfo harrumphed. "I do not need a charlatan or a witch."

Esperanza immediately regretted her comment and tried her best to control her anger. "That's why I need to examine these works. They will show me the way."

Adolfo did not respond. Taking his silence for acquiescence, she said "All right then, I will begin right away. What do you hope to gain from these books?"

"Aside from the medical texts, there are other writings of literature, history, and poetry. Before I die, I would like to have a taste of the knowledge an educated man has. I want to die a cultivated man, not the ruin of an old thief." His Adam's apple bobbed, and he drew a deep breath. "And I would like you to heal me."

A hollow grew in the pit of her stomach. She was both humbled and exalted. No one had ever placed so much faith in her. Yes, she was dependent on him for food, clothing, and shelter, but he was also relying on her. Her instincts told her that his ailments were grievous, and her heart opened a little wider allowing a sliver of hope to creep in.

Day after day, Esperanza buried herself in the treasurers of literature at her disposal; and day after day Adolfo grew weaker, sadder, and more discouraged. So did she. With all these resources from the great healing traditions - Indian, Greek, Persian, Galenic - she was not producing a plan. As the days grew cooler, she began to worry she might not be able to help him. Had she lost her intuitive talents?

One day as she sank into an ornately embroidered armchair on the loggia, eyes closed. With the feeble rays of a dying autumn sun caressing her face, she made a decision. *I will go back to the basic herbal medicines I learned with Amika, roaming over the hills of Ponferrada, and from Master Cohen in Burgos. I will think this through. First, I must unravel his symptoms. The poor old man's ailments are baffling.*

She rose and went to him. She found him in his office, his head buried in his hands, ledgers and parchments scattered over an untidy oak desk. She knocked lightly on his door.

"Come in, dear girl." He sounded tired and dejected.

"I want to help you, but I need more information," she declared. "Tell me which ailments trouble you the most."

"You are nothing if not straight forward." He smiled indulgently. "Come sit next to me." He clasped her wrist and pulled her into the chair beside him. "My eyes trouble me the most. They burn, and my vision is blurred."

"Yes, I can see that. The whites are very red." Esperanza said.

"I live in fear of losing my vision."

"Do you feel pain or pressure in your eyes?"

"Yes, but more worrisome are the blurred vision and the halos I see around candles or bright objects."

"I will see what I can find to soothe them. Are there other symptoms that distress you?"

Alfonso pulled up his stockings revealing his legs from knees down. His legs looked like sausages, with ankles as fat as his calves.

"They hurt. I can barely walk. And look at these." Adolfo pulled off his shoes. Esperanza sucked in a great gulp of air and struggled to suppress a wave of nausea.

"And these?" Esperanza choked out the words lightly touching the vicious-looking open ulcers and dark purplish skin that ringed ankles.

"We called it jungle rot. We often slogged through water on deck, and our feet and legs were soaked much of the time. Most of us developed these pustules; they festered when we sailed in tropical areas. In those hot, humid climes we were also plagued by mosquitoes. The more mosquitoes we encountered the more the men suffered from the pestilential fumes of the swamps. Men with fevers, shaking, chills, muscle aches died all around me. We needed to replenish our ranks by 'recruiting' men from other trading vessels or snatching them from the squalid dockside neighborhoods."

Esperanza spoke up, trying not to sound horrified and accusatory. "So, you kidnapped sailors?" she asked.

"I did no worse than what was done to me. And I was only a child when I was taken." Adolfo bristled defensively.

"It's a wonder you reached the fullness of years you have. You are a survivor."

"Yes, I am a survivor, but my luck can't last forever, and I fear that the end is fast approaching. I have never followed any religious practice, but I know when I meet my maker I must account for my misdeeds." He looked directly into Esperanza's eyes, almost begging her to forgive his crimes. His expression held guilt, and remorse, but his strongest emotion was fear.

"I will do the best I can. I have a thorough knowledge of herbal remedies, but I have never encountered the exotic malaise you have described."

"I hope you will find answers in the books and manuscripts I have given you."

"Yes, I too hope to solve these mysterious illnesses. Beginning today, I will move the books to my quarters, as you suggested. I would be lying if I told you I could heal all your ailments. But I will study diligently to do so."

Esperanza buried herself in the task. Visions of Rabbi Beneviste, hunched over his podium at the School of Translators in Toledo, nose to nose with ancient works, inspired her to be diligent and tenacious. Esperanza picked up a small, square book with ornate gold characters. She had seen this graceful Arabic script previously. In this case, the Latin translation was written beside the Arabic. 'Rumi, Sufi Poet,' she read. *I will bring this to Adolfo tomorrow. If he wants to be an educated man, this will be a good place to start.*

The following morning, she tapped at his door; he called for her to enter. "I found this book of poetry. I thought this would be a good way to start your education."

She let the book fall open in her palm to a page with the translation of a short poem. She began to read aloud to Adolfo.

'O soul, if thou, too, wouldst be free,
Then love the Love that shuts thee in.
'Tis Love that twisteth every snare;
'Tis Love that snaps the bond of sin;
Love sounds the Music of the Spheres;
Love echoes through Earth's harshest din.

The world is God's pure mirror clear,
To eyes when free from clouds within.
With Love's own eyes the Mirror view,
And there see God to self akin.'

Rumi, Sufi Poet

"That was lovely,"
She whispered more to herself than to Adolfo.

"Yes, it was. I had no idea words could be woven so beautifully, like gold threads in an elegant cloak." Adolfo was genuinely appreciative. The palliative of poetry like this was exactly what he had hoped to find within these works, words to comfort and encourage him.

"I will study every day, then after the evening meal, I will read you more of this magical language called poetry. We will both get an education," Esperanza promised.

13

THE MIDNIGHT OIL

WINTER 1264

Esperanza's bedchamber and the collection of works now occupying her ante chamber marked the boundaries of her world at the Villa Marino. Apart from the occasional visit to the loggia, she was not allowed anywhere else in the villa nor on the grounds. There were workers present during the day - the kitchen maid, the incongruously brawny majordomo who dealt with anyone who knocked on the door, and the equally strapping gardeners and orchard workers; but they returned to their homes in the village after work each day. During the long evening hours, Dolores, who was both housekeeper and cook, Esperanza, and Adolfo were the only inhabitants of the enormous villa.

Restlessness, as irritating as a rash, prickled her flesh, inflaming her desire to leave her elegant jail. Without freedom to roam, she immersed herself in the task of healing Signore Adolfo, searching the literature of disparate medical traditions for cures. She layered her new knowledge atop what she had learned from Master Cohen's amalgam of Hebrew practices, and the bedrock of herbal healing she learned from Amika, who gleaned them from millennia of Wise Women of the ancient tradition.

She could look out over the fields and orchards down the Bay of Napoli, but she was as constrained as a prisoner chained to the cell walls; and Dolores, always aloof and curt, was her jailer.

Esperanza watched Dolores with growing interest as the weeks dragged by. She never deviated from her rigid schedule, did not vary the menu, never smiled, never complained, or talked much at all, as she attended to her duties. By the time winter arrived with cool, windy days and frequent saturating rains, she was desperate for conversation and the companionship of another woman. Perhaps she could replicate the warmth, affection, and security she enjoyed with Amika and Gabriela. Finally, she asked Dolores if she could join her in the evenings, when all the day's tasks were done, as she sat before the fireplace in the kitchen.

"Do as you wish," Dolores responded, avoiding eye contact or any semblance of hospitality. Esperanza no longer cared whether Dolores was hostile or friendly. She had her own conundrum to deal with. She needed to devise a new strategy to accomplish her tattered and bruised dream of reaching the Scola Medica in Salerno, a goal that was more difficult now that she didn't even have the freedom to walk the grounds.

"I'm curious, Dolores. Are the Signore, you, and I the only people living in this Villa?"

"Yes."

"But there must be others to manage the orchards, the horses, and the grounds, isn't that correct?"

"Yes, but they don't live in the villa. Do you ever get lonely?"

"No. I have no need of companionship."

"We have been sharing this home for several months, and I would like to know more about you. I was hoping perhaps we could become friends."

Esperanza knew it was highly improbable that Dolores would return the sentiment, but she thought this forthright approach would draw her out of her iron-clad shell. There was no point in beating around the bush with Dolores. Dolores drilled her with a long, searing stare. Esperanza felt like a butterfly pinned to a collector's display board, yet she held her gaze. Dolores was the first to look away.

"I'm sure you have no interest in the details of my existence." Her voice was expressionless and cold.

"You are wrong in that regard." Esperanza replied. "I find you fascinating. Nothing appears to tie you to this place or prevent you from leaving, yet you remain here."

"Hmph. You know nothing about me."

"Yes, that's right, and now I would like to remedy that situation."

"So, you want me to tell you my story?" Dolores' voice was flat and thin.

"Yes, I really want to know more about you. I've never met someone quite like you."

Minutes passed, with only the sound of soft breathing and the crackling fire filling the silence.

"I can tell you my story," Esperanza offered, "how I came here against my will and am now trapped."

"Don't bother. I'm sure your story is like all the others, and you will be gone after winter storms have passed."

"What others? You just told me that we are the only ones here." She paused. Dolores had hinted at the presence of "others" many times. But Esperanza stored that mystery away for another time. Today, she just wanted to find the human being behind Dolores' hard shell.

"How did you come to live here, alone with an ailing old man?"

Dolores sighed, and sat still as stone, back ramrod straight, staring down at her work-worn hands neatly folded in her lap. Moments passed slowly and neither of them spoke. "If I tell you about myself, will you leave me alone?"

"Certainly. I will never trouble you again if that's what you wish."

Without any fanfare, Dolores began. "I was from a good Sicilian Muslim family."

"Really? You don't look like the other Muslims I have met." Esperanza focused on Dolores' thin dishwater blonde hair and blue eyes, her hawkish nose, her skeletal, angular body and her pale, almost translucent skin.

Dolores' icy glare silenced Esperanza. "You know nothing! My family has been in Sicily for many generations, but we were originally from an ancient settlement on the Black Sea north of Constantinople. We were proud of our light complexions. It set us apart, and for hundreds of years we did not mix with the swarthy Muslims around us. When I came of age, my family found a suitable husband for me in the Muslim caliphate of Granada, so they sent me alone on a voyage to meet the man I was to marry. His family had an excellent reputation, and I had every expectation of becoming a good wife and mother. My mother, bless her sainted soul, explained everything I needed to know about marriage so I would be prepared for my matrimonial duties. I learned the practical skills needed to run a household from her. She also warned me of the risks of the voyage. She was a strong woman, not prone to emotional displays, but tears stood in her eyes as we said goodbye. 'Do not be weak,' she told me. 'Life is full of uncertainty, and whatever happens, you must show only your strength.'"

Esperanza's heart was shot through. These were almost the same words Master Cohen had said to her, *'I know you will make the best of it, whatever your future brings. Life can be unpredictable.'* But he was far less honest about her prospects than Dolores' forthright mother.

"When Signore Adolfo's pirate crew threw their grappling hooks over the rail of our ship, I knew Allah had another plan for me and for all the others on board. The crew, raised to a seafaring life, knew what to expect; they would be sent to the castration houses in Venice to be sold as eunuchs to wealthy Arab emirs in Granada. They fought ferociously, desperate to save their lives as men, but were no match for the marauding pirates. There were several women on board, either promised to husbands as I was, or already married. If they were beautiful, the pirates would sell them to wealthy Muslims as concubines for their harems. If they were plain, as I was, they would bring a profit when sold into servitude in the slave market." She took a long breath, taking shelter behind her emotionless armor. "Rather than debasing myself as a whore, I threw myself overboard." She stole a sideward glance at Esperanza, gauging her reaction before continuing.

"Adolfo saw me clinging to a trunk, kicking furiously to distance myself from the ship. He told me later he admired my fortitude and strength of will, so he rescued me and made me his servant. He has never threatened to marry me off or sell me, and for that reason, I have rewarded him ever since with my loyalty." Dolores remained stoic; not a trace of self-pity revealed itself on her face or in her demeanor.

Dolores' stark, unembellished story stunned Esperanza. "Your mother would be proud of you; you display no weakness. Are you satisfied with your situation here?"

"I have no choice, so yes, I am at peace with my lot. I do what I must."

They sat in silence, the blaze in the fireplace slowly waning. Esperanza picked a log from the stake of firewood and stoked the dying embers hoping to prolong the conversation.

"You said I would be like all the others. What did you mean? Were there other women here before me? Where were they?"

Dolores' curtain of frigidity descended; her eyes resumed their blank stare. There would be no further conversation. "You promised you would leave me alone when I had told my story. Now, please do so." She rose and moved toward the door. "Follow me." She led Esperanza back to her room, her steps clacking briskly on the marble floors.

She is like me, brought here against her will, expecting a different life. She is indeed strong, but she has lost the spark of hope or happiness, if she ever had one. I will not surrender so easily. Somehow, I will find my way to Salerno. Esperanza stoked the smoldering remains of rebellion stirring her defiance into a fire, but her resolve was burning low.

The bed was comfortable, the pillow deep and soft. The luxury of the villa was a temptress beckoning her to stay. Until opportunity showed itself, she needed only to live from day to day. Tomorrow she would try again to find treatments for Signore

Adolfo's many illnesses. But she promised herself she would keep her eyes open for her chance to flee.

The days began to fall into a regular pattern. As mid-morning terce bells rang from the Cathedral Santa Maria calling the faithful to prayer, Esperanza met Adolfo in his rooms. The Signore was compliant as she examined his eyes and asked a series of questions. "Do you have eye pain or pressure, headaches, colored halos?"

"My eyes don't hurt, but I feel pressure from the inside like an overfilled wine skin, and my vision is blurred, and is getting worse."

Symptom by symptom she catalogued his complaints - fatigue, swollen, painful joints, open sores on his ankles, chest pain, and a mysterious grippe that appeared and disappeared periodically. Every part of his body screamed for relief, entangling Esperanza in a snarled web of bewildering symptoms.

"I will do whatever I can, but I am a simple healer, not a master physician. I will search for treatments in your collection of medical texts."

The absurdity of her situation was ironic, almost ridiculous. She found herself in this remote villa surrounded by manuscripts of healing the traditions of Persia, Hindustan, Greece, Germania, yet was unable to find a remedy. There must be a golden thread binding this tapestry together. She spent night after night exploring Adolfo's collection of watermarked Egyptian papyri, and leather-bound books like a traveler searching for a mystical crossroads where all paths crossed. Many days, as the mid-morning bells wafted up the hill, Dolores found her asleep, sprawled on the library floor, surrounded by oil lamps burned dry. No one was happy. Dolores was annoyed by her profligate waste of oil and Adolfo was frustrated by her lack of progress as he continued to deteriorate.

"My patience is not limitless," Adolfo grumbled. "I was misled; I thought you could help me. If you cannot, I will give you back to Ibrahim. He can fetch a price for you adequate to repay the expenses I incurred in bringing you here."

"No, Signore Marino! I promise you; I just need a little more time. I am so close to putting the pieces of this mosaic together. The pattern is revealing itself. Please, a little more time." Panic tinged her voice; the consequences of failure loomed ominously.

That night, Esperanza's dead mother came to her in a dream. She was whole and beautiful again, like the mother she knew when she was very young, before she crumbled into a helpless husk ravaged by leprosy. Even as she died in Esperanza's arms, along the Camino de Santiago, she promised to take care of Esperanza. The fear, grief, and deep sense of abandonment she experienced on that day roared over her again, like a malevolent wave determined to drag her out to sea. Esperanza had been seeking the love and security she lost in the moment of her mother's death ever since.

In her dream, her mother was a beautiful apparition who spoke to her with great tenderness. "Esperanza, I am here; I see your struggle. You can accomplish anything you set yourself to achieve. You are making this too complicated, my child. Think. What are the basic principles of good health? Look."

Her mother swept her outstretched arm before her in a broad arc. A shimmering scene of aching beauty appeared, and Esperanza saw herself as a little girl running through tall grass on a sun-bathed hillside, laughing, surrounded by the vivid colors and aromas of the plants she loved. Her mother beckoned her to share a simple midday meal.

"We didn't bring anything to eat," Esperanza said.

"But we have everything we need all around us."

One by one, the plants approached, glowing with the blessings of health and happiness, proffering their gifts to Esperanza. The tansy, flax, blackberry, fox glove, snakeroot, yarrow, angelica offered to help her.

"You see, my girl? All these healers came to the same conclusion. It is simple. Though they took many paths, they all arrived at one destination."

Esperanza awoke bathed in tears; her grief as fresh as if it had happened yesterday. Her mother had died a leper along the Camino de Santiago, desperately trying to reach the Cathedral to beg the saint for a cure. For centuries Saint James had performed miracles there, and her mother was convinced if she could only reach the saint's tomb, she could throw herself on the altar, plead for her life, and be cured. Instead, she died in her little girl's arms on a rocky hillside along the Camino de Santiago path.

As her spirit departed, she performed her own miracle. She promised Esperanza she would be endowed with the power to heal. From that time on, when Esperanza came close to an ailing person, she would feel her mother's presence. It would manifest itself in a burning or tingling sensation behind her eyes and a buzzing in her ears. At those times, she would receive uncanny insights into the illnesses that troubled them. Her insight would guide her healing hands.

The next morning Esperanza did not appear at the first meal but rifled through her books searching for the magic concept binding them together. She began to list the world's healing traditions and outline the basic principles of each. There was a lot to learn. She already knew from her years with Master Cohen, the chief medical principles of the Talmud, written, as tradition taught, a thousand years ago by the hand of Moses, and inspired by God himself. God's purpose was clear. He intended man to manifest both the natural harmony of body and the spirit.

She had also learned something of Galen's principles from her explorations of Master Cohen's collection. In a spidery scrawl on ragged parchment, Esperanza could imagine the hand of a devoted monk, hunched over his scriptorium, as he labored to translate "On Diseases and Symptoms" from Greek into Latin. The translator of the book she now held in her hands had attempted a commentary on the similarities of the philosophies of Galen and the Talmud.

Both the Talmud and Galen agreed that the principles of good health included exercise, a moderate and healthful diet, and hygiene. It was a wonder to her how two writers, from such different traditions, could codify the same principles.

Galen's work, 'On Diseases and Symptoms,' frequently referred to an earlier Greek luminary named Hippocrates, who had written over seventy works on all aspects of medicine. Judging from the reverential terms Galen used to describe Hippocrates, he considered him the founder of Greek medical practice. Esperanza scavenged without success through the disorganized treasure trove of ancient medical writings searching for anything written by Hippocrates. She found only a quotation from Galen's book in which Hippocrates emphasized natural causes and natural treatments of diseases that stressed the convergence of bodily health, mental health, spiritual health, and a healthy lifestyle.

Another scrap of a document, in even worse condition, caught her attention. It was titled in both Latin and Greek, 'The Ayurveda.' She puzzled over this for a long time. At length she discovered that this title referred to a set of medical beliefs, written many centuries before Christ's arrival on earth, originating in the lands of the Indus River, a place about which she knew almost nothing. She imagined it as a dreamlike, land of wonders, mysterious arcane knowledge, and exotic women entrapped in harems. She pored over the difficult Latin, her mouth moving in concentration when she realized, with a growing excitement, that the mysterious principles of Ayurveda mirrored those of both Galen and the Talmud.

She shivered with delight; certain she would not sleep that night. Indeed, her days' exploration seemed to reaffirm what she had already suspected. To achieve bodily health, one must achieve physical, mental, and spiritual harmony.

Just as she was ready to go to bed, exhausted but exhilarated, she caught sight of a hefty tome peeking out from beneath a mound of papers. Its spine was ornamented with an elegant but indecipherable gold leaf script in characters that looked like worms contorted into curving, rounded shapes. In hand-written print, beneath the books' title, she recognized the Latin words 'Avicenna, The Cannon of Medicine.' She let the book fall open in her lap. The left page was written in a script she imagined to be Arabic, and the facing page was in Latin. Her heart beat faster with the possibilities. This was what she had been searching for, the key to unlocking the secrets of Arabic medicine. It was too much to take in.

Finally, she turned her attention to a manuscript by a German writer, again translated into Latin. She judged this person to be at least a near contemporary and, to her amazement, a woman! The book's cover read *Hildegard von Bingen's Physica: On Health and Healing*. She leafed through page after page of plant names accompanied by delicate drawings, each one with a detailed description of its medical benefits and how to prepare it for use.

Her spirits soared with intense satisfaction. The path to wisdom from cultures as different as puppies and plow horses, all reached the same conclusion. The key to well-being consisted of a healthful diet, a regimen of regular physical activity, and spiritual nourishment.

It was just as her mother had told her in the dream, she had found many paths to the same destination. She paused in her excitement to ponder for a moment the strange journeys these separate documents must have taken to finally nestle together under the same roof in Signore Marino's villa. She fell to her knees, hands clasped.

Thank you, mother. You have shown me the way. The priceless wisdom all these traditions teach is that the road to good health winds along one path. Now I can help Adolfo.

The following morning, she woke up late. The wan winter sun cast its eggshell yellow light through the fog, lifting from the bay. She found Dolores at the wash basin on the wooden bench in the kitchen, cleaning the dishes.

"You're too late; I am almost done here. There will be no breakfast for you."

"I am not here to beg for a tardy breakfast. I have discovered something far more important, the secret to healing Signore Adolfo. Look at this," she shook a scrap of parchment in her Dolores' sullen face. Dolores stared at her blankly, never glancing at the written page, then looked away.

Esperanza stopped abruptly. "Oh, I'm sorry. I should have realized you may not have had the opportunity to learn to read." Trying to shake off the awkwardness of her insensitivity, she blurted out. "I've made an important discovery searching through all those manuscripts. All the wise men of the past reached the same conclusion about what makes a healthy life, and Adolfo is doing none of these things." She was almost quivering with delight at her discovery. "We can heal him, Dolores!" She lightly touched Dolores' arm. Dolores looked at the shaking fingers on her arm as if they were maggots but said nothing. "I will need assistance. Dolores, will you help me?"

Dolores did not respond. Esperanza suspected she would need to ponder this in her slow, methodical way, so she did not press. Dolores simply picked up a scrap of wool on the wooden bench and began drying the dishes. The dishes were dry by the time Dolores spoke.

"And what is this marvelous discovery you so cleverly identified?"

"He needs three things: physical activity, a nourishing diet, and something to engage his mind and spirit. What does he do now? He eats too much, and the foods he eats are too rich."

"I prepare the foods he prefers. It's not my place to decide for him."

"But he eats meat for nearly every meal and very few vegetables. He is physically ponderous; and carrying around all that extra weight is taxing his body. He does not read or busy his hands with any productive work. He has probably never had a spiritual thought in his entire life. In addition, he has symptoms of several diseases. Now that he can see death approaching, he is afraid."

Another long pause ensued, but Esperanza resisted the impulse to fill the silence with chatter, leaving Dolores to deliberate in silence.

"I can find no fault with your reasoning, but how do you propose to lure him into making these changes? He is expecting medical treatment from you, not merely a change to his routine."

"You are right. The changes to his habits will help him feel better in general, but first we need to lure him into trying them. We can also work to treat his other ailments. We will need to do this together. He will resist and will try to foster contentiousness between us. But I cannot do this without you. Will you help me?"

Dolores's lips were closed but Esperanza sensed her mind was open.

"You choose and prepare his food. You could gradually make some dietary changes, gradual enough that he might not complain. Perhaps we can get him to leave his chair and walk around the grounds. He has expressed an interest in learning, and a fondness for Rumi's poetry. I think his soul is troubled by the lawless, unprincipled life he has led. If he is meant to die, we can at least help him die a happy man."

A flicker of a smile danced across Dolores' stern visage. Esperanza knew she had found a co-conspirator. Now it was time to diagnose and treat his symptoms.

14

AFFLICTION

SPRING 1265

"Look at this," Esperanza said, waving a small book made from cheap rag pulp paper overhead. Though unwelcome, she often insinuated herself into Dolores' kitchen, calling out over the clatter of dinner preparations.

Spring was just over the horizon, chasing the damp, chilly spirits of winter away, tempting all to believe her promises of warmth. April flowers crowded the hedge rows between the orchards and farmers' fields, flushed with spring-green rye, oats, and millet.

"Put that book down and help me pluck this chicken." Dolores' hands were a mess of chicken juices and clinging feathers. Suspended downy feathers circling in the air around her head created a halo; she looked like the patron saint of chicken pluckers.

Esperanza choked back her laughter, coughing to cover up her guffaws. Dolores shot her a sharp glance, warning Esperanza not to mock her. But then, everything about Dolores was sharp. Her bony elbows might inflict knife-like wounds if she ever deployed them as weapons. Her scapular bones protruded from her back like thinly veiled wings, counterbalanced by clavicles that sliced across her chest. Her every action was abrupt, the way she chopped vegetables, the way she plopped the Signore's dinner before him on a thin bread trencher. The angel who endowed some women with fluid, graceful movements utterly overlooked Dolores, whose jerky actions were as graceless as the dead chicken she now held out toward Esperanza.

Esperanza tucked the fragile little book into a pocket of her apron taking care not to crumple its edges as she reached toward the headless chicken.

After an interval of sullen silence, Dolores' curiosity defeated her annoyance. "Alright, then, tell me. What did you find?"

"These are the writings of Hildegard von Bingen. She was a Benedictine Abbess and a master of herbal medicine. She was from Germania, not from ages ago, like the ancient Greeks and Romans, but from the recent past. She says eyebright, you know, the flower eyebright..." She trailed off.

Dolores rolled her eyes. "Of course, I know what it is."

"Have you seen it growing around here?"

"Yes, it grows in the untamed hedgerows separating the fields. What about eyebright?"

"Hildegard von Bingen says we can infuse warm towels with a tea made from the flowers and use them as compresses to relieve Adolfo's eyes.

"Hmph."

"Perhaps you could pluck a handful and bring some back for me. Or I could prowl around and find some on the grounds near the villa."

Dolores paused and sighed, resting her hands on the bloody cutting board. "You know you are not allowed to leave the villa."

Esperanza's eyes twinkled. "Who will be the wiser if I leave for a short time?"

"It's not allowed, and that's that."

"The Signore will never know. He rarely leaves his chambers."

"He will find out, mark my word; he has eyes everywhere. And you won't be happy with the consequences."

A sly smile crept across Esperanza's face. She reached around her back and withdrew a small bundle of flowers from her waist pouch. "See!? You didn't know I was gone and neither did anyone else." She flourished a bouquet of eyebright in Dolores's face.

"You are treading dangerous waters. You will be punished, and I will be called to account. Signore seems mild-mannered until his ire is aroused."

"I'll be careful."

Dolores slapped her palms down on the cutting board and glared at Esperanza. "No! If you want something, you must ask me. I will do what I can." She began plucking a second chicken, ferociously pulling out great clumps of bloody feathers.

"I see. I will prepare a list of treatments. I'll need . . . "

Dolores interrupted her chatter. "If you are not going to help, then get out of my kitchen."

Esperanza dropped the topic of getting medicinals for Adolfo and joined Dolores, plucking a chicken she would boil along with cabbage for dinner.

After the faint music of sext bells wafting up to the villa had faded, Esperanza knocked lightly on the door to Adolfo's suite.

"Enter." Adolfo's grumbled. "He sat sprawled in his upholstered chair, with a map of the Middle Sea splayed across his lap. "I have sailed all over this great expanse of water, as hale and hearty as any ship's captain" He spoke without looking up from his map. "And now I am barely able to walk beyond my rooms."

"I understand how you feel. I have been similarly hobbled; though I am vigorous and healthy." Adolfo shot her a menacing glance; so, she let that thread of conversation die and directed his attention in a more useful direction. "I have prepared medicine for your eyes. Just drop your head back and I'll start."

Compliant as a spring lamb, Adolfo let the map slide to the floor and did as he was told. Esperanza picked up a warm towel infused with tea of eyebright. "Now, just rest with your eyes closed. This should relieve the pressure and pain."

"Will it restore my eyesight?" Adolfo sighed and relaxed.

"Possibly. If it doesn't, I'll search for more efficacious remedies. If I had permission to leave the villa to continue to search for herbs and plants among the hedgerows and untamed forest verges, I could do much more to relieve your suffering."

"If you could *continue* to search? Are you telling me you went out and collected herbs by yourself?"

He pounded his fists on the arms of his chair with a percussive jolt, seized the warm towel from his eyes and flung it to the floor. "You are not to leave this villa, do you understand?"

Adolfo narrowed his eyes and studied her suspiciously. "If you ever try something like that again, I will put one of my men on you to keep track of your every move. In case you are entertaining any idea of running away, they are armed. I will have a little chat with Dolores about this matter. Does she know you are sneaking out?"

"No, Dolores is blameless. She knew nothing of my little foray."

"I *will* talk to her, and I *will* remind her emphatically that she is not to let you roam," Adolfo's voice boomed in anger. "And there will be no fraternizing with Dolores or any other of my people."

Esperanza picked the now-cool towel off the floor and left the room. *This is a lesson. Dolores was right. This man can be compliant, but he also has a quick temper. He is needy and mild mannered, like a child, when not aroused, but volatile. Did he say armed guards? His men? He was a pirate. Are 'his men' crewmembers he brought with him to this place? This is not something I anticipated. All the more reason I need to escape.*

Then it became clear. The brawny majordomo who ushered her into the villa when she arrived - she suddenly realized that she had never seen him again. Sailors' skills, like boatswain, quartermaster, cooper, carpenter, surgeon, blacksmith would all correlate to the functions needed on an estate. It was likely that half of the skilled workmen in the village were once Adolfo's crew. Even the gregarious driver, who delivered her to the front door, could have been one of Adolfo's men. Perhaps he was the boy who climbed the rigging as comfortably as a spider on its web.

When she returned to her 'library,' her materials had been neatly organized, books in one stack, vellum manuscripts in another, loose parchments in a third, completely regardless of their subject matter. Esperanza would need to return the works to an order that supported her research. Dolores had no doubt tidied her library. Esperanza interpreted the gesture as a sign of support, a message that she would be willing to help.

Esperanza buried herself in her research. She mentally catalogued Adolfo's ailments: redness and pressure of the eyes, swollen legs, ankles with those loathsome open sores, fatigue, weakness, shortness of breath, aching joints. She recognized the latter from his stiff gait and the excessive amount of time he spent in his chair. Something shimmered on the edge of her perception, just beyond her reach. Whenever she approached Adolfo, she felt the familiar tingle behind her eyes, and ringing in her ears. He harbored some deeper malady that evaded her. Whatever it was, she had a vague sense she had encountered it before but was unable to recall where or when.

One by one she tackled each of his infirmities. He had used the term jungle rot for the livid sores around his ankle. It was crudely precise, a name a sailor would use, direct, practical, and vivid. Since there were no jungles nearby, Esperanza supposed he may have contracted it in tropical regions of his voyages. Which of her sources contained information about tropical diseases? She shuffled through her stacks of documents until she found the work called Ayurveda. The translator included a foreword, explaining that these were ancient traditional medical practices of the people of the Indus valley. Though she had only the vaguest concept of geography, she deduced it must be far away, perhaps somewhere tropical. After shuffling through her papers, she discovered something that sounded sufficiently exotic. There it was - "jungli jaldi bemari" - an Arabic word defined by the translator as a disease of the skin causing it to decay or rot. The treatment began with cleaning the wound with vinegar or wine, then preparing an ointment by adding various curative ingredients to butter.

She searched in Galen, Hippocrates, and Hildegard, for plants with wound healing properties. Not surprisingly, all of them had preparations for injuries. After all, men would always make war, and warriors would always be wounded. She was already familiar with yarrow. Every healer since the time of Achilles knew its ability to stop bleeding. But there were many more: angelica, balsam, lavender oil, curcumin, myrrh, chamomile, calendula. Which of those would be available in the market in this season?

The following morning found her once again sleeping sprawled on her library floor, the oil lamp burned dry. She arose groggy, but buoyant with expectations of progress. Today she would begin treatment of his sores.

Esperanza hustled to the kitchen and took a place next to Dolores at the table.

"What can I do to help?" she asked.

"Why are you here? Have you appointed yourself my little helper? What do you want from me?"

"Yes, I'm here because I would like to help you; and I would also like you to help me." Esperanza knew insincere wheedling would not sway her. She had learned to wait for Dolores' long-suppressed curiosity to overcome her reticence. Dolores needed time to formulate her questions.

"I think I have found a treatment for Signore's ankle sores and his other ailments too. We can try them if we can find the ingredients. We will need plants from the market." She waited to go on.

"I knew you were up to something. All that oil wasted in the library every night."

"It isn't wasted. I have found ways we can help him. He will credit you with getting the medicines that make him better."

"He's not a fool; he will realize it was your talent as a healer that guided my purchases." Dolores would not be swayed by flattery. "But yes, I will bring home what you need - on one condition." She hesitated so long it seemed she had nothing more to say. "You must promise on the soul of your mother that you will not leave the premises. Is that clear?"

Esperanza sighed. After all these months, she was still a prisoner. The dream of becoming a bonafide Doctor of Medicine at the Scola Medica, still burned within her; but she needed to live within her strictures as long as she was here at the villa.

"Yes," she reluctantly conceded defeat. "I promise." She felt as hollowed out as a drinking gourd.

Esperanza retraced her steps to her chambers. By the standards of her childhood, they were opulent, but it was not home. Though Dolores' attitude toward her was softening, their relationship was nothing like the close bond she enjoyed with Amika and Gabriela, or with the Cohen family in Burgos. She wondered if they missed her, if they thought of her at all, after so many months. Remembering her past prompted a rush of nostalgia, recalling how meticulously she had packed her trunk. Yes! Her trunk, of course! She bolted to the chest. She threw open the lid and rooted around like a ship rat in a flour bin. There at the bottom was the answer to curing Adolfo's ulcerous flesh. As an afterthought, when she was packing, she had tossed in a salve she'd concocted from beeswax, infused with oils of lavender, yarrow, and chamomile. First, she would wash his wounds with vinegar, then apply her balm, leaving them open to the air so the ulcerous flesh would dry. If that didn't work, she would devise a compress of flaxseed oil.

Next day she knocked, as she always did, at Adolfo's door.

"Enter." His voice was harsh, like pebbles grating underneath the wheels of a farmer's cart.

"How are your eyes today?"

"I can't see any better, but they hurt less."

"It will take time. And if, after two weeks, there is no significant change, I have something else we might try."

She knelt at his feet and gently lifted his heels. "Do these sores bother you?"

"What do you think?" he snapped. "How would you feel if they were on your ankles?"

"Of course," she said, "That was a stupid question." He was going to be in an irascible mood today, not amenable to casual conversation, so she got right down to the business at hand. "I brought something with me that I think will help." He looked at her intently but said nothing. "I created it when I was still with Master Cohen's beloved family in Burgos, when I thought I would be attending the Scola Medica." She glanced surreptitiously up at him gauging his reaction.

He did not reply, but red blotches rose on his drooping, jowly face. The pot was about to boil over. She dared not press the issue further.

"Would you like to try it?"

When again there was no response, she bent her back to the task of bathing his ankles and feet in vinegar. She removed a small jar from her pouch and dabbed the fragrant, waxy ointment on his ulcerous sores.

"I brought a few of my herbal remedies with me from Burgos, but if I am to really heal you, I will need other medications. Dolores won't know what to look for in the market or what to pluck from among the hedgerows."

"Teach her then! You are not leaving the villa."

Today was not the day for innuendo. His black mood did not make the ailing, old man tolerant. She finished treating his ankles, slunk off to her library, slumped into a chair, buried her face in her hands and cried. Discordant emotions finally broke through the dam of defiance and denial she had built around her heart to protect her from despairing because of her helplessness. Frustration festered within her, and rage boiled like a witch's cauldron. Her heart was as shattered as glass thrown against a wall in anger. *I don't care what he says. It doesn't matter that I am lonely, heartsick, and sorely betrayed. I have no one to rely on but myself. I will leave here one day to pursue my vocation.*

In the late afternoon, when the air cooled, she wandered to the loggia. As the sun slid toward the horizon the fragrant spring fields below overtook her senses, drawing her out of her sulk. Tangy, delicate smells of lemon blossoms swirled in the air, chasing the lily-sweet fragrance of the tiny olive flowers. That was where Dolores found her, with her eyes closed, head thrown back, lips slightly parted looking like an ecstatic saint lost in heavenly visions.

"Signore would like you to read to him." Dolores ordered

tersely and turned to go. Then she hesitated. "He is not as bad a person as you think. He is terrified of you running away. That is what the other girls did, or at least that is what they tried to do."

"Wait! What other girls? Why did they run away? Who were these girls?"

"You will have to ask him yourself. He likes you; you know. 'No' is not always his final answer."

"He expects me to cure him, but he won't let me out of the villa. I will need your help. Can we meet tomorrow after breakfast, and talk about what ingredients we will need?

"Yes, fine." Dolores grudgingly agreed.

Dolores led Esperanza to the Signore's anteroom and knocked softly.

"Enter. What have you brought for me tonight?" His tone was casual, as if no harsh words had passed his lips, as if he hadn't once again locked the gates to Esperanza's prison.

Dolores turned and left as Esperanza entered. Adolfo's chambers consisted of a spacious anteroom with an embroidered overstuffed chair and matching footstool, a side table, and a desk. The bedchamber was spacious enough to accommodate a four-poster bed, so tall, one needed a footstool to climb into it. At the foot of the bed rested a round-topped storage chest covered in hand tooled leather. Esperanza had seen Adolfo's rooms before, but their opulence still gave her pause.

"I found a poem by Francis of Assisi, 'Praise of God's Creation,' in Italian so I won't need to translate. And we will end with Rumi."

"Whatever you wish." His face was pale, and his body immobilized by lassitude; he nodded vaguely.

"From now on, I will be in your suite at mid-day to administer treatments, and again in the evening to read to you."

Adolfo waved a hand feebly, as if bothered by a fly. Esperanza studied him. Her ears were ringing persistently, and her eyes burned so much she could scarcely focus. He was getting worse. She and Dolores would need to implement a plan soon.

15

EDUCATING THE PIRATE

WINTER 1265

"How long has Signore been taking his meals in his quarters?" Esperanza's brain was churning with ways to apply the lessons she'd learned from studying the diverse medical works in Signore's collection.

"Oh, I don't know, for many years." Dolores paused to string together her memories.

"He was taking his meals in his cabin on the *Sultana* soon after he rescued me; that was four years ago. The crew was starting to grumble about having a woman, on the ship, so he retreated to his cabin to escape their complaints. Also, many did not take well to the transition from life as a freebooter to life as merchant seamen, especially if it meant sacrificing a share of their plunder to taxing authorities.

"Let me figure. Since he rescued me, he lived four years as a pirate, four years as a merchant, and two years here in the villa. How much is that?"

"That makes ten years," Esperanza said. "Did he end his merchant trade and when he moved to the villa?"

Dolores' face darkened; her eyes shuttered as she retreated into her shell. "I need not answer any more of your questions, you will have to ask him yourself."

Conversation ceased. They dried the oak table, wet from cleaning dishes, draped the towels on a line to dry, and returned to their respective stations - Dolores to the kitchen and Esperanza to

169

her library. The hour after dinner found them once again at the wash basin. Esperanza turned the conversation to Dolores' offer to help. This time she would carefully avoid damaging their fragile truce.

"When I lived in Ponferrada, where I lived with Amika and Gabriela, we sold various remedies along the Camino de Santiago. We had a beautiful mahogany apothecary cabinet. I loved its intricate warren of compartments and drawers crowded with ointments, elixirs, and infusions. Bundles of herbs hung from the ceiling. The air in the room was a symphony of spicy, citrusy, fruity, and minty aromas. Think of the good we could do for the Signore if we had a cabinet like that."

"Very interesting, but you will never have such a thing." Dolores said dryly.

"I know, but perhaps if we persuade the Signore to allow us to use one of the villa's many unused rooms, we could create a smaller version. Maybe we could enlist a carpenter to build some shelves and . . . . "

"Preposterous," she said emerging from her iron-clad conversational armor. A flash of curiosity flickered in her eyes. "But you might talk to him about it. You can be quite persuasive." A corner of her lip tilted upward in a tiny smile. "I advise a subtle approach, and you'll need to catch him at a compliant moment."

Their days fell into a rhythm. Breakfast was in mid-morning, dinner in early evening; and shared moments of amity and quiet conversation, standing side by side at the wash basin, followed each meal. The evenings were quiet; each of them retreating to their separate quarters. Esperanza did not know how Dolores filled her hours. She didn't seem like the devout type who would settle herself with praying rosaries, nor could she read. Sometimes Esperanza could hear her thumping around in the kitchen, but she dared not intrude on her private time. Esperanza and Adolfo, however, filled these lonely hours with reading lessons and Esperanza's recitations from the manuscripts.

Esperanza's days were full and sometimes rewarding, with

occasional flashes of happiness. Despite her comfort and complacency, Esperanza still suffered icy pangs of loss. No matter how often she mentioned the Scola Medica to Adolfo, he slammed the door on her dreams. Sometimes he scoffed, or pointed out how impossible it would be for an unprotected woman to make the journey, she had no money, no referrals, no proper educational background. Despite her skills in Latin, Hebrew, Greek and Italian, and her wide knowledge of the classics, she would not be qualified to study there. Sometimes he was disparaging, or derisive, and sometimes amused. But most often such conversations made him angry.

The notion that she could recreate the marvelous apothecary she had in Burgos invigorated Esperanza. She started sending her own shopping list with Dolores to the market. In mid-winter she could expect to find salted, pickled, or dried plants. But it was a start; and their collection grew quickly. In their shared hours, after kitchen chores were finished, they bent their heads together over their growing assortment of tinctures, oils, and balms Esperanza created from the ingredients Dolores brought home from the market. Dolores did not know their uses, and her curiosity was beginning to nag her.

"Look at all these herbs and concoctions," Dolores marveled sweeping her arm in a wide arc over the table. "Wouldn't I be more useful if I knew their uses?"

Esperanza lit up like a firefly in July. "Excellent idea! We should create an inventory of what we have collected so far." Her eyes darted around the room looking for a place to start. "Let's begin by inventorying the herbs in my chest, then we will catalog what we have collected at the market. Tell me which of these plants you know. It will be helpful if you understand their uses. She laid them all out and quizzed Dolores.

Dolores picked up what looked like a dry stick and lifted it to her nose. "This smells like licorice."

"Excellent, and what is it used for?"

"My dear mother would place a sliver under my tongue when I

had a stomachache."

"Very good, and it is also useful for coughs and head colds."

"Do you know what it is called?"

"Certainly, that is licorice." Dolores concluded with a satisfied smirk.

One by one, she ticked off the herbs laid out before them - ginger, rose water, lavender, sage, flaxseed, oregano, dried rosehips, and dill. Dolores identified all of them. It was a good start. All Esperanza had to do was tutor her in their uses.

"God did not put a single plant on this earth that has no use, even if its use is for animals, insects, or simply to add pleasure to our days. If we wish to create a true apothecary, there are additional items we will need, like bottles, jars, and gauze. I have been learning so much from the priceless medical tracts Signore poached from his victims. Now we can take the next step, enumerating Signore's ailments and matching them to these remedies. What do you think?"

Dolores looked up from the table and narrowed her eyes, in concentration. She hadn't expected to be consulted as an equal.

"His eyes hurt, and his vision blurs more with each passing month. This is his most persistent complaint. But you have treated that issue with eyebright, so that issue is less pressing," Dolores said. "He complains of headaches. Also, there are those nasty sores on his ankles; and his legs and his feet are so swollen he can hardly walk. He is lethargic and has no energy. Some mornings it looks as though he hasn't slept at all, with puffy, purple pouches under his eyes, and he is frequently irritable. His mood changes wildly from moment to moment, from placid to enraged. I suppose there are no cures for irritability and lassitude. That's just his manner; changeable, moody, and angry. How can you heal a person's disposition?"

"I don't know if we can, but many medicines alter mood. We can try some of them. All the ancient philosophies reached the conclusion that health is more than the absence of disease. A healthy man also needs a healthy diet, exercise, and something that nourishes the mind and soul. Signore loves poetry and literature, and he wants to be an educated man. Since he cares not at all about religion, maybe opening the door to higher thoughts by reading classical works to him will suffice. It will be a challenge."

"Getting him to leave his room to take the fresh air will be another problem," Dolores reflected. "Perhaps if he is feeling better, he will be more willing," she trailed off.

* * *

"What is this! I want real food when I break my fast," blustering and red-faced, he held up a boiled carrot. "This is food for hares or sows, not for people. These are all root vegetables, radishes, beets, turnips. Only peasants eat this silage. Give these to my horse. Where is the salted pork I like? I gave you enough coin to buy meat. Did you pocket the money and buy this peasant food instead?"

"As you wish, Signore." Dolores removed the unwanted vegetables and came back with grapes, a pomegranate, and a pear drizzled with honey, several slices of hard salami encrusted with ground black pepper, and a slab of the whitest bread she could find. Only the wealthy enjoyed the luxury of eating white bread made with wheat flour rather than rye or oats.

"That's better," he said calmly. "I will also take a salted pork rib as well."

The evening meal was more peaceful. Dolores gave the Signore slices of pork loin bathed in a rich wine sauce, along with a clear gravy made from the pan drippings with added pepper, garlic, coriander, caraway. Dolores knew that would please him. Then she added a dose of more healthful foods - a small serving of fava beans and a shallow pewter bowl of mushroom and lentil soup, flavored with pepper, and curls from lemon rind.

"How did that go?" inquired Esperanza. "Did he object to the mushroom soup?"

"It was better than breakfast. I think if we disguise the

vegetables in flavorful soups, he will not object. And he seemed to relish the sweetened fruits I served. We can gradually increase the proportion of vegetables and fruit as we decrease the meat."

Esperanza began to knock on Adolfo's door each evening with a glass of wine. He was calmer, more tractable when the intense sun's eye gazed down with sidelong glances rather than the searing directness of midday. A little red wine took the edge off his temper. If she was ever to find time to ask for favors or raise difficult subjects, the hour before bed was the best time. She gently knocked on his door.

"Enter." His voice was flat; she discerned no mood or emotion of any kind. He spoke like a man only half alive.

Esperanza set his wine on the side table next to his chair, knelt, and gently lifted his feet. "I see the sores are healing. We can take that as good news. Within a month or two, they should be entirely healed." She looked up, but his face was impassive and blank. "I have devised a regimen of herbs and oils to reduce your pain, improve your general well-being, and cheer your spirits. Day by day your vigor will return."

He watched her intently as she bathed and salved his ankles. "I know what you're up to," he said, "you are going to ask once more for leave to go to Salerno, and once again I will reject the proposal. When can we stop this tiresome charade? You are here to help me, and I can see you are sincerely trying to do that. I am not an ungrateful person. Ask me for something else."

Esperanza carefully slipped his foot back into its calf skin slipper. She looked down her hair hanging past her face, hiding her smile. "That is very kind of you. I have been thinking; it would be very helpful to have a room with sturdy shelves lining the walls to store the remedies I need to treat you."

"Yes, that's good. I can do that. Call the carpenter."

Soon sturdy oak shelves lined the walls of their new apothecary. The hours before the midday meal belonged to Esperanza and Dolores and they did not waste a moment but dove right into the task of stocking the sturdy shelves with all the articles they had accumulated.

Though the cooling autumn temperatures diminished the number of summer herbs available each week, Dolores succeeded in bringing many discoveries back to the villa. Like Caesar entering Rome after conquering the Gauls, Dolores strode proudly into the apothecary with cranberry, yarrow, angelica, wintersweet, valerian, and willow bark.

The market of Napoli often had exotic goods brought by traders who plied the Middle Sea, and sometimes those specialties found their way to their little village on the flanks of Vesuvius. Rarities like green and black teas, turmeric, ginger, myrrh, and cayenne did not appear often, and when they did, the high price reflected the great lengths to which traders had gone to deliver these rarities to this remote place; but the Signore did not flinch when Dolores asked for more coins for medicines to cure him.

The next step in his therapy, raising the old man to his feet to get him moving again, would need to wait until he lost weight, and felt better. They agreed to devote their efforts first to his most immediate needs and address the rest next spring.

* * *

The weather cooled and Adolfo wrapped his fur-lined robe around himself and straightened in his chair. "What have you brought this evening for my edification?" He looked forward to the reading hour more than any other part of the day.

"You told me you would like to learn to read, and I promised to teach you. Would you like to learn your letters?"

"Yes, yes, I remember saying that, but the time for that has passed. I am too old and tired to learn to read. I am satisfied to listen to you read to me as you have been doing."

Esperanza continued, ignoring his remark. "You are fortunate your native tongue is so much like the Latin used by scholars for over a thousand years. First, I will teach you the letters. After you know letters, you will be able to construct words. After you learn words, you will be able to string the words together like rosary beads to create meaningful sentences. Then the doors of knowledge will be open to you."

A shard of hope pierced Adolfo's heart. He had always nurtured a seed of embittered jealousy for men of learning. The seed grew every time he pilfered manuscripts from the vessels he plundered. "If only I had grown up under my mother's tutelage instead of my father's, who knows what I might have achieved?"

"Those are the words of a man disheartened by a plague of ailments, not a man who is at ease in his body, mind and soul. When you start feeling better, you will look forward to the lessons as much as our nightly reading sessions. In fact, you will be able to read Rumi for yourself.

Adolfo was an apt student. He had previously learned enough to read a ship's manifest but had no grasp of how to use words to express thoughts. Esperanza started slowly, building on the vocabulary he already knew.

"A barrel of apples purchased in Venice cost one lira." Esperanza began. "How would you write that?"

With difficulty Adolfo lifted his quill, dipped it gingerly into the ink pot, and wrote "One barrel apples. One lira."

"Yes, good. That conveys the meaning, but can you write the word 'cost?" Adolfo shook his head. "As I thought. Let's try another. 'I study literature,'" Esperanza said. "Can you write that phrase?" He stared at her blankly. "Good. Now we have our starting point. We will start with verbs." She drew a chart:

I am we are
you are you (plural) are
he, she, or it is they are

"Let's try again. Apples are red."
"What is the word for apple?
"Poma."

"And the word for red?" He hesitated. "Rubrum?" he said uncertainly.

"And the word for 'are'"? He shook his head. "Look at the chart. Do you see the word for 'are?'" His head bent low to the page, lips pressed firmly together, like a diligent schoolboy and he tried again.

"Poma sunt rubrum."

"Excellent!" Adolfo blushed like a child. "Every day we can add new verbs to your vocabulary. They are most important for understanding a writer's meaning." And so it began, the long road to literacy that he so craved.

There was another task, in addition to mental stimulation and an improved diet, Esperanza and Dolores needed to accomplish. Adolfo needed to move his body out of that chair of his. When the weather was fine, as it often was in winter, Esperanza tried to tempt him to enjoy some fresh air.

"Let us relax on the loggia," Esperanza suggested. Dolores stood by her side, back as straight as a well-made arrow. Before he had an opportunity to shower them with a chorus of complaints, Esperanza on one side of his chair and Dolores on the other, slung his arms over their shoulders and lifted.

"Come on now, stand up. Where is that strong pirate body to match the pirate soul within in you?"

He knew his arguments would be defeated, so he made the attempt to stand. His legs quivered; his knees buckled; his head swam with vertigo. And his feet! Though the swelling had abated, and his sores were merely blotchy red reminders of the livid wounds they once were, they screamed in renewed pain. He staggered as if he was drunk on Arab al-kohl. The thought of those wild times with his untamed men lit his fire and he manfully staggered on, heaving deep breaths, until they gingerly lowered him to a seat on the loggia.

The winter fields flowed out to the bay of Napoli like water over a fall. Faint scents of lemons and olives lingered in the cold-harden orchards. A bracing breeze filled his lungs. His eyes closed, and he sucked it in like a thirsty man in a desert. How long had it been since he last gulped air fresh? Esperanza and Dolores, standing behind his chair, exchanged meaningful glances. Another milestone accomplished. They had treated his body, mind, and spirit, and given Adolfo a reason to go on drawing breath each day.

Esperanza studied treatments for headaches, mood swings and melancholia. The more she learned, the more she believed that these ailments were related. She decided to try two remedies. The first recipe, recommended by Hildegard von Bingen, called for grinding aloe and myrrh to a fine powder. To these ingredients she added wheat flour and poppy oil. Now she had something that resembled bread dough.

When she entered Adolfo's chambers and explained this would help with his headaches, he laughed out loud.

"You see?" Esperanza smiled, "It's working already, you're laughing. What harm is there in trying? The aloe reduces inflammation, the poppy has been used as a sleep aid and a powerful pain reliever for a thousand years. It also elevates one's mood, and the bread dough is a handy way to spread the mixture out over your entire head where it will seep into your skin." She unceremoniously plopped the dough on his head, spread it out, and covered the whole mess with one of the knit caps he wore as a sailor.

"You will wear this for three days and three nights. Then we will take stock of its efficacy. After three days and nights, we will use a combination of plants prescribed by As-Akhawayni, a Persian healer, made from celery stalk, fennel stalk, and cucumber. He says this combination will lift the spirits and banish dark thoughts."

Esperanza and Dolores brought Adolfo to the loggia every day the weather permitted. The Bay of Napoli, festooned with boats bobbing in the harbor, mirrored the skies, transforming the bay from a dusky slate when clouds loomed, to a shimmering cobalt when bathed in sun. The spectacle of sky reflected in water provided an ever-changing spectacle. The effort of moving the

Signore became easier as he shed some of his extra weight. Dolores found the magic balance between foods he loved and foods that promoted fitness and well-being. Each small success encouraged them to believe that they could coax the irascible old pirate back to health.

16

CLOSED DOORS

WINTER 1265

Over a year had passed since Esperanza first glimpsed the imposing villa from the carriage that deposited her at the front door. She had been awestruck by the symmetry and elegance of the two-story mansion. Wings to the right and left of a broad central loggia reminded Esperanza of encircling arms. When she had arrived, a steward ushered her into the entrance hall. Her eyes were immediately drawn upward to the exquisitely ribbed vaulted ceiling, like those in basilicas. Above it, an upper-story open-air gallery, adorned with beautiful frescoes, caught the breezes drifting up from the bay.

Since her arrival, her world had been reduced to the south wing of the villa. On the first floor of the south wing, a well-equipped kitchen and pantry serviced an expansive dining hall. The great hall held a banquet table commodious enough to seat twenty people. Above those rooms, three suites of sleeping chambers occupied the second floor – one for Adolfo, Esperanza, and Dolores.

Esperanza grew accustomed to gliding over terrazzo floors under arched ceilings, past frescoed walls. She lingered over the frescoes depicting gauzy landscapes, formally posed aristocrats, and scenes from Roman mythology. No two were alike; they portrayed very different scenes, like peaceful pastoral idylls, fisherman with dozens of fish slung over a shoulder, peasants with broad-brimmed hat hoeing a grain field. Some were not so soothing, but presented violent scenes of soldiers on war horses, charging at each other with swords held high. One of the frescoes captured her attention more than the others. In it Galen and Hippocrates sat together, engrossed in discourse, texts open before them on their laps.

She wondered if the north wing was equally lavish. Why were the doors to the north wing locked and barred? Curiosity niggled away at her until one day she could stand it no longer.

"Dolores, I've noticed that no one ever enters the north wing of the villa. The doors are blocked. What is over there?"

Dolores' tone turned icy. "Ask the Signore. It is not my place to discuss that part of the villa."

"It's such a simple question. Why can't you just tell me?"

"Go ask the Signore. He will tell you as much or as little as he sees fit." Dolores shrank into her impenetrable shell, and Esperanza knew there was no point in asking again.

That evening, after tending to Adolfo's feet and ankles, Esperanza read him one of Rumi's soothing verses.

"O Friend! we are near you in friendship,

Wherever you set foot, we prostrate ourselves like earth.

How is it permissible, in the religion of love,

That we should see your Creation and neglect to see You?"

Adolfo sighed contentedly, moved by the sentiment and the beauty of the words.

"I was wondering, Signore, about the other wing of the villa" Esperanza maintained a voice as smooth and melodious as the voice she used to read poetry. "Why are the doors to the north wing sealed?"

"Those rooms are not in use now so there is no reason to maintain them." His eyes slid sideways toward Esperanza. With the instincts of a bloodhound, he sensed her curiosity was leading him into the troubled waters of his pernicious past.

"The rooms are not important. They were intended for house

guests who came to the villa and sometimes stayed for weeks or even months. The rooms are comfortable, but not elegant so as not to entice visitors to overstay their welcome."

It was the truth, as far as it went. Customarily, owners of grand villas hosted lavish feasts and celebrations that could go on for weeks. The host provided rooms so the party would not be interrupted. Or guests might be detained by bad weather and need extra rooms.

Adolfo had no parties or banquets however, so his "guests" were not at the villa to enjoy aristocratic life. Esperanza could not cajole him into divulging his secrets. He did not suffer any compunctions about his trade, but Esperanza was certain to pronounce judgment on his "merchant" activities. He had grown to respect Esperanza. He admired her curious mind, her earnest studies, her breadth of knowledge, her diligence in caring for him. As much as it irritated him, he also admired her determination to achieve her goal. He did not want Esperanza to think badly of him, nor did he want her to flee, as she so often threatened, so the discussion of his "guests" and their rooms remained off limits.

He deftly changed the subject. "I would like to ask you a question in return. You have been here for how many months now?"

"It has been over a year," Esperanza replied.

"Over a year, and I still know little about you. I've told you my story, now it's only fair to tell me yours. Where were you born?"

Esperanza felt an uncharacteristic shyness; she was defensive, as if her privacy had been invaded, but she could not think of an excuse for withholding her story. She had nothing to hide, nothing to be ashamed of, so she began.

"I was born in the Basque country where the craggy mountains mark the boundary between Francia and Iberia. My family were poor sheep farmers, and when I was very young, I was sent to the summer pastures to tend the sheep. My only companion was a golden sheep dog named Dabi who took care of me, and my sheep. He was friendly, faithful, and fearless.

I hardly knew my father. He died when I was a baby. My mother was an angel, caring and kind. When I was young, perhaps five or six years old, my mother took ill with a dread disease. The townspeople called her a leper and drove her out of town with blows, kicks, and harsh language. I could not understand why this was happening to us. One kindly old neighbor lady took pity on us, gave my mother a scallop shell on a string and tied it around her neck, giving us the only advice she could offer.

"'Follow the trail down from the mountains until you find Saint-Jean-Pied-de-Port. A sacred walking trail starts there. The scallop shell will show people you are on a holy pilgrimage to Santiago de Compostela, and they will help you. The townspeople along the Camino de Santiago believe they gain indulgences toward their own salvation by helping pilgrims. It is a long, arduous walk, and might take you several months to complete, but Santiago performs miracles for those who have faith." She dropped a few coins into my mother's hand, gave us her blessing, and sent us on our way.

"She was right, the road was long; it seemed never ending. Day after day we walked, first down the slopes to the foothills of the mountains, then through fields and forests, over rivers and across ancient bridges built by the Romans centuries ago.

We walked for a long time, moving as quickly as a sick woman and young child could, making steady progress toward our goal, but my mother's disease moved faster, until it caught up with us. One night, as we sheltered from the rain under a rock overhang, she died in my arms. Before she died, she promised me that, though she would not be present in body, her spirit would always be with me, giving me the power to intuit the maladies of others. She promised I would not be left alone on that sodden hillside, that someone would soon come to save me. A short time later, my two saviors appeared. I know it sounds suspicious, but two pilgrims, Amika and Mateo, found me and took me under their wing."

Adolfo interrupted her implausible story. "Fine," he said, curt and unsympathetic. "How did you go from a bedraggled orphan to a well-educated healer. I think you are deceiving me."

Esperanza sighed. "I can understand why you might think so, but hear me out. Along the way, Amika suffered a grievous injury and stayed behind in Ponferrada, while I traveled with on to Santiago with Mateo. He was on a mission to deliver legal papers to the bishop in Santiago, and I traveled with him to the great city. When we arrived, he found work teaching at the Cathedral's monastery school and enrolled me in the girl's convent school adjacent to the Cathedral. I lived with the sisters at the convent for two years where I studied classic literature, learned to pray, recite my catechism, and to read and write in Latin. The other students considered me an outsider, one of the primitive Basque *hasieraks* or "mystery people," and branded me a heretic. I suffered insults, small and large, from the more "cultured" students. They tread on my toes, elbowed me on the stairways, pushed me into the fountain, whispered about me behind my back, so the most important lesson I learned was how to stay clear of bullies and take care of myself."

"Ah, I see," Adolfo interrupted. "That is where you learned your defiant attitude."

Esperanza ignored his remark. "After Mateo completed his duties at the monastery, he took me to Ponferrada to be raised by Amika and her friend, Gabriela. Together we sold herbal remedies along the Camino. They were like mothers to me. I learned everything I know about herbs and plants from Amika; I can never repay my debt to her. We roamed the hills, gathering healing plants. She taught me their uses, and dangers.

"One day, a customer misused the bella donna I sold her, and she died. The Count of that district blamed me for her unfortunate death. I had to flee the wrath of the Count. Once again Mateo rescued me, taking me to Burgos where he entrusted me to the care of his friend, a Hebrew physician, who raised me with his own children and treated me like part of the family.

"I helped the Master in his medical practice and had the privilege of reading from his extensive medical library. When his own children grew up and began lives of their own, my caretaker did not know what to do with me, so he consigned me into the care of Ibrahim the trader who promised to take me to Salerno to study medicine. They betrayed my trust, and instead of taking me to Salerno, Ibrahim brought me here to you."

Esperanza recited her story as if she was speaking of someone else. But her brave façade crumbled when she looked at Adolfo, her enslaver. She felt her heart break anew and buried her face in her hands, her shoulders shook but she made no sound. "All I ever wanted was my mother, a family, and a peaceful life as a healer."

Adolfo stared at her in silence. She felt like a cast off, unwanted and unloved. She could feel the weight of his judgment fall on her. She gathered herself, straightened her spine, and lifted her chin. The muscles in her jaw clenched. "And one day that is what I will do. I will have a peaceful life as a medical doctor."

Adolfo waited until her paroxysms of grief passed. "I see," he said. Esperanza hoped he would be moved by her predicament, but he remained dispassionate.

"Now will you let me go?" Esperanza's smokey grey eyes drilled into his shuttered ones.

"Are you not satisfied with my library of tracts and treatises? Haven't I given you full access to all the documents I possess? Look around you. You are surrounded by classical literature, medical knowledge from all cultures, treatises on herbal cures. They are all right here. What more do you expect to learn in Salerno you can't learn here?"

Esperanza glared at him, radiating defiance. "There is so much more to know. The students at the Scola Medica learn mathematics, rhetoric, disputation, astronomy, history, and literature. The students are both men and women. I might find friends. I could build a life and career of my own. I could earn the designation of 'doctor of medicine.' With that credential I will be able to make my own way in the world."

Adolfo's attitude softened. "I understand your motivation; and your determination is impressive, but I still need you here. We are not that different. When I learn to read, my ailments abate, and I can live my life as an educated man, I will help you achieve your goal. You must have patience; I still need you."

Next morning, as they prepared the first meal of the day, Esperanza filled Dolores' ears with details of her conversation with the Signore. "He said he would help me, but I can't trust him. After all, he and Ibrahim tricked me into coming here. I asked to be set free, but he won't let me leave here until he is well and can read well enough to educate himself. He needs to learn Latin to read the works in his library. Who knows how long that will take?"

"What did he say about the locked door to the north wing?" Dolores asked.

"He diverted my questions about the locked door as deftly as a street performer tricks the eye into choosing the wrong hand holding a stone. I know you understand why rooms are locked. Dolores, please. Why won't you tell me? There must be a reason they are kept locked. He said they not used."

Dolores looked at Esperanza, "he said they are never used?

"Yes, that's what he said."

Dolores's brows furrowed, concentrating harder on scrubbing the dishes. She shifted her weight from foot to foot, clearly agitated.

"He lied to me, didn't he? Those rooms are used for something, aren't they, and you know, don't you?" It was clear to Esperanza that Dolores was torn between her conscience and her loyalty to Adolfo.

"Yes, I do," Dolores admitted. "But if the Signore wishes to wait until he is well and can read, then I must respect his wishes."

Esperanza stamped her foot. "No! I won't have it. I have a queasy feeling about those rooms, and I want to know now!"

Finally, Dolores leveled a gaze at her that would stop a viper. "You are acting like a petulant child. You need patience. You must cure him, teach him. That's what he wishes. He promised to help you if you fulfill your part of the bargain. The path to your future is clear, and you should consider yourself lucky."

Dolores's sharp tongue no longer surprised or offended her. Dolores was right; she needed to put her months of study to use treating Adolfo's symptoms and teaching him to read. The question of the closed doors hung between them like an unfinished book waiting for the writer to end the story. Esperanza decided to ignore her forebodings about the north wing. What difference did the north wing make to her? She did not intend to stay at the villa one day longer than it took to return Adolfo to a semblance of health and teach him rudimentary Latin. Then Adolfo and Dolores could do whatever they liked, and it would not affect her in any way.

Esperanza turned her attention to completing her make-shift apothecary. She and Dolores had accumulated dozens of dried herbs, tinctures, teas, balms, and oils. She set about painstakingly labeling them with their names and uses: Tincture of sage, steeped in vinegar - reduces inflammation relaxes the internal organs. Foxglove - strengthens the heart. The inventory went on and on. Fennel - cures indigestion. Oregano - stops infections, Hyssop - loosens chest phlegm. Dill, cumin, comfrey, vervain, flaxseed, willow bark, oregano, fennel, valerian, snakeroot, allium, hawthorn. All of them sat labeled and arrayed on the shelves ready for use.

Esperanza prepared the labels with care. They were for Dolores's benefit, since she would be Adolfo's only caretaker when Esperanza left. She did not have Esperanza's experience and intuition and needed to be taught which medicines alleviated which ailments. When Esperanza left, she wanted Dolores to have what she needed, so she could leave with a clear conscience, knowing she had fulfilled her duty.

17

THE ERUPTION

SPRING 1268

Esperanza lounged on the loggia eyes closed, head thrown back, enjoying the balmy spring breeze. Her body was relaxed but her spirit was as anxious as a sinner on judgment day. Her life with Dolores and Adolfo had flowed along untroubled and steady over the past winter, yet she sensed that something was wrong. The previous night she had a dream. In the dream, she was sleeping in her home-made apothecary. The ground around her began to tremble; bottles and jars jittered to the edge of their shelves and hurled themselves at her head. Terrified, she ran out of the house and saw Vesuvius coming to life. Smoke and ash belched from its long-dormant cone, enveloping the landscape until she couldn't see through the miasma. Its fierce rumble got louder and louder until the mountain convulsed into a violent eruption, throwing her into the blood-red sky. Esperanza jolted out of bed breathing heavily, her heart pounding like a blacksmith at his forge.

She made her way to the window. A benign, tawny moon reflected off the bay, turning the entire landscape a mellow bronze; the view was as tranquil as a lily on a silk-smooth pond. She tried to shake off her anxiety, but she knew something, or someone, was about to disrupt her peace.

By spring, Adolfo was a new man. He had proven to be a diligent student, absorbing as much as he could in his studies. His Latin was tortuous but serviceable. His ailments were under control, with one exception. He occasionally experienced squeezing, pressure, and heaviness in his chest. But the pain passed quickly, and he thought no more about it. His clothing hung loosely around his slimmer body, and though he was still robust, folds of fat no longer drooped around his waist. It was time for Esperanza to claim her freedom.

In the almost two years she lived at the villa; their isolation had been nearly complete. Gardeners, deliverymen, and skilled workers came and went, but they never had guests. Neither Dolores nor Adolfo seemed to have any friends, and their neighbors were far flung. If the residents of nearby villas and villages pursued social lives, Adolfo was never included. So, it was surprising when one day a carriage trundled up the road, and an unanticipated guest knocked on the door. Since no one was expected, Adolfo had not arranged for one of his men to stand in as steward, Signore Adolfo himself opened the door to greet the visitor.

"Ibrahim! What a surprise to see you. Come in, come in." Adolfo laid a hand on his back and propelled him into the house.

"Come sit with me in the loggia. The spring breezes are delightful today."

Esperanza panicked when she recognized the visitor's voice. She heard them coming up the stairway, but she did not flee. If there was going to be trouble, she wanted to face it.

Esperanza could hear their chatter as they climbed the stairs. Ibrahim took one step into the loggia and stopped abruptly. "Well, look at this?" He surveyed Esperanza as if she was a piece of fabric he meant to buy. "Is this the ragtag girl I gave to you, what was it, two years ago?"

"Yes, she is the one. She has matured nicely. Don't you agree? She has been most helpful to me." Adolfo sounded like the owner of a prized coursing hound.

"I can see the results of her ministrations, Adolfo. You look very healthy; you are slimmer, your color is high, and you have more energy than I've ever known you enjoy. There is nothing like a good concubine to bring back a man's zest for life."

Adolfo said nothing, but looked intently at Esperanza, who came close enough to confront Ibrahim. Color rose in her neck and face as she reached her boiling point.

"I am no concubine." Esperanza stood her ground. "Signore Marino has been a perfect gentleman and is a better educated and much healthier man than he was when I arrived."

Ibrahim chuckled into his beard. "I see you are as brazen and discourteous as ever. No matter, you are already too old to serve in the harem. But I'm sure I can find a less luxurious position for you." He turned back toward Adolfo. "What do you think she is worth now?"

Adolfo remained mute, looking at his toes, recoiling from Esperanza's piercing stare. Here rain-cloud eyes flashed with lightning.

"Adolfo!" Esperanza barked. "What sort of arrangement did you have with this charlatan?"

"You are a fool, Esperanza!" Ibrahim sneered. "Did you think you would stay here forever, living in chaste domestic bliss? It is only because our friend was ill that you escaped the fate of all the other girls."

"The other girls?"

"Do you mean to say you don't know?" Ibrahim looked back and forth from Adolfo to Esperanza. "Didn't you see the cubicles in the north wing where we housed the hapless girls we captured from ships at sea?

"No, I didn't!"

"How can that be?" Again, he turned toward Adolfo. "Where did you keep her? Don't tell me you gave her a suite! She must be so spoiled by now that she will be ungovernable. She already had a tart tongue. Now she will be useful only as a scullery maid or laundress working under a master with a hard hand. No one will want her. She is too old for the trade."

"Adolfo, those other rooms," Esperanza faced him eye to eye. "Did you keep girls captured for the slave trade in them? Are you a "merchant" who buys and sells young girls?"

"Well, no, it wasn't like that."

Ibrahim let out one gravelly guffaw. "Adolfo, you are lying to her. It was exactly like that. You made a good commission re-selling the girls I brought you. And you had the added benefit of free access to them whenever and however you wanted."

Adolfo glanced one last time at Esperanza and stood erect, arms akimbo. He shed his façade of respectable merchant like a sheep sheds its winter coat in spring. From under the disguise emerged the hard-hearted pirate. She had glimpsed it occasionally, as when he failed to sympathize with her sorrow-filled life story. She suddenly saw why he refused to talk about the closed rooms.

Esperanza's world shattered once again. *Fate keeps teaching me the same lesson over and over. Never put your trust in another human being. Is there no end to the betrayals I will suffer? Will I be spit out like a well-chewed cud by everyone I trust?*

Adolfo saw Esperanza's surprise grow into disgust, even hatred. How dare she judge him! Hadn't he given her everything? He no longer needed her and would not let her shame him.

"Yes, you are right. It is time for her to move on. Whatever use you can make of her is fine, she is no longer of any use to me. I have gotten what I wanted from her, and she has trained Dolores to maintain my care."

"But Adolfo!" Esperanza shrilled. "You promised me you would help me get to Salerno."

Without a word, he turned away from her, approached Ibrahim and guided him down the stairs. "Let's go to the dining room to continue this discussion without interruption. Dolores will prepare a wonderful dinner for us. She has proven to be of lasting value. I will ask my men to keep watch for a run-away."

Now she understood the meaning of her dream of an erupting volcano. In less time than it takes to dry the breakfast dishes, her world had exploded, throwing her into a red sky of fear and chaos. She felt dizzy, heartbroken, furious, confused, betrayed as she had been by every man she had trusted.

There was no time to bemoan her fate. As she watched Adolfo

and Ibrahim walk away, a paralyzing mix of emotions overtook her; her mind shifted from shock and dismay to panic and terror. She hurried to the kitchen where she found Dolores.

"Ibrahim is here. They intend to sell me into slavery."

Dolores turned her cool eyes on Esperanza. "I know."

"You knew that Ibrahim was coming to kidnap me?"

"No, but I knew it was only a matter of time before he came for you, just like all the other girls. As soon as I saw his carriage riding up the trail, I knew he would leave with you in tow."

"Dolores, please help me! I must flee. I won't be a slave."

"You are already a slave; you have been a slave for the past two years. You just didn't know it."

"But you knew! Why didn't you warn me?"

"Why do you think I resisted your friendship for so long? I knew you would go, just like the others. But Esperanza," she laid a hand on Esperanza's shoulder, the most intimate gesture she ever offered her. "You are not like the others. You have a special gift, and you have never given up hope, nor your resolute vision of going to Salerno. You are stronger than the others."

"Dolores please, if you have ever cherished a dream and had it ripped away, then you would understand. Please help me."

"Follow me." Dolores led Esperanza to her chambers, where she searched under her bed and retrieved a solid wooden box. "Here, take this. She quietly opened the box to reveal a profusion of coins, gems, and jewelry." She pushed the box toward Esperanza.

"Where did you get these? How could you possibly have hoarded this much wealth?"

"There is much you do not know about me. When Signore rescued me, he gave me a job. It was my duty to keep his stolen girls under the strictest confinement. They were not allowed to leave their rooms, speak to each other, or even look out their windows. I had total control." She drew a deep breath, exhaled, and continued. "Signore employed a cadre of men who helped him with his "merchant" trade. It was almost impossible for me to keep the men away from the girls, so I didn't. Instead, I levied a price for access to the girls."

Esperanza dropped her head as tears welled up. Shock silenced her.

"You don't understand; the men would have suffered serious consequences if Signore found out that they used the girls in that way, and so would I. We established an unwritten pact of mutual silence. It was a devil's bargain. They were allowed to visit the girls surreptitiously, and they paid me for the privilege. I don't expect you to understand, but I was doing the girls a service, truly. I made sure the girls were not mistreated or abused, just used to slake the men's desires."

"Oh, Dolores! How could you?" Esperanza was horrified, yet here she was, about to accept the ill-gotten money. She could hardly condemn Dolores when she herself was about to benefit from Dolores' scheme. "I see." was all she could say.

"Fine." Dolores maintained her calm demeanor. "You must understand. I could not have saved those girls, but I can save you. Now we must dress you in something less ostentatious, a disguise to protect you on the road to Salerno. I will send the stable boy with you; he knows the road. Who do you wish to become, a widow, a nun from the convent, a man?"

Esperanza was astonished by Dolores' resourcefulness. "I will be a nun, in a Franciscan habit."

Dolores dug around in her sea chest and handed her a coarse, loosely woven brown robe, completely unornamented except for a heavy belt of rosary beads.

"Where did you get these?" Esperanza marveled.

"The Signore sometimes needed to ensure his girls would not be recognized. The costume he used to enslave others we now use to free you."

Esperanza pulled the habit over her tunic, drew a tight-fitting wimple that covered her head, neck, and sides of her face over her hair, and pulled the cowl over her head. She picked up the box and headed for the door but turned abruptly to embrace Dolores with the fervor of a child being pulled away from her mother. She hurried out to the stable where she mounted the old, sway-backed mare. The stable boy gaped at her in bewilderment but did not question her when she told him she needed to leave.

Her life had accelerated like a wild horse escaping a blazing stable, her brain could barely keep up with the speed of events. She was grateful for her experience living at the convent, in Santiago and hoped it had adequately prepared her for this impersonation.

"I am going to Salerno," Esperanza muttered.

"I know the road. My family lives in Salerno, and I am allowed to visit them twice a year." He was a youth, already worn down from years of relentless toil. "This is the first time I have been asked to escort a nun. Don't fret. Everything will be fine; I will get you to your destination."

Esperanza took slow, regular breaths as she rode into a run-colored sky.

18

SALERNO

SPRING 1268

Esperanza stood gawking up at the bewilderingly complex web of intersecting arches, as tall as two-story buildings, looming above her. The stable boy guided them to Salerno's city center, where they paused to stare at the aerial architecture.

"The people call these aqueducts the Bridges of the Devil," the boy said. "They say the builder, Barliario, built them in a single night with the help of demons," he explained grinning with pride for his hometown.

"The name is appropriate," Esperanza responded. "They certainly look sinister, looming over the street." Then, turning to face him she asked "We've come all this way together and I don't know your name. It was thoughtless of me not to ask."

"They call me Benito, the blessed one." He chuckled. "My mother was happy to finally give birth to a boy. After she achieved perfection with me, she stopped producing babies." A gap-toothed grin spread across his face.

Esperanza smiled warmly. *What a charming boy he is. It was fortunate he was my guide and not some loathsome brute.*

"Where does your family live?"

"My family lives in an ancient home in the oldest quarter of the city where the Romans first built this town. We have occupied our home for so many generations no one can remember living anywhere else. But we are poor, we own no land, and it is difficult to earn enough to sustain us. So, my family sold me to Signore Adolfo."

"Sold you? You are a slave?" Esperanza was shocked and dismayed.

"I wouldn't use that word; it sounds so degrading. The Signore treats me well and I never go hungry. Now and then he allows me to visit my family, trusting my sense of loyalty to bring me back. I have never disappointed him. Why would I leave him? I live like a king compared to my kinfolk here in Salerno."

Benito gestured vaguely toward the city walls. "You will find the Monastery of St. Benedetto in that direction; they take in pilgrims and the sick." He eyed Esperanza up and down. "Even a Franciscan mendicant can find refuge there." He gave her an impish wink and walked away, leading his horse through the labyrinth of ancient streets.

Refuge is what she needed. She and Benito had slept rough the previous night, hidden in a copse of trees, with only a couple of apples to share for nourishment. All night they kept one eye open, and an ear to the ground listening for the drum beat of horses. If Adolfo or Ibrahim were pursuing her, they would not be looking for a person wearing the tattered robe of a Franciscan nun.

With the old mare trudging along behind her, she drifted in the direction of the wall. Before long she found a simple church tucked fast against the city wall. Its stone façade was embellished only by a massive oak door and a small circular window in the choir loft. Abutting the church were two sizable, enclosed cloisters, one on each side like a limestone bird with outspread wings. Esperanza shuffled to heavy oak door and pulled the bell cord. A small, square panel slid open; a pair of dark eyes, perched atop a beaky nose, peered out at her.

"May God be with you. What is your business here?" The masculine voice addressing her was as smooth and soft as a ripe peach.

"I am in danger. I need a refuge." It was a simple explanation, uncomplicated but urgent.

"Tie the horse to the post. Someone will bring it to the stables."

The massive door groaned on its iron hinges as it opened a crack. Esperanza slipped sideways through the narrow opening.

"I will show you to your cell." The owner of the dark eyes and prominent nose materialized into a tall, skeletally thin Benedictine monk. Two-story, colonnaded hallways bordered the courtyard. Esperanza followed the monk, enshrouded in his black robe, down the hallway to a door tucked into the far corner.

"The dormitory where Benedictine nuns and the lay women who stay at the monastery is through this passageway. They occupy the western section of the property, while monastery for the monks and the male employees is in the eastern section. Men and women have separate entrances into the church. We eat in the same refectory, but at different times. Everyone here, male or female, has a task. No one wiles away the hours in leisure." He didn't bother to turn around to see if she understood him. Esperanza trotted along after him, barely able to keep pace with his long strides.

"When the bell for dinner rings, you may leave your cell and follow the other women to the refectory. The fare is simple but filling. We observe silence during our meals. You will find a prie dicu in your cell. I suggest you make use of it this evening. Kneel and give thanks to God for directing your footsteps to this place of respite. I suggest you pray for forgiveness for the sins that brought you to seek refuge here at our monastery. Someone will talk to you in the morning. Until then, you will not intrude on the peaceful silence of our community."

My sins? she thought, *my only sins were to trust Adolfo and Ibrahim, and my refusal to be treated like a slave. How strange that he would assume a woman seeking refuge is somehow guilty.* He opened the door to a tiny cell, dark even now, in the light of a spring afternoon. An unseasonable chill clung to the thick rock walls. The straw pallet on the floor smelled fresh, and the coverlet was clean. An enormous olive-wood crucifix, as tall as she was, hung on the rough limestone wall. The wood was almost black from untold years in a damp, dark cell. The kneeler before the cross was the only touch of beauty in the room; its cherrywood frame glowed, even in the dim light.

There was nothing to do now - no reading, no studying, no concocting medicines - so Esperanza knelt to pray as the monk suggested. She had never cultivated the habit of prayer; the closest she came to religious devotion was while living with the Cohen family, though even they were not unduly strict in their practice. She was grateful for the prie dieu, at least its unyielding kneeler would be more comfortable than the rock floor. With the suffering Jesus on the imposing cross looking down on her, she closed her eyes, relaxed her body, quieted her mind, opened her heart, and breathed deeply. She felt lighter as the weight of distress evaporated.

As she knelt, her body began to vibrate, and all other sensations fell away. She heard a voice; "YOU ARE LOVED," it said. She perceived the message as clearly as if a voice was whispering into her ear. But it was not a voice. It was more like the hum of a beehive. But it was not a beehive. She sensed it in every part of her body, inside and out. Her body tingled. "YOU ARE LOVED," the disembodied voice insisted.

"Mama?" She usually felt her mother's presence only when it manifested itself as burning eyes and tingling ears. But this was different, more powerful, more emphatic. Then she lost the connection, and the sensations ceased. Fear and anxiety dropped from her like rain running off a tile roof. Despite all evidence to the contrary, she was loved.

Thank you, mother, you still look after me, even as the distance between us grows. A warmth suffused her cold cell, and she prayed as she never had before. She was safe, and ready to face her new life eagerly and with confidence.

The dinner bell came and went, but she did not leave her cell. The following morning, as promised, a middle-aged woman, in the coarse brown robe and black veil of a Benedictine sister, came to her cell.

"You were not at dinner," she said simply. "Were you not hungry?" It was a straightforward start to a complex conversation. "Come, follow me to the refectory we will break our fast together."

Her gentle demeanor and pale blue eyes beckoned Esperanza to follow. The refectory held long rows of tables and benches. Nearly fifty heads bowed over the breakfast porridge, eating silently. Some of them wore the Benedictine habit; and some wore the every-day clothing of common people.

"The monks and their lay guests, most of them workers from the town, have already eaten," Esperanza's guide explained. Though we share the same refectory and church, we maintain physical separation. One of us will come for you tomorrow and you can eat with the other lay women.

After the other women had eaten and returned to their daily routines, Esperanza's guide held her back with a gentle but firm pressure on her arm, indicating that she should stay seated at the bench. "Did you sleep well? Are you free of hunger, Are you free from fear?"

Esperanza nodded. She thought it was a sensitive, but unusual, way to begin an interview.

"Let me introduce myself. I am Sister Annunciata. Now, tell me what brings you here. Why you are in danger?"

Esperanza briefly considered giving a misleading explanation, or an abbreviated version of her plight, but decided she should tell her story truthfully, fully revealing the threat that propelled her flight.

"The story of how I came to you is confusing and complicated. I was orphaned at a young age. Eventually, I came to live with a family in Burgos for several years. They were gracious and welcomed me into their family. The master of the house, a well-respected Jewish physician, allowed me to help him in his practice. I prepared medicinal tinctures, elixirs, and balms. Master Cohen knew that I ardently aspired to attend the Scola Medica in Salerno, and he generously arranged for me to attend, at least that is what he told me. But I was deceived. Instead, he entrusted me into the care of a Muslim trader, a friend of his, who had no intention of bringing me to Salerno. On the contrary, he sold me to a pirate slave trader, Signore Adolfo Marino, who lived in Napoli. Adolfo was sick and wanted someone to heal him. I lived with him for two years and helped restore Adolfo's health. When he no longer needed me, he threatened to sell me off. I ran away; and now I believe he is pursuing me. I fear for my life if he finds me."

The nun peered at Esperanza. "So, you are not a Franciscan sister? I would ask how you came to us wearing the Franciscan habit, but it is clear enough that it was a disguise, and you are not a member of the Little Sisters of St. Francis." Not waiting for an answer, she got straight to the heart of the matter. "What are your intentions here? What do you want from us?"

"I don't really know. My aim was simply to save my life; but I think I could be helpful." she plowed on. "I have useful skills. I am educated and could teach sisters who wish to learn to read and write. And I am an herbalist and can maintain an apothecary. I have a gift for diagnosis. My dream has always been to attend classes at the Scola Medica and become a medical doctor. I heard that the Scola conferred this title on women students who qualified."

Sister Annunciata showed no overt reaction to Esperanza's story, no judgment, no disapproval. "That is a very interesting story. I don't believe we've ever had a woman here who aspired to such a high station. I will need to talk to my Mother Superior. In the meantime, you might be useful in our gardens. I will take you to Sister Lucinda, and she will put you to work. She is always in need of willing hands to help in the gardens. Come with me."

Esperanza followed Sister Annunciata through a portal in the monastery walls. Only then did she appreciate the monastery's majestic setting. Below them, the land rolled down to the cobalt Bay of Salerno shimmering under the exuberant spring sunshine. Lush, terraced gardens rolled down the hill to the bay. A series of ponds and waterfalls flowed through the gardens, bathing herbs, exotic plants, flowers, and orchards in sparkling rivulets. The resplendent scene rendered her speechless.

Sister Annunciata did not interrupt her rapture. She simply stood at Esperanza's side as she absorbed the beauty. After a few moments, a small, sprightly young nun joined them, and broke the spell.

"God has blessed us with this glorious day. It's lovely, isn't it?" She was incandescent with energy. Esperanza wondered how she stayed still long enough to endure the daily round of religious observances and prayers. Her face was round like Esperanza's but scarred with pock marks; her olive skin shone with sweat.

"Sister Lucinda, this is Esperanza. She came to us yesterday seeking refuge. Her future is unclear at this time, but she professes a knowledge of herbal remedies, so I thought she could be useful here in the gardens with you."

"I could surely use some help. Spring has produced a profusion of unruly new growth needing to be tamed lest our beautiful garden turn into a wild jungle." Then, looking directly at the newcomer she asked, "Are you a sister of St Francis? I thought your territory was in the north, near Assisi. We are Benedictines here."

"No sister," Sister Annunciata explained. "She wore the habit only as a disguise. She will work with you today. I will go back to the cloister and find more suitable clothing for her." Sister Annunciata turned and walked back through the portal into the convent.

"There is so much to do. Let me see," Sister Lucinda said. "You have knowledge of herbs you say?"

"Yes, in my old life" she paused, settling into the realization that the past few days had utterly ended her previous life. "In my old life, I had an apothecary of my own."

"Wonderful. If you can tell a carrot top from parsley, you will do for a helper." She smiled brightly. "Come with me." They descended to the garden's lowest terrace.

"This is the first level garden. What do you notice about this garden?" Like a true Socratic instructor, Sister Lucinda encouraged her new student to reason out the answer, rather than expounding facts.

Esperanza studied the large garden plot before her. "It is quite lovely, arranged in a large circular design."

"Yes, that's correct. What else do you notice about the circle?"

"It is divided into four sections, and there are different types of plants in each section." Esperanza stepped closer to peer intently at the plants – ginger, turmeric, curry, garlic, basil, marjoram mint and dill all grew in one quarter of the circle. In another section camphor, eucalyptus, jasmine, peppermint, rose, and tulsi flourished. In the third section were thistle, yarrow, calendine, and sage; and the fourth and final section contained cinnamon, bay laurel, thyme, fenugreek, camphor, and hyssop.

"What do the plants in each of the four plots have in common?"

Esperanza closed her eyes and pinched the bridge of her nose in concentration. "This makes me think of the teachings of Galen, or Hildegard von Bingen." She paused again. "I know! The plants in each of these plots correspond to one of the four humors, cold, hot, wet, and dry. Each of the humors is tied to personality types and the curatives in each of these sections is most suited one of these types," Esperanza lit up, elated that she had recognized the pattern. "I've studied these ideas, but I have never seen a garden laid out to correspond to the theory of the four humors."

"Very good," Sister Lucinda nodded enthusiastically. "Now I'll introduce you to the orange and lemon groves."

The perfumed air of the garden mingled with sea-salted breezes drifting up from the Bay of Salerno below. "This is heavenly, all of it. The view of the bay the waterways and rivulets running through the gardens, the ingenious arrangements of plants, the symphony of aromas, all of it delights the senses."

"I agree. We are truly blessed; but the garden serves a higher purpose. We take our vow to share God's graces with those less fortunate very seriously. Our brothers, the Benedictine monks, operate an infirmary for men, and we sisters maintain one for women.

"We are all dedicated to advancing the medical profession. We share the knowledge we have gleaned from all the healing traditions. Naturally this approach attracts students from many countries – from the distant Indus River, north Africa, Iberia, Gaul, and even the islands in wild north seas. If you were to sit in on the symposia these students attend, you would see a marvelous array of clothing, skin colors, and languages. The students are from diverse backgrounds, but most discussions take place in Latin. The exchanges are lively. The mixing of all these scholars creates new ideas, and innovative techniques. This garden is a proving ground for their theories."

"This is so exciting," Esperanza broke in. "In my studies, I learned Frederick II of Sicily declared that only physicians holding a medical degree from the Scola Medica could be called medical doctors. The Scola's reputation is well known everywhere. That is what brought me here. I wish to become a medical doctor."

Sister Lucinda's demeanor sobered. "It won't be easy, you know. It will take much more than enthusiasm. The curriculum includes mastery of the seven liberal arts, before you are considered ready for medical studies. The regimen takes several years. In the final assessment, the students must demonstrate their knowledge by submitting to an oral examination before a panel of faculty judges."

Esperanza squared her shoulders. "I knew the course of study would be rigorous. I am prepared. I am conversant in Latin, Greek, Castilian, and Hebrew, and have studied with a scholar from the Toledo School of Translators."

Sister Lucinda took a step back, reappraising Esperanza, still in her tattered Franciscan robe. "As you know, the Scola Medica does accept some women students, but of course there are very few who qualify. I will discuss this with Mother Superior, she will be the judge of whether to sponsor your application to the Scola." She shook her whole body, like a dog emerging from the water, and focused her attention on the garden. "Now you can help me thin those carrots. They are growing so thickly none of them will thrive until we make more room for them."

Digging her hands in the loamy black soil, smelling the fecund odor, working side by side with an agreeable companion elated Esperanza. She felt the wounds of her past begin to heal, and the door to her future open.

19

THE INTERVIEW

AUTUMN 1268

Stained glass windows punctuated the walls of the Chapter House. An austere stone bench built into the wall bordered the circular room. The only concession to comfort was a pillowed armed chair where the Abbot sat. Each morning the monks shuffled single file into the building to sit in contemplation while the lector read a chapter of the Rule of St. Benedict. When he finished the reading, the Abbot initiated a conversation regarding the details of daily monastic life. Brother Jerome, the Prior, led the discussion. Settling disciplinary issues and routine business fell to him. One by one, the brothers voiced the transgressions of their fellow monks.

"Brother Alexus fell asleep in the bake house and caused the fire in the oven to burn out. For this reason, our rations of bread will be reduced tomorrow, and Brother Alexus will go without bread and make a public apology to the brothers."

"Brother Theodoro callously walked past an old widow woman begging alms at the well. He will deliver food to her for the rest of the month and beg God's forgiveness."

"Brother Julius, the cellarer, found Brother Maximo drunk among the barrels in the wine cellar. He will drink only well water for a week, and we will all pray that he may resist the temptations of the devil."

"Brother Salvatore, the steward, has returned from his

inspection tour and will report on the status of our outlying estates and villages tomorrow."

With the minor matters deal with, Abbot Jerome spoke. "The final matter is more troubling." Brother Jerome's voice dropped. "Sister Annunciata has granted refuge to a young woman fleeing from a dangerous situation. The young woman is highly educated, is conversant in several languages, well versed in the classics, and has an in-depth understanding of herbal medicine. She wishes to be admitted to the Scola Medica and attain the rank of medical doctor. Sister Annunciata brought the matter to us for deliberation."

Nicola, the infirmarer, rose to give his opinion. "This woman is surrounded by many unanswered questions. We know almost nothing about her background and education. Though we all know that the Scola Medica admits women, her acceptance might take the opportunity away from a deserving young man. If she is to be admitted she must be exceptionally well-qualified indeed. I say the Abbot should interview her in person to gauge her suitability."

"Are there any dissenters?" Brother Jerome scanned the group for tacit signs of objection, a man shifting restlessly in his seat, a man looking intently at the floor at his feet, but no one showed doubt or grievance. "As there are no objections, I will arrange an interview with Abbott Jerome when his schedule allows it."

A week passed, and each day Esperanza followed Sister Lucinda through the portal to the gardens. Together they pulled weeds, thinned overcrowded beds, harvested selected herbs as they reached their seasonal peak. They turned and enriched the soil to accept new plantings. She reveled in the sweet, dark earth between her fingers, watching new seedlings unroll their leaves to greet the sun, and the rich mixture of herbal aromas. She tried to let her immersion in the garden comfort her, but a persistent anxiety hung over her head like the sword of Damocles, until one day Sister Annunciata came to her with the news that Abbot Jerome had ordered her to the Chapter House to be interviewed regarding her admission to the Scola Medica.

On the appointed day, Esperanza entered the room and stood in front of the Abbot's chair to wait. A plain undyed tunic, belted at the waist with a simple leather thong, cloaked her from chin to toe, and a white veil covered her head. She hoped her downcast eyes and lack of adornment would strike a discreet, modest tone, neither boastful nor pretentious. The Abbot's heavy footsteps announced his entrance. A slight moan escaped his throat as he lowered himself into the chair. *He is in pain* she thought, *perhaps his bones are arthritic.*

"So, you are Esperanza, the woman who begs admittance to the Scola Medica."

"I am she."

"Please list your qualifications."

Esperanza cleared her throat, took a deep breath, and began. "I have a thorough knowledge of Latin, Greek, Castilian, and Hebrew, and have studied with a scholar from the Toledo School of Translators. I have worked in an apothecary since I was a young child, and I developed and maintained my own apothecary."

"That is all interesting and rather unique for a woman, but you must realize that if we admit you another candidate will be unable to attend."

"Yes, of course, I do understand; but attending the Scola Medica and becoming a doctor has been my lifelong dream."

"So, you came to us without credentials of any kind. You have no letters of recommendation, no accreditation from any educational institution, no distinguished advocate who can testify to your character. And I assume you have no money or lands you can contribute to the Abbey, nor any endowment to offer."

"That's true, Abbot, but I have skills and knowledge. I could be useful. Since I arrived, I have been working with Sister Lucinda in the magnificent gardens. I could attend to patients in your hospital; I would be willing to do the most menial jobs. And I have studied all the great medical practitioners of the ages, Galen, Hippocrates, Avecina, Hildegard von Bingen." She stopped herself, not wanting to appear desperate.

Abbot Jerome stared at her for a long while, taking in the

details of her appearance, clothing, demeanor, and her strange accent. Before him stood a young woman, comely but unassuming. Nothing about her set her apart from the most mundane housemaker.

"Where are you from? How did you come to us, seemingly from out of nowhere?"

Esperanza sighed. She knew her strange story conformed to none of the bounds that constrained the life of a typical woman. If she were typical, she would long ago have been married, and by her age would have produced several children, or died in the process. She wanted to go straight to the heart of the matter and not get bogged down in the details of her unconventional circumstances which could only distract from her earnest desire to be admitted.

"I am an orphan. I have suffered great loss and known great kindness. God laid out a complex path for me which has led me from the Basque Pyrenees, to Ponferrada, Burgos, Napoli, and lastly here to Salerno. Life has taught me to rely on my own resources, and to face whatever happens with fortitude and confidence. I know my own mind and abilities. The Scola Medica has been the guiding light that led me through many dark days. If you give me this opportunity, will not disappoint you,"

The Abbot sat in silence for many long moments. She was not at all the woman he expected; the other women scholars were from entitled, prosperous families with more intelligence than most, excellent references, and plenty of money. This Esperanza did not fit his picture of what a student should be; she was poured from an entirely different mold; he would need to apply a different measuring stick to her circumstances.

"I will consider your case thoroughly. The Abbey's reputation is affected by the quality of the candidates we recommend. I will pray for God's guidance and see you again in one week." He rose from the chair and swept out of the room, his black robe billowing around him.

For another week Esperanza and Lucinda tended the verdant

gardens. As they walked, Lucinda hummed a simple hymn in her sweet, pure soprano until they reached the garden plot they would work that day.

"Here are our late spring vegetables; they are beginning to reach maturity. See how we have put plants that live in harmony with each other together in the beds." She bent to examine the developing broccoli heads. "Oh no, look at this." She sounded concerned.

Esperanza saw the problem at once; cabbage worms were beginning to burrow into some of the vegetables.

"We have planted beets, celery, cucumbers, radishes, in the same bed." She ran her fingers over leaves and stems. "They deter moths that lay their eggs on the crucifers, but they nevertheless manage to lay some eggs. So, we must pick them off and put them in our sacks to feed the chickens."

"I understand this problem," Esperanza said. "My foster mother taught me which plants are companions and love to grow near each other and which inhibited each other's success. We planted beans near beets, radishes, peas, and strawberries, for example, but never onions or garlic. Celery loves chives, cilantro, and leeks, but not parsnips."

"Right! That's exactly what we do here with our vegetables." A broad smile lit up Lucinda's round face and she nodded her head.

"Look, there." Esperanza switched her focus to a covey of young men. They were wearing every manner of costume. Their clothing, headwear, and dress were embellished with exotic adornments. The group crowded around each other as they made their slow, methodical way through the grounds following a lumbering giant of a man, tonsured and clad in Benedictine robes.

"Oh them." Sister Lucinda off-handedly flicked her wrist at the group. "Those are the scholars from the Scola Medica. They study in these gardens, learning the herbal medicines that you and every other herbal healer have used for millennia. The difference between them and ordinary healers is that these students can experiment on their hospital patients and compare the effectiveness of their cures. I must admit that this experimentation appears to improve the outcomes for some of the patients."

Esperanza studied the young men as they bent to inspect various plants, gesturing at one another chattering like a tribe of magpies. *There they are*, Esperanza thought, *the privileged men whose position allows them access to this education as part of their birthright. They can't possibly appreciate the opportunity they enjoy born, as they were, to wealth and entitlement.*

The longer she watched them, the more one student stood out from the crowd. He had ginger hair and stood tall and regal, square-jawed, square-shouldered, and long-legged. He looked up and, quite accidentally, his eyes met hers. At first it seemed he was looking past her, gazing off into the distance, not registering her presence. Then he smiled, and she experienced the strangest sensation she'd ever felt. Her throat tightened and her stomach clenched. She turned and looked behind her to find out what he smiled at, but there was nothing there. He nodded his head in her direction, then re-focused his attention on the garden and his teacher. Confusion and agitation overtook her. She knew her reaction was irrational. They hadn't spoken, she wasn't even sure he was looking at her. She shook herself like Lucinda had done days before, as a dog shakes water from his fur, trying to put the encounter out of her mind.

"Be careful, Esperanza," Lucinda warned. She had seen the interaction between Esperanza and the man. "Nothing will get you expelled faster than associating with the male students."

"Yes, of course." Esperanza replied. "Seeing them here just surprised me."

Lucinda shook her head. "I understand. But the look I just saw wasn't merely surprise; it was attraction. Just be careful. I suggest you spend some extra time tonight with your knees on your prie dieu. Do you think just because we sisters wear these robes we are not prey to sins of the flesh? On the contrary, knowing we will never fulfill our maternal nature only exacerbates the natural attraction to men. We are experts in redirecting those instincts into prayer and work. After a certain age, the longing evaporates like morning fog on the river, and we wonder what the excitement was all about and go on devoting ourselves to our vocation."

"Certainly," Esperanza demurred. "I understand. I have every reason to mistrust men. And I have no time for them in my life. I am as devoted to my calling as the good sisters are to theirs."

Esperanza and Sister Lucinda worked in amicable harmony. The week until her next interview with the Abbot passed swiftly, and once again Esperanza stood looking modestly at her feet when Abbot Jerome sailed into the Chapter House his robes billowing around him like sails in a brisk wind. He settled himself in his chair and began without any preliminaries.

"Well, young lady, I have considered your case carefully. I must admit yours is a perplexing quandary. This is how I perceive your circumstances. You came to us boldly requesting admission to the most prestigious school in the country, the only medical school that will admit women. You have no roots in our country. You have no references, no notable person to vouch for you, no certifications to verify your education, no prestigious family connections. You say you have been educated by a Jew and are otherwise self-taught. It is doubtful you have in-depth knowledge of the seven liberal arts - a prerequisite to studying medicine. You are from the lower classes, so you have no endowment to offer as reimbursement for your education. Are these statements correct?"

His eyes drilled into her. She resisted the temptation to lower her gaze under the heavy weight of his judgment. She straightened, squared her shoulders, and did not flinch. "Yes," she admitted.

"Yes," he repeated. "Not only that, but you appeared at the monastery's doorstep begging for shelter. Since then, the sisters have provided you food, clothing, and shelter for these many weeks without any compensation whatsoever." He took a long breath. "And to top it all off, you are a WOMAN."

Despite her resolve to remain strong, she felt herself beginning to wilt.

"The audacity of your boldness is staggering. Yet it is that very pluck that makes me think you might be the kind of woman who could endure the rigors of the course of study."

"Yes." Esperanza struggled to suppress all emotion, and make her face immobile a marble statue.

"Here is my offer. You may continue to live in the cell the convent provides you. As payment for their generosity, you will continue to work in the gardens, assist in meal service, and do whatever other task they ask of you, no matter how menial." The Abbot paused, trying to detect any reaction to these terms, but the young woman remained stoic.

"In addition, you will assist the Scola by working in the women's wing of the hospital doing laundry, disposing of waste, changing the bedding as needed, or whatever other task they give you regardless how unpleasant."

"Yes."

"Those employments will keep you quite busy. However, if you find any unoccupied hours in your day, you may choose one of the colloquia to attend. You will wear the robes of a postulant to signify that you have dedicated yourself to God and are not available for marriage."

"Yes."

"And one last thing. If I hear one word, one whisper, that you have caused any disruption or distraction among the scholars, you will be immediately evicted from both the school and the convent."

"Yes, I understand."

The Abbot's gaze bore into her one last time, then he turned and glided out of the room, satisfied that he had set the standards for this upstart so impossibly high, that she would be gone within the month.

Esperanza, on the other hand, was ecstatic. If these tasks were the price of admission to the Scola, then she was happy to do whatever they asked in both the gardens and the hospital. Her education had begun.

20

LA MAESTRA

SUMMER 1269

After finishing her morning duties, Esperanza ran from the monastery to the south portico of the Cathedral, her postulant's robes undulating behind her like pennants in a stiff breeze. She charged, sweaty and disheveled, into a room crowded with men ensconced behind rows of lecterns, quill pens in hand, parchments sprawled out in front of them. All eyes rested upon Esperanza as she tucked herself into a corner, mumbling an apology for the distraction. She shrugged off the unwanted attention and soon all eyes returned to the Maestra, a woman, at the front of the room. Esperanza chose this class because it convened near the monastery during one of the few breaks she eked out between chores.

The Maestra interrupted her lecture, calling attention to Esperanza's awkward intrusion.

"The young lady who arrived tardy will speak to me after class," she said pointedly, then glanced down at her notes and resumed her lecture. "Let me see, where was I? As I was saying, you can analyze the patient's ailment by closely examining his urine." Esperanza found her place in the manuscript she brought with her. "Quoting from my book 'On Urines,' I write *'The physician who wishes to be considered an expert must consider the following things . . . health or illness, strength or debility, deficiency, excess and balance. These can be determined with certainty by examination of the urine.'"*

The Maestra Guarna inspired Esperanza's awe, not only was she a physician, but also an author, and a teacher at the prestigious Scola Medica. She conducted empirical tests to discover new medical knowledge and her discoveries were fast becoming the new standard of medical practice. Esperanza could put this knowledge to practical use caring for patients in the Monastery hospital. The Abbot hoped to punish her by assigning her the menial job of emptying bed pans; on the contrary, he gave her the opportunity to apply Maestra's teachings to the care of actual patients. While Esperanza engrossed herself in the Maestra's lesson, one of the young men in class was equally engrossed with this bewitching girl tucked into her corner of the room. The tall, ginger-haired student had first noticed her in the gardens as he and his classmates examined the vast collection of medicinal herbs. Though she wore a postulant's garb, she did not emanate the humble, self-contained, demeanor of a woman dedicated to convent life. Even from a distance, she exuded fervor, intelligence, and the intensity of someone who had more at stake than simply growing vegetables. He realized she had also noticed him that day in the gardens when their eyes met; but today he could not catch her attention. She was intent on attracting as little notice as possible. Curiosity tantalized him. What brought her to this place, and to this class? She never mingled with the few other women in the Scola, who were highly placed daughters of the privileged class. She was as out of place here as donkey on the racetrack.

After class, Esperanza waited nervously for Maestra to castigate her for her late arrival. In truth, she was more worried about arriving late at the Monastery for her chores than she was about the dressing-down the Maestra would dole out.

The Maestra shuffled her papers at the podium until all the other students left. With a nod of her head, she summoned Esperanza to her rostrum.

"Don't you know it is ill-mannered, and an insult to the instructor, to arrive late to class?"

"Yes Maestra, of course. I got here as quickly as I could after finishing my morning duties."

"Your duties? What duties?

"My situation is not traditional. The Abbot at the Monastery Benedetto allowed me to attend one class if I continued to work in the monastery's the garden and hospital."

"Working? You are working at the Monastery?" The Maestra huffed. "Are you a postulant at the convent?" She surveyed Esperanza's rumpled habit. "I have never seen a postulant in one of my classes."

"I know; it is confusing. I am not actually a postulant, but the Monastery allows me to take shelter with them as I have no other place to live. It's a long story."

The Maestra impressed Esperanza even more at close range than her illustrious reputation suggested. Her appearance was neither young nor old, probably not past child-bearing age. Her clothing was elegant in its detail but simple in its design. She wore a deep russet gown with a black cloak, a common form of dress, except for the luxurious ermine fur around the hood, and the flashing gold brooch that closed her cloak. Fine lines radiated from the corners of her amber eyes, and vertical creases ran down her cheeks. Esperanza imagined they had been endearing dimples when she was a girl. But most impressive of all were her brilliant intelligence and the magnetic pull that made it impossible to turn away from her.

"The Abbot usually informs me when a new student will be joining my class. There are protocols to be followed, letters of recommendation to be reviewed. Students don't just drop in unannounced." her irritation made it difficult for her to remain civil.

"I'm sorry, Maestra. I assumed the Abbot had told you about me. He set the requirements for my participation so high he might not have expected me to attend. But he did not appreciate the fervor with which I aspire to become a medical doctor."

The Maestra tilted her head then shook it. "Did you think it was acceptable to just walk into my class? Your presumptuousness is astounding. I will talk to the Abbot tomorrow. In the meantime, you will tell me how you weaseled your way into the Scola without the usual formalities."

"I'm sorry, Maestra. I would love to explain everything to you, but I am expected at the Monastery hospital."

The Maestra's eyes widened, and her cheeks reddened at the thought that this young woman would dare to defy her. "No, you did not hear me. I gave you a direct order. I want your explanation *now*. I will deal with Abbot Jerome tomorrow."

Once again, Esperanza retold the story of the unlikely odyssey that brought her to the Scola - her education at the Cathedral monastery in Santiago, all she learned when she lived with Amika and Gabriela selling herbal remedies along the Camino de Santiago, the crisis that forced her to flee, the excellent Hebrew education she received with the Cohen family, her more recent immersion in the classic literature and texts of ancient Greece, Arabia, and north Africa, and the deception that resulted in her present situation.

"The Abbot allowed me to attend one class after I completed my assigned tasks in the monastery kitchen, gardens, and hospital. If he did not inform you of the arrangement, he probably did not think I would find time to attend class.

The Maestra's amber eyes focused on Esperanza with the intensity of a hawk hunting its prey. "Interesting," the Maestra said coolly. "You tell me you have a superior educational background, and I don't disagree, but I am not convinced it is appropriate for a student of mine. I would be willing to wager that you lack the basic prerequisite of having studied the seven liberal arts. You probably cannot identify a logical fallacy, analyze Latin grammar, or compute solutions in geometry; and I doubt you understand astronomy or music. The students in my class today were required demonstrate their suitability by presenting letters of reference attesting to their mastery of these studies. My class covers many intricacies relating to a physician's practice. In addition to my manuscript detailing the diagnostic value of studying urine, I have also written books about fevers, the unborn embryo, the malformation of fetuses, and wound care. This is a complex course of study, and each student is responsible for mastering it.

"As I said, I will talk to Abbot Jerome. In the interim, you may attend until I tell you otherwise. We meet twice a week, here in the Cathedral. You are not qualified, but if nothing else, you have grit. I like that in a woman." She turned and swept out of the room.

Esperanza sat in stunned silence. She felt as though she had been held up by the heels and shaken. Every secret, every inadequacy, lay exposed on the cobblestone pavers. Every accomplishment she struggled to achieve, each scrap of knowledge she accumulated was dross compared to this woman's brilliance. She had broken every convention, breached every barrier to excel in many disciplines and now she stood at the top of her profession. She was the epitome of a talented, educated woman, a woman Esperanza would be proud to emulate.

Once again Esperanza waited in suspenseful anxiety not knowing if she would be banned from Maestra Guarna's class. But the bad news never came. She continued to assist in the kitchen, work in the garden, and help the patients at the hospital. Only now, she must also study the lessons she learned in Maestra's class. Her unforgiving schedule left no time for reflection, yet every night when she dropped onto her pallet she was filled with gratitude. Every day brought her closer to her goal.

When it became clear to the other students that she would be attending class regularly, the atmosphere around her changed. When she entered the classroom, the handful of women students bent toward each other, glancing at her surreptitiously over their shoulders, shielding their mouths so she would not hear their conversation. The men, on the other hand, ogled her boldly, snickering and nudging as she slipped quietly into her corner. Despite the hostile undertone that surrounded her, Esperanza carried on. What other option did she have? She had nowhere else to go and she was, after all, living out her dream. The other students would never be her friends, coming as they did from their privileged backgrounds, but Esperanza found a friend in Sister Lucinda. Even Sister Annunciata, though she maintained her cool demeanor, did not treat her unkindly. Her happiest moments were spent in the garden with Sister Lucinda and in the hospital caring for the sick. Many of the women in the hospital suffered from problem pregnancies or had fragile newborns struggling to survive their critical first months. She held the sweaty hands of unhealthy women, swabbed their fever-warmed brows with cool cloths, spooned nourishing bone broth into their mouths, changed their soiled bed clothes. She examined their urine as she carried it away to dispose of it, diagnosing their illnesses, applying what she learned in Maestra Guarna's class to the patients she cared for.

The medical doctors and their students made regular visits to the hospital, consulting and vigorously debating the proper treatments and cures for the patients. The student doctors explored the monastery's libraries searching for guidance in the copious collections of Arabic, Hebrew, and Latin writings. They frequently turned to the Scola's collection of wisdom written by their own luminaries over the years. The primary text the Scola had produced, the 'Handbook of Healthcare,' was a collection of treatises on diverse subjects like hygiene, dietetics, anatomy, surgery, and wound care. They often consulted over even older books written by the most legendary scholar of Salerno, a woman practitioner named Trotola, who set the standard for knowledge about an astounding variety of illnesses and conditions.

* * *

The exuberance of spring tempered, turning into a torrid summer. No one expected rain in this season of arid of unrelenting sun; and no one escaped the oppressive blanket of heat. Many farmers, travelers, and those who spent too much time under the sun were brought to the hospital with heat-related illnesses. The symptoms were easy to diagnose – confusion, shivers, exhaustion, cramps, sunburn and heat rash. Esperanza packed cool cloths into the victims' armpits and groins, brought them water and wine cooled in the root cellars. Though the hospital practiced a strict regimen of handwashing and fastidious disposal of feces, some patients inevitably brought their intestinal parasites with them from the farms and fields. The medical practitioners treated these persistent pests with bitter, purgative cures such as wormwood or gentian.

No matter what the illness, Esperanza toiled tirelessly at their bedsides, suggesting effective therapeutics to the medical doctors and the nursing sisters who assisted them. She did not call attention to herself and tried to make her suggestions as discreetly as possible, yet her reputation among the hospital staff grew. The doctors gloated over their successes, never crediting Esperanza when they followed her suggestions, but the nursing nuns exchanged knowing glances, tacitly acknowledging that their successes owed a lot to Esperanza's counsel.

The more experienced doctors traveled through the rows of beds with a flock of students at their heels, hanging on their every word. The students Esperanza encountered in the gardens in spring had now progressed to treating the sick. They tried out remedies, experimented with oils and herb teas, and created new compounds to counteract the effects of illness.

Whenever their paths crossed, Esperanza and the ginger-haired man's eyes sought each other out. One day the inevitable overlapping of their schedules brought them together over an elderly patient, a woman with swollen ankles, shortness of breath, fatigue, and weakness.

"I have seen this condition before," Esperanza placed her hand on the woman's inner arm both to reassure her and so she could feel the woman's pulse beating against her palm. "A man I worked for suffered from the same symptoms," she spoke softly to the woman.

Esperanza did not notice the ginger-haired man coming up behind her. "Yes, I have too," he said, looking over her shoulder at the patient.

A flush of heat raced through her body. "How did you treat the case?" Esperanza asked, not daring to look at him.

"I used leeches," he said, reaching past Esperanza to lay a hand on the woman's forehead.

"I have never used leeches. I used foxglove." Esperanza's breath came in short spurts, and her heart pounded like a butter churn, but she tried valiantly to maintain the professional manner of a doctor, not as one who merely empties bedpans.

A flush of energy passed between them, as unmistakable as the convent bells tolling the Angelus. He smelled like lemons and honey. She cringed, guessing that she exuded a far less wholesome aroma. His wrist brushed her arm as he withdrew his hand from the woman's forehead. He let his hand rest on Esperanza's arm. She did not move, did not snatch her arm away. He leaned further in, and she felt his skin radiating warmth next to hers as they peered at the patient. After a few moments Esperanza gently pulled her arm away, lightly sliding her fingers across his hand as she did so. She felt him shiver at her touch.

"I will take your suggestion and try foxglove tomorrow." He hunched over the patient longer than necessary, looming over Esperanza until he finally straightened. Esperanza looked surreptitiously around the room, hoping no one had observed their encounter, then she rose and faced him. "My name is Tomaso," he said.

"And mine is Esperanza." She stood motionless,

She hurried out the hospital door to a shady place where the ivy climbed, and an old cherry laurel shaded the stone wall. She stood for what seemed a long time waiting for her pounding heart to slow, and her breathing to return to normal.

She heard the door open and close behind her, and again the lemony, honey aroma scented the air. This time she turned to face him.

His voice was low and mellow with a distinctly aristocratic accent. "Meet me tomorrow in the garden. Keep to your regular gardening schedule, but go to the plot where the shrubs grow. I will be waiting for you among the echinacea, lavender, and lemon balm. Our meeting will be as sweet as our bower's scents. The Maestra has much to teach you, but I have more." An endearing lopsided smile softened his face.

"No, I can't." Esperanza stiffened in alarm.

"I understand you can't, but you will."

Esperanza fretted all that night, caught between blissful dreams of meeting Tomaso in the gardens and abject terror. In those dark hours, she finally resolved not to respond to his summons. What kind of and arrogant man would order her to meet him, expecting compliance as if she were a pet dog? The more she thought about him, the more his presumptuousness repulsed her.

The next day, she found herself on her knees, spading fork in hand, loosening the rich soil earth beneath a thicket of bushes. She concentrated assiduously, ignoring everything but the task before her. Absorbed as she was, she did not hear Tomaso's footsteps or the soft rustle of his clothing as he crept up behind her and knelt at her side. Abruptly she was aware only of him; all her senses focused on his scent, his warmth, his overpowering presence. She felt her heartbeat in her throat; and her body froze, paralyzed by shock and indecision.

When she turned toward him, he pulled the garden fork from her hand, and brought her palm to his lips. His gentle kisses traveled, one after another, up the inside of her arm to her neck. Esperanza's face glowed as rosy as a ripe apple, and she grew hot all over. *I should say something; I should resist, push him away, display outrage or anger.* But she did none of those things. By the time he pressed his lips to hers, all thoughts of resistance melted like butter in a hot pan. Tomaso turned Esperanza toward him until they looked directly into each other's eyes. The rest of the world disappeared as he placed his hands on her shoulders, then let them glide slowly down her arms to her hands. Every strand of hair raised up to meet his exploring hands. Once again, he brought her palms to his lips, his blue eyes never leaving hers.

"Meet me here again tomorrow. I would like to know you

better." His meaning was not lost on Esperanza. Even if they never uttered a word, he would know her better.

The next day Esperanza nearly ran to the garden. Her dedication to the garden became obsessive. Tomaso found her there almost every day. Together they sought out the most secluded corners of the magnificent garden. There were copses of trees, thickets of shrubbery, patches of tall grass that offered islands of privacy. Small affections quickly grew into intimate embraces and ardent lovemaking. Esperanza's entire world revolved around her lover, and his passion for her also grew as the weeks passed.

The world beyond their corner of the garden disappeared for them, but they did not disappear from the notice of the Scola students or the nuns who also worked there.

21

BANISHMENT

AUTUMN 1269

The time skimmed by as fast as the shearwaters gliding across the surface of the Bay, Esperanza hardly noticed the days gradually shortening. The citrusy tang of maturing lemons and the mellow, woody scent of olives filled the air. The sun's intensity moderated, and velvety breezes caressed her skin with the gentleness of a lover. At least that was Esperanza's love-struck perception.

She had never sought a man's affections, nor had she ever expected to capture a man's attention. Least of all, had she envisioned a liaison with one of the medical students. It was dangerous and imperiled her already tenuous position at the monastery. But ginger-haired Tomaso's combination of tenderness and power entrapped her in a spider's web of desire.

"What will become of us?" Esperanza's cooed as she lay in his arms under the evergreen leaves of a boxwood. Her words stabbed Tomaso's conscience but at this moment he had no desire to allow the future to intrude on the pleasures of the present. He would rather bury his nose in her sunshine-scented hair and caress the soft, supple skin of her shoulders, and nuzzle the curve between her neck and shoulder.

"I will take you home with me to Perugia and introduce you to my family." It was a lie, and he knew it; but the deceit came easily as curling his body around hers.

As the second son of an aristocratic family, Tomaso's future was pre-ordained. Though he would not inherit the estate, he was nonetheless assured of a share of its income and a villa in which to live. As the only man in Perugia to achieve certification as a licensed physician, his status would command respect for him individually and reinforce his family's influence among the region's prominent citizens. Respect and admiration were important tools in maintaining his family's power in the ever-shifting struggles among the Duchy's aristocracy. Besides, he had been betrothed to Ariana since she was born. Tomaso was only five years old at that time, and they grew up knowing they were promised to each other. Their family ties spanned generations, and the marriage contracts had been signed long ago. Their mutually beneficial marriage was a foregone conclusion.

Esperanza basked in his promises knowing full well that she, a woman of humble position, with no money, no connections, and no family, would never be acceptable. She wondered at how easily her practicality and strength of character melted in the glow of his incandescent magnetism.

The days became months and the romance ripened like the fruit of the trees. Tomaso's affection was genuine, and Esperanza's devotion to him was as steady as the tides in the bay. When the inevitable confrontation came, it did not surprise either of them. One buttery warm autumn day, after their garden tryst, Esperanza re-joined sister Lucinda tending the vegetables. Instead of simply greeting her with a disapproving side-long glance, as she usually did, Lucinda abruptly stood up, her dirt-encrusted hands pressed firmly to her hips and planted herself squarely in front of Esperanza.

"What do you think you are doing out there in the bushes with that depraved lordling? Have you lost your senses?"

"What, what do you mean?" Esperanza's feigned innocence fell flat and shriveled at Lucinda's feet.

"Do you think the sister gardeners and the medical school students are blind? For heaven's sake, do you take us for idiots?

Do you two think you sound like nightingales, thrashing about in the bushes? It's a wonder you haven't been thrown out of the convent, the hospital, and the entire premises by now."

"I . . . . I . . ." Esperanza stuttered. "It was only one time. . . ."

"Oh please, Esperanza. Don't make matters worse by lying. You disappoint me. I thought we could be friends." She lowered her voice and moved closer. "Sister Annunciata is on her way right now to speak to Abbot Jerome. I would have tried to stop her, but your blatant disregard for all we hold holy finally disgusted me so much, I didn't even try."

"But what will we do?"

"We? You are even more deluded than I suspected. Do you think anything at all will happen to your Tomaso? Do you think he hasn't despoiled countless other girls before you? His aristocratic position entitles him to leniency. Certainly, he may be reprimanded, though even that is doubtful. The Abbot will shrug, perhaps even reminisce about his own youthful conquests, and Tomaso may even endure a short lecture about discretion, but his life will go on as before. Yours most certainly will not."

Esperanza knew she was right. Of course, she knew. That evening, none of the other convent women spoke to her. Before she left her cell at the dinner hour, there was a knock at her door. One of the postulants laid a bowl of soup on the floor and quickly left before Esperanza had a chance to speak a word. There could be no clearer message she was not welcome among them. She asked herself over and over why she had carried on with Tomaso like an alley cat, throwing caution to the wind. She had acted like a love-struck girl; she had not even attempted to resist. She sighed at the thought of him. Of course, she knew why she lost her heart to him. He gave her something she had never experienced. He made her feel beautiful, special. She was convinced his sentiments for her were sincere. But what if they were? It would not matter in any case, he was not free to choose his future any more than she was. Though he had more freedom than she, his family had decided his future long ago and he had little chance of changing it.

Finally, she understood. In Tomaso's embrace she felt loved. He didn't feel sorry for her as Amika and Gabriela had, nor was he motivated by generosity like the Cohen family. Neither did he feel responsible for saving her as Mateo did. Tomaso didn't want to exploit her talents as a healer like Adolfo or treat her as a product to be bought and sold like Ibrahim. It was no wonder that she found Tomaso irresistible. She knew the consequences of being found out would be disastrous, and yet she was compelled to take the risk. As calamitous as she knew the outcome would be, she did not regret loving him.

She was filled with a sudden, forceful anxiety, and panic began to build. She could not simply wait patiently for the tongue-lashing, or worse, that Abbot Jerome would delight in dispensing. She realized her time at the convent had ended the day she took Tomaso as a lover. The next day, before the rising sun spread its rose-colored rays across the bay, she donned her postulant's robe, tucked the box of coins Dolores had given her under her scapular, and prepared to walk away. She did not know a single soul in Salerno except Benito, the boy who brought her to the monastery, but it didn't matter. She had to leave, and quickly.

With nowhere else to go, she walked to Benito's neighborhood asking everyone she met where she could find the charming youngster. She did not know how he could help her, but he had connections. After all, he said his family had lived in Salerno for untold generations. Perhaps he knew a family who wanted a tutor for their children, or a hostel for travelers that needed help in the laundry or kitchen. She wandered the narrow, meandering streets and alleyways where stone hovels crowded shoulder to shoulder, and the smells of the butcher shop, the tannery, and the blacksmith's forge overpowered the lemony smell of the countryside. Everyone seemed to know the beguiling Benito, but no one could tell her where to find him.

"He went searching for someone. It seemed quite urgent." The butcher volunteered the only information she got.

By midday she was tired, hot, and beginning to despair of

finding him. She dropped heavily onto the steps of the old church of Santa Maria, fighting off the dark mood descending upon her.

"This is truly remarkable." She recognized the voice and looked up to see Benito standing over her. "I just left the convent, asking for you. They did not know you had gone. I was about to retrace our steps back to Napoli." He cocked his head, bursting with curiosity, but was too polite to ask why she decided to flee again. "I have a letter for you," he said, handing her a piece of folded linen paper, its seal still unbroken. "The last time I was in Napoli, Dolores made me swear I would find you and give this to you."

Esperanza stared at the missive as if she had never seen a letter. She recognized the red wax seal of the Villa Marino.

"Aren't you going to open it? Dolores is expecting an answer."

She cracked the seal open, unfolded the page and began reading.

Dear Esperanza,

I hope this letter finds you. I tell Benito to look at San Benedetto Monastery in Salerno. He say you might be there still.

Here at the villa, Signore Adolfo's is worse. He is almost blind now, and his heart grows weak each day. He lays in bed and thinks he will die soon. He lives in fear, worried that he will meet the Almighty to answer for all sins of his lifetime.

He hears voices and sees the ghosts. The girls he and Ibrahim sold come to haunt him. He wails loudly to God and begs you will return. He wants to make amends to you. He forbids Ibrahim from seeing him.

I welcome you back with an open heart. I never had a friend before you in my life. I miss you.

I told Benito to find you and to not to come back if he did not give you this letter. Please forgive my poor writing. Is bad, but good enough I think, so you understand. I thank you for opening the door to reading and writing. I care for Signore Adolfo best I can, but now he needs a true healer. He needs you.

May God's grace guide you back to us,
Dolores

Esperanza dropped her head into her palms, wracked with deep, ragged breaths, her shoulders heaving as if she was crying, but she made no sound. Benito watched in fascination. Was she feeling anguish, relief, or grief? He could not be sure. When she finally looked up, she asked "Did you bring a donkey for me to ride?"

* * *

Esperanza expected a short, peaceful ride back to Adolfo's villa overlooking the Bay of Napoli, with Vesuvius at its back and orchards, groves and farms rolling down to the sparkling water. But as soon as she mounted the little burro, she felt queasy. They had walked only to the edge of town when she slid off the burrow and wretched into the grass at the side of the trail. Her stomach was empty but despite that, greenish brown bile dribbled from her lips. It was peculiar; she rarely suffered stomach upsets, but the last days at the monastery were filled with anxiety, so perhaps this was her body's reaction. She remounted and soldiered on, clinging to the reins, taking short, shallow breaths. Bouts of nausea roiled her stomach, but she managed to control the spasms. By the afternoon she felt better, weak, but not nauseous.

They rode in silence for several hours until Benito grew restless and bored.

"Dolores gave me a few coins and ordered me to feed you, so I bought us salami, some peaches, and grapes. That should keep body and soul together for the next two days. Would you like to stop and eat? You look a little pale." Benito twisted around to look at her. "Are you well?"

"Yes, I'm fine, I just had a bout of the vapors."

They dismounted in a field of grain. The burros indulged themselves, burying their muzzles in a field of farro. Benito helped

Esperanza down, bracing her against his slim body as she nearly rolled into his arms and dropped heavily onto the ground.

"You really don't look good. Maybe you should lie down for a spell."

Esperanza needed no further encouragement. She curled up and drifted into a half sleep as Benito ate his lunch. When she revived, Benito again offered her something to eat something.

"I'm fine, I'm fine," she said, trying to convince herself it was true. But she did not feel fine. She felt her stomach could betray her again at any moment, and she was so sleepy it took an act of sheer willpower to propel herself back into the saddle. "I think I just need something to drink," she said.

Benito handed a wine skin up to her. "It's well watered down, so it should be refreshing."

"Thank you. Let's move on."

For two days they plodded along the narrow road, retracing their steps back across the winding cliffside above the twinkling, aquamarine waters of the Amalfi coast. Esperanza had never been especially prone to vertigo, but this time she had to avoid gazing over the cliff edge to the restless waters below, lest she have another bout of nausea.

After two days on the trail and two nights sleeping in roadside hedges, the Villa came into view. It was just as she remembered it, the open-air loggia connecting the two wings of the villa beckoned her. The well-tended grounds, with their flowerbeds, shrubs and formal gardens spilling down the hill, were as lovely as ever. A tangle of emotions gripped Esperanza. Unlike her first arrival, when all she could see was the elegant villa, this time the dark secrets of the north wing tarnished its beauty. The spirits of the lost girls who passed through those hallways, each ill-fated soul locked in her tiny cell, now haunted the man who had imprisoned them.

Esperanza and Benito ascended the gravel path to the front door. Benito waited and watched as Esperanza pulled the bell cord. The ringing had barely begun to echo down the hallway when Dolores flung the door open, engulfing Esperanza in her angular embrace. The gesture was so unexpected and uncharacteristic of the normally chilly Dolores, that Esperanza staggered backward.

"You're here!" She placed her bony hands on Esperanza's shoulders and held her at arm's length. "You are thinner, and you look a little sallow. Are you well? Didn't they take care of you at the convent?"

Esperanza opened her mouth to speak, but immediately turned her head to the side and threw up on the entry's Italian tiles. "Oh, my dear! What have you been eating?" She turned her eyes toward Benito. "Did you give her moldy cheese?"

"No, absolutely not, Signora. In fact, she barely ate anything at all because every time we stopped for food, she fell asleep."

Dolores draped her arm across Esperanza's shoulder and shepherded her to the dining room. "Sit here. Benito, get her some fresh water from the well."

"How long have you been unable to keep your food down?"

"It only started recently, after I had to leave the convent."

"You had to leave? Why? What happened?"

Esperanza's face reddened and she dropped her head. "I violated their standards of behavior."

"What on earth do you mean? Just be honest. How bad could it have been that they wished to expel you?"

"I was a fool!" Esperanza laid her head in her hands. "You see, there were medical students at the Scola Medica. I was allowed to attend a class if I could find time away from all the chores they gave me. It was my dream come true. But I was a fool. There was this one young man. Tall, ginger-haired . . . ."

"Oh no, Esperanza, did he violate you?"

"No, it wasn't like that. I wanted him and he wanted me."

Dolores leapt up from the chair, walked to Esperanza and slapped her across the face.

"Not you! No, you couldn't have! You were the strongest young lady I ever knew. And now you come back to me, not as one person but two!"

"What do you mean?" Esperanza was shocked. Then she froze. Suddenly she knew Dolores was right. She was with child. She groaned, put her hands to her face, and convulsed with sobs. This time they were not silent. She could barely breathe between her howls. Dolores stayed at her side, not speaking until Esperanza's wails died.

"Don't worry, child. I will take care of you,"

"But I am not a child. I am a grown woman, and I should have known better. What will Signore Adolfo think?" She realized she was so absorbed in her own sorrow she hadn't given him a single thought,

"Adolfo," she said. "How is he? Shouldn't I go to him right away?"

"No. I will tend to him tonight, as I have been doing these past months. He will be neither better nor worse tomorrow. Collect yourself tonight and rest. I will bring you some more suitable clothes to wear, a basin and ewer, so you can clean the grime of the road off, and I will take you to him tomorrow."

22

REDEMPTION

AUTUMN 1269

The Signore's room had the sickly odor of imminent death. He preferred the curtains closed, even though they blocked the rich autumn scent of maturing orchards and fields. Dolores had adjusted to the rank smell little by little as the Signore's health declined, but it hit Esperanza with full force, overwhelming her senses as she entered his room.

She squinted and winced as the odor hit her. Constant exposure to the sick every day in the Salerno hospital had dulled the edge of her intuition, but upon entering Adolfo's room, her eyes burned like hot coals and her ears buzzed as if infested by a thousand bees.

"I brought you a surprise with your breakfast," Dolores said as she proffered his food.

"I don't like surprises." Adolfo grumbled. "And I don't want breakfast." His gnarled hand shook as it reached to push the bowl away.

He removed the cloth that lay over his eye and tossed it on the floor. Eyes that had been red when Esperanza fled from the villa now looked like the eyes of a demon, permeated with a network of red veins so thick there was almost no white.

"Are you still using eyebright?" Esperanza asked, turning toward Dolores.

"Who is that?" Adolfo grumbled. "You brought a visitor? In my condition? And you didn't ask my permission?"

His once round face was now gaunt, his cheeks sunken, his lips a thin line beneath a scruffy gray beard. The outline of his body tucked under the bedding was no larger than that of a slim youth. Esperanza steadied her nerves and approached the sick bed.

"Yes, Dolores brought someone with her this morning. It's me, Esperanza." She had seen enough sickness and disease that almost nothing shocked her, but Adolfo's eyes were the worst she'd ever seen. "I have returned to help Dolores take care of you."

"Dear God in heaven above! You have answered my prayers! You brought her back to me." He thrashed about trying to throw his covers off. "I must get down on my knees and thank the Lord."

Dolores pushed his shoulders back against the pillow. "No Signore, you can thank God as easily from your bed as the floor. He will hear you either way."

"Yes, I have returned." As she spoke, waves of resentment boiled up in Esperanza. This man, pathetic as he now appeared, was the same man who confined her, kept her from her one great goal, the one who was willing to sell her, enslave her, the man who had done the same to countless other young women.

"I returned for Dolores' sake, not yours. You did nothing to earn my affections. You made me your slave and tried to sell me. You kept me from pursuing my dream. Do you think I should now be delighted to see you again?"

The old man thrashed round in his bed. His exertions winded him. His heart raced, his breath became short and shallow, until a bout of coughing overcame him, and blood-tinged mucus dripped from his mouth.

"I am going to die, Esperanza. Can't you spare some mercy for a dying man?" He gripped his chest and groaned in pain. "I will not live out the year."

"I can see that. It's hardly worth my time to treat you." Her rejoinder was so cold-hearted, she shocked even herself. Now that she was in a position of power over him, her vengeful side rose like a hissing serpent; she wanted retribution. "I've got to leave." She ran from the room, racing to the nearest chamber pot and heaved until she was exhausted. She could hear him calling after her.

"No, no, don't leave."

She walked to the loggia so she could sit in the sun to settle her stomach and her nerves.

That night, she wished she had her prie deux so she could beg forgiveness. *What have I done? I have been running from one disaster to the next my whole life. Now I have circled back on myself. For all my experiences since being torn away from Amika and Gabriela, have I learned nothing? Have I turned into a spiteful fury? I must drive away the demons of vengefulness. I hurt myself when I indulge these vindictive feelings.*

That evening, just before she closed her eyes to sleep, Dolores tapped lightly at her door. When Esperanza answered, Dolores entered with two small glasses of red wine.

"This vintage is from the grapes harvested the year you escaped from here. Luckily, they are sweeter than your memories of this place." Esperanza motioned her to the upholstered chair sitting just where she'd left it, as if waiting for her return.

"You bear him a great deal of ill-will, don't you?" Esperanza nodded. "You needn't love him, but you must try to treat him with forbearance. He's right, you know, he is going into his final decline. We must allow him his repentance and encourage his search for redemption. We are not his judges, only God can do that."

"I know; you're right. Wrath overpowered me at just the same time as a wave of nausea struck. You might wish to judge me as I judged him, and it would be justified. Look at me, unmarried, pregnant, and banished from the life I longed for. I am as guilty as he. I beg for tolerance from you as he begs it from me. I am not without sin, so I should not cast the first stone."

"No, Esperanza, I do not judge you. Nature is a primal force that drives us, whether we are saints or sinners. I am surprised though, I fully expected you to come back to me as an accredited physician."

Esperanza ground the heels of her palms into her eyes, trying not to burst into tears again. After sitting in silence for many moments, she raised her chin, squared her shoulders, and swore to herself that she would make the best of her situation. At least she was not out on the street. She had been welcomed back into the lovely villa like the prodigal son.

"I would like to go to our apothecary and see what needs to be done."

Dolores' thin lips stretched into a tight smile. "Yes, it will need some tending. Tomorrow we will deliver Signore's breakfast, and you will apologize for your harsh words. Then we'll revisit our little apothecary and see what needs to be done."

* * *

"The sun has risen. Helios is riding his chariot across the sky toward its apex. Don't you want to see it?" Esperanza entered Adolfo's room with as cherry a disposition as she could muster. She went to the drapes and began pulling them apart.

"No! The light hurts my eyes."

"Then I will open them just a bit," Esperanza said. "Natural light is healing. It will be good for you." Adolfo grumbled but did not stop her. Esperanza moved to the edge of his bed, looking down at the diminished man.

All through the previous night she wondered what she could do to alleviate his suffering, even if she could not save him. In her dreams, Galen, Avicenna, Hippocrates, Hildegard, Maestra Guarna, and Amika all danced forming a perfect circle. She stood in the middle, whirling joyfully until they closed in on her. Voicelessly they asked her, 'Did we ask if you were worthy of learning? Did any of us withhold bestowing our knowledge on you because you were a sinner?'

When she awoke, her antagonism had vanished and, though she still could not love or forgive him, she could use her accumulated knowledge to alleviate his suffering. The next day she began diagnosing his condition.

"I am going to lay my head against your chest and touch your arm. It may feel inappropriately intimate, but it is meant only to help me assess your condition." What she heard was alarming. His heart was galloping unevenly, like a wounded horse.

"Can you save me?" he begged piteously.

"I don't know. Your heartbeat is irregular, and your eyes are very red. Dolores and I will go to our apothecary and choose the remedies most suitable for your symptoms."

Esperanza and Dolores fell easily into the old rhythms, and, after cleaning the kitchen, they made their way up to the little room they called their apothecary. The shelves were still well-stocked except for a few items. There was only a little willow bark left because Dolores had used it liberally for tea. Many other staples were still there – yarrow, angelica, lavender, flaxseed.

"We will try foxglove first. His heartbeat is wildly irregular. The heart is the center of emotions, actions, and desires. His fear and worry over his life of sin could certainly have imbalanced his humors. He has too much bile and that is known to affect the heart. If we can't bring his system back into balance, I'm afraid we may not be able to help him."

"I expected you to say that. Day after day I have seen him decline, but we can try." And they did try.

They prepared baths with sweet smelling herbs, working together to move him to the soothing water and back again. They swabbed his eyes with a mixture of milk and honey, and when that did little to reduce the redness, they tried castor oil. One by one, they tried potions, and balms of snake root, wall flower, and oleander. For several months he held his own against his many infirmities, and even recovered slightly. He looked forward to his baths, and after a while he was able to sit up in bed. When his eyes improved, he agreed to open the blinds a bit more, reducing the gloom of his surroundings.

Two things brought him joy above all else. One was lying peacefully in his bed with cool cucumber slices on his eyelids, and the other was Esperanza reading Rumi's poetry to him. It gave him exquisite pleasure to watch Esperanza changing before his eyes. After a few months she rushed to the chamber pot less frequently. Her face became rounder, her hair glossier, and her belly expanded. At first a small bump protruded, barely showing beneath the folds of her dress. Then the bump grew into a graceful curve. To Adolfo it looked elegant, and appealingly shapely. By the time the lemon pickers swarmed the orchards and the farmers' scythes swept back and forth felling the barley and rye, her bump dominated her entire torso. She leaned back as she waddled through the hallways and had difficulty rising out of a chair. Still, she glowed angelically, until the month when she could no longer sleep through the night. Her eyes drooped and sunk into their sockets, and she became as tired as an overworked dray horse pushing her enormous belly before her as she waddled through the villa.

Dolores worried more each month as Esperanza's time drew near. "I have never attended a childbirth," she fretted. "I have no idea what to do."

"Don't worry. I am healthy and a good age for childbearing, neither too young nor too old. I have attended many births in my time at the monastery's hospital. I will tell you what to do." It was true, she had attended many births. She knew that many did not go smoothly, and that there was a fair chance either she or the baby, or perhaps both of them, would not make it through the ordeal.

Esperanza's pregnancy gave Adolfo something other than himself to worry about. He asked after Esperanza's health every day when she tended to him. She was frank with him, explaining her progress, beginning with the first flutters of life she felt. When the baby was big enough to move inside her, she placed his palm against her belly so he could feel the little feet and fists push against her insides. He was mesmerized and insisted Dolores take good care of her, feed her whatever foods she craved, and make sure she was not on her feet all day.

"Who would ever believe that old pirate would be so solicitous of you and the baby." Dolores chuckled.

"It's a wonder, isn't it? The juxtaposition of old life waning and new life waxing is a marvel – for me as much as him. If I am honest with myself, I must say I'm glad I have the old pirate to take care of. It gives me less time to dwell on the uncertainty of what is in store for us."

"Have you thought about what you will name the child?"

"No, it's bad luck to pick out names before the birth. If all goes well, there will be plenty of time. Would you like to help pick a name?

Dolores' thin-lipped smile spread across her face. "Yes, I'll start thinking right now. You look like your time is very near. When do you expect the baby to make its appearance?"

"I expect I will be waiting until the end of September - another month or so."

* * *

That night, Dolores dreamed a demon got into the house and was screaming through the corridors, racing from one room to the next seeking out a special target for his spear. The screaming went on and on until she heard it call her name. She jerked awake and recognized Esperanza's voice wailing from the next room. She leapt from her bed and ran to her. By the time she got there Esperanza had already been laboring for hours. Dolores found her drenched in sweat, a puddle of blood and fluid pooling between her legs.

"It's coming, the baby is coming!"

"But it's too early!"

"Yes, early." Then another shriek tore through her. She panted short, hot breaths as she tried to give instructions. "Boil water, fast! Get the towels and rags we prepared."

Dolores turned in tight circles, not knowing what to do first.

"No! No time! It's coming, it's coming." She howled like an injured animal. She tented her knees and threw the covers off. "Get down between my knees. Get ready to support the baby as it comes." Her words stopped. She panted and wailed, panted and grunted, panted and pushed with all her might.

"It's early! It's not my time yet." Esperanza whimpered between her contractions.

She shoved her fear and panic aside. No time for that. Dolores did as she was told, positioning herself between Esperanza's knees. Another enormous push and a shriek and a round bald head bulged between Esperanza's legs. It seemed far too large to be coming out of this slight woman.

"Put your hands under its shoulders and when I push, you gently pull the baby out." Another scream and Esperanza pushed again. The baby slid out dragging its cord with it.

"It isn't crying. It should be crying." Then Esperanza collapsed back against the pillows, delirious with pain and desperation.

"Its head is covered. There is a film of slimy skin over its whole head and it's not breathing." Dolores croaked, as agitated and afraid as Esperanza.

Esperanza knew at once. The baby was born with a caul, a thin film of flesh enshrouding its head. "Pull the film away, hurry! Get it out and make it start breathing! Hurry!" Esperanza's words came out as an urgent, husky whisper. She used every bit of her strength to maintain consciousness and the ability to speak.

Dolores hooked one finger under the bloody, slimy film of skin and delicately lifted it from the baby's face. With eyes squeezed shut and its little arms and legs curled up, he opened his mouth wide, gasped for air and let out a wail almost as loud as Esperanza's.

"A boy, it's a boy!" Dolores' voice was unrecognizable.

One more heaving push and the afterbirth slid out.

Dolores wrapped the dark purplish red creature in the sheet Esperanza had thrown off. For a moment he looked deeply into her eyes, then started wailing again.

"Help me sit up," Esperanza directed. "I'll take him." She reached out her arms to the baby. One by one, she uncurled his tiny fingers, each one with a minuscule nail. She bathed him in tears as she put him to her breast. With only a little encouragement, he latched on and greedily sucked down his first meal.

As Dolores gazed at mother and baby, her near panic evaporated, and a flood of exquisite joy coursed through her. She bent and kissed the baby's head, then set about cleaning the mother, the baby, and the bed. A boy, she thought. Now we have a boy.

Two days later, mother, baby and Dolores crept into the dying man's room.

"Here he is," Esperanza cooed. She held the tightly wrapped bundle out for Adolfo to inspect. Adolfo turned his head toward the baby and trembled like a guttering candle. He tried to reach out for the child. Esperanza laid the baby next to his head so he could take a closer look. Adolfo inhaled the baby's ineffably sweet scent, then sighed, and closed his eyes. A single tear slid onto the bed sheet.

"It's a boy. Good." Pleasure suffused his face. "What will you name him?"

"He will be called Mateo. He was born with a caul." Esperanza said as she bent to lift the baby from Adolfo's bed.

"Aah, an omen of good luck. Yes, he was born to good luck. I will see to that. Dolores, call the notary," Adolfo said. The glow of pleasure drained from his face, replaced by profound fatigue, and his whole body wilted.

"Would you like us to bring Mateo to see you tomorrow?" Esperanza asked.

"Yes, bring him to me. I would like to see my heir as long as my heart still beats."

23

ORPHANS

AUTUMN 1273

Two women and a curly-headed toddler trundled down the slope through the lemon grove to the village cemetery. They carried bouquets of purple gentians and yellow tansies to lay at Adolfo's grave outside the walls of the village church, in the place set aside for the poor souls not worthy of a religious burial inside the walls. Unphased by his frequent tumbles, the little boy hauled himself up and trundled on. After a particularly hard fall, Esperanza hurried to his side prepared to comfort him, but found him sitting on his diapered bottom marveling at something he had found on the ground. He bowed his head over the small treasure, his auburn curls framing his round face.

"Mama, mama," the little boy reached out to show his discovery to his mother.

"Well, look at that," Esperanza cooed. "What did you find?"

"Roccia, roccia,"

"His vocabulary grows every day," Dolores beamed. "He is such a bright little thing."

"It's not a rock," Esperanza explained as she examined it closely, turning it over in her hand. The profile of a curly haired man was embossed on one side, and a bounding deer on the other. It was worn smooth, with the date, CCCX barely visible. "Look, it is imprinted with the year 310. This is an old Roman coin."

"Mine, mine." The pudgy hand reached up to take back his treasure.

"It is a lucky day for you little man," Dolores tousled the boys hair. "You discovered a treasure."

"Yes Mateo, it's yours, but I'll put it in my coin purse until we get home, so it doesn't get lost." Esperanza reached down and took the gold piece from his hand.

Mateo stuck out his bottom lip and emitted a little whine but did not protest. Soon the coin was forgotten, and he toddled down the hill on his pudgy little legs. When they reached their destination, Esperanza and Dolores knelt to place their bouquets on Adolfo's gravestone, a simple rectangular marker bearing his name, an image of a ship, and the date of his death, September 1267.

Mateo plopped down next to the headstone and reached for the flowers Esperanza and Dolores had placed there. "Mine, mine."

Esperanza pulled one purple and one yellow flower from the bouquets and handed them to the boy.

"Here, these are yours." Esperanza said to Dolores. "You've got to pick your battles with toddlers. I'll save my fights for something more important than a couple of flowers."

"Yes, something more important, like a real Roman coin!" said Dolores, gazing down at the gravestone. Her tone became pensive. "His soul rests with the Lord, I just know it," she said. "For all his evil deeds, in the end he repented and made amends by bequeathing his estate to

Mateo. He could not have left it to us because we are women without men, but he could leave it to a child. It was his way of thanking us for making his last years on earth bearable."

"He was enchanted by Mateo." Esperanza mused. "As irascible as he was, he never got flustered or irritated with him, even when the baby wailed at night, even when he was suffering and near death. Mateo brought an unexpected joy into his life. I am grateful too. I never expected to have the security of living in the villa, unafraid of eviction. It's too large for three people, and sometimes

I wonder how we could make better use of all those haunted rooms in the north wing."

Mateo wobbled to a stand, grabbed his two flowers, and tottered along the wall. When Esperanza and Dolores caught up with him, they found him kneeling next to a girl flung across a mound of freshly turned earth, the side of her face and her tunic caked with damp soil, her body shaking with sobs interrupted by violent coughing. Looming over her was a burly man with a grizzled beard and unruly hair protruding from under his peasant's cap. His deeply creased face was contorted with the effort of remaining patient.

Dolores and Esperanza reached Mateo just as he was offering his two flowers to the girl.

"No cry, no cry" he said, his chubby hand thrusting the flowers at her. This compassion was a side of their little cherub Dolores and Esperanza had not seen, the sweet sympathy of one innocent child for another.

The women approached the desolate girl slowly. Bouts of violent coughing interrupted her hoarse sobbing. She could hardly gulp a breath of air without exploding into another fit. She finally noticed the little boy and the shadows of the two women hovering above her. Bright red patches bloomed on her sunken cheeks. Her head scarf sat askew, her stringy mouse-brown hair dangling limp and lifeless around her dirty face.

"Who do you mourn here?" Esperanza asked.

"My mother," she blurted in a croaking whisper. "Is this man your father?" she asked motioning to the man behind standing behind the girl.

"No," a booming voice erupted. "I am her uncle. Her father died years ago of the bloody flux. Who are you to be asking all these questions?"

"How did your mother die?" Esperanza ignored him and talked to the girl. She dropped to one knee and placed a gentle hand on the girl's back. *She is like me, motherless, fatherless, facing a hostile world without a parent's love.*

"She died after many months of coughing, and now I am coughing as she did," the girl continued. "I am doomed to die like she did. I doubt I will see my tenth year."

"Stop this interrogation! Can't you see she is upset enough? I am her uncle. Who are you? Stop bothering the child." He huffed like a horse after a brisk trot. "I am taking her to my family. Never mind that I already have seven children and can barely feed my own. I am her mother's brother, so I will do my duty. If I cannot feed her, I will take her to the nuns at the dell 'Annunziata convent."

The girl sat up and stared at Esperanza with desolate brown eyes but did not move until Esperanza spread an arm across her torso and lifted her. Beneath her hand, Esperanza could feel thin ribs. Prominent lumps bulged from the girl's neck beneath her jaw, her skin was warm and clammy, and a dribble of blood escaped from the corner of her lips. Esperanza's eyes burned and her ears buzzed. *This girl has scofula. The orphanage will not want to take her in.*

"What is your name?" she asked the sprig of a girl.

"Filomena," she said studying the clay beneath her feet.

"Filomena, 'one who is loved.'" Esperanza smiled at her. "That is what your name means."

"Well then, I am misnamed. There is no one who loves or wants me." Another burst of swampy coughing mingled with wet tears shattered Esperanza's heart.

"That's enough," the uncle pushed Esperanza out of the way. "Get out of here, you are meddling. This is none of your business." He reached out, grabbed Filomena's thin wrist, and jerked her away from the grave. "She is coming with me, at least long enough to see if she can pull her weight in our household. My wife could use the help hauling water and cleaning the ashes from the hearth."

The man tugged the stumbling girl after him as he disappeared into the village and headed back to his home.

"That poor girl," Dolores commented. "I know these peasant families. They work their children like oxen, feed them little, and get them out of the household as soon as they can."

Esperanza picked up little Mateo and carried him back up the hill to the villa hugging him and whispering 'I love you little man' into his ear.

"Don't cry, girl. Don't cry." He laid his curly head on Esperanza's shoulder and cried his own hot tears.

* * *

For the next three weeks Mateo was subdued and lethargic. Esperanza and Dolores tried to reassure each other that he would soon forget the incident. After all, didn't young children have short memories? But Mateo's spirits never lifted. He sat talking to the corn husk doll Dolores had crafted for him whispering "Don't cry, girl. Don't cry, girl."

"This has been going on too long." Dolores' voice was thin and strained. "Little children should not carry on this way. It's not good for him."

"You're right. It breaks my heart to see him this way. He is truly worried about Filomena. We don't know where her uncle lives, so we can't find her there. I can only imagine that her life would be sad and exhausting with that heartless man. She must be growing weaker as her disease worsens." Esperanza paused for only a moment. "But we know where dell'Annunziata orphanage is. We can try to find her there" Esperanza said.

* * *

A diminutive sister on duty at the orphanage door stood on tip toes to speak through the sliding peep hole. "May God be with you."

"And also with you, sister. I am looking for a young girl of about seven years who may have been brought here. She has a serious cough, was thin and sad."

"Wait here. I'll get Mother Superior."

Mother Superior did not open the door to the visitors, yet even from the doorway they could hear a cacophony of wailing of children.

"Yes, we have her, but she is confined to her room. She cannot have visitors. I know that terrible, hacking cough too well. I had to isolate her, or within days, all our children would have been infected with the coughing disease. I cannot endanger others. As you can hear, we have more children than our poor sisters can adequately care for." She stopped explaining and turned her suspicious eyes toward Dolores. "Do I know you?"

Dolores remained stolidly silent.

"Aren't you the one who cared for the recluse in the mansion above town? You stayed away from townspeople, but the people knew you worked for that odious man in the villa on the slopes of Vesuvius. Whispers followed you everywhere you went."

"He has passed away. His soul is in the hands of the Almighty, but he left the villa to us."

"How dare you pawn this girl off on our exhausted sisters?" Mother Superior hissed at Esperanza and Dolores. "You sent your lackey, here to deposit her on our doorstep; then he fled. He was a gruff, bristly man with filthy hands and deep creases across his swarthy face."

"We did not send her here," Dolores bristled. "That man was her uncle; she was supposed to go with him when her mother died, but he dumped her here. We met him in the cemetery where poor Filomena was crying over her mother's grave. The uncle made it clear he was reluctant to take her to his home, and threatened to bring her here if she could not work. That's why we are here. We were afraid he would relinquish her to your care. We wish to take her home with us so we can care for her properly."

"So, the old scoundrel is dead. What are you doing with all that space?" She pointed up the slope to the villa. "I heard there is an entire wing of the villa with small rooms for the many girls he stole to sell as slaves." The sharp gaze she turned on Dolores could have shattered glass, but Dolores stood her ground. She was shocked that this woman knew so much about their secretive existence.

"And you, young lady," her steely eyes focused on Esperanza. "You must have been one his slave girls." She spit the words out as if they tasted wretched on her tongue. Although she did not call Esperanza a whore, the implication hung in the air.

"I was not a slave!" Esperanza stomped a foot. "I am a healer. He brought me here to care for him in his declining days. I have studied at the Scola Medica in Salerno!" For many long moments no one spoke. The silence was so profound they could hear the ground squirrels scratching in the leaves.

"Come in," the nun said ushering them into the cloister. She narrowed her eyes and glared at baby Mateo who fidgeted in Esperanza's arms, his face buried in her hair.

As Mother Superior turned to go, Mateo said. "Girl cries. Don't cry, girl."

The nun stopped, turned slowly, and looked at the tot. "This baby has feelings for the girl?" she asked.

"Yes, he hasn't stopped worrying about her for weeks. And, as you said, we have a lot of room in the villa. We can easily make a good home for the poor girl, and Mateo wants to see her happy."

"My poor sisters are overburdened with all these children, as you have noticed. The girl is diseased and miserable. She can't be exposed to the other children. I'll go get her." Mother Superior turned and strode down the portico, her robes swishing against the tiles as she walked away. When she returned with Filomena, the girl wrinkled her forehead and squinted trying to piece together what was going on.

"Aren't you the ones from the cemetery?" she said as recognition dawned on her. "And this is the little boy who gave me the flowers." A wan smile spread across her face, until she bent over in a paroxysm of coughing.

"They have come to take you home with them." Mother Superior nodded toward Esperanza, "Do you want to go with them?"

"What will my uncle say if he comes, and I am not here?"

"If he comes for you, we will come and get you at the villa." She pointed up the slopes. "Until then, you may go with them if you wish." Filomena brought her shoulders up to her ears, as if she was retreating from the world, like a turtle withdrawing into its shell. After a few moments, she straightened and nodded uncertainly. Fear gripped her; she felt like a dead fish in the market being passed from hand to hand. But at least these people seemed to want her.

"Yes, I'll go with them," she said in a barely audible whisper.

Esperanza approached, lowering herself to one knee and looked into the girl's eyes. She took the girl's clammy hand in her own. "I understand how you must feel. I was an orphan like you and just about your age when my rescuer came for me. I know how terrifying it is to live in uncertainty and fear. Don't worry, we will take good care of you."

Mateo leaned out of Dolores' arms reaching toward Filomena. "Don't cry."

Filomena came to Esperanza's side and stood quietly beside her.

"You know," Esperanza said to Mother Superior, "You were right about us having much more room than we need. Dolores and I have been wondering how we might put our villa to a better purpose. We have all those small rooms in the north wing, like cells in a monastery. We could take your sick children to our villa and care for them until they are well. We have a well-stocked apothecary, and I am a trained healer. I attended the Scola Medica for a time. I worked in their hospital and learned the practices of the healers of many cultures. If we cared for your sick children, you would be able to devote yourself to the education of your healthy children. When they are old enough to leave the orphanage, they would have some skills to help them make their way in the outside world."

Mother Superior leapt at the suggestion. "Dear mother of God, that would be so helpful. We can establish a partnership. I will ask the bishop if he would provide funds for our sick orphans' upkeep while they are with you."

"Excellent." Esperanza looked down at the fragile girl and at Mateo nestled in Dolores' arms. "Now we have a new addition to our family. We will work hard to restore her health."

Mother Superior turned to Filomena. "Today you start a new life with these good people. Most of our orphans are not as fortunate as you. God has truly blessed you; your name suits you. You are one who is loved."

24

FAMILY

1279 to 1281

Filomena flourished under the Napolitano sun, maturing into a serious young lady. Now thirteen, she was healthy and strong. The scrofula raking her lungs when she arrived had been banished years ago by the careful ministrations of Esperanza, who had administered a saltwater gargle each morning, followed by honey-sweetened lemon water, and peppermint tea. At midday Dolores had brought her a bowl of soup, fresh greens from the kitchen garden, and echinacea tea. When her energy waned, she slept; day by day her wracking cough disappeared. When she was well enough to sit up in bed, Esperanza began teaching her letters, followed by words, and sentences. She diligently applied herself to the task, soaking up as much learning as Esperanza could give her.

Every night Mateo and Filomena snuggled side by side while Esperanza read them Aesop's Fables, and ancient folk tales like – The Little Geese, the Crystal Rooster, the Haughty Prince. As she read, she trailed her finger along the lines of writing until, by the age of five, Mateo could decipher most of the words. Mateo was devoted to Filomena and followed her everywhere. Despite their six-year age difference, they were inseparable.

When the orphan children were ill, Esperanza nursed them back to health, but as they recovered Mateo and Filomena took over their care. When they were healthy enough, and if the weather was fair, the children in the infirmary went outside to play on the grassy lawn encircled by the arms of the curved entry staircase. Nine-year-old Mateo and was close enough in age to join in their games, but also responsible enough to intervene with all the officious authority of a bossy big brother when altercations cropped up. And at fifteen, Filomena could read to them from the books Esperanza had read to her. And Dolores worked with the children in the garden. They loved burying their fingers in the rich, black loam, learning the right time to pull the carrots and leeks, how to make the bean plants cling to their ladders, and how much water from the bucket to dribble on them.

The children who were still weak from their illnesses played with clay marbles, fired in the oven until they were as hard as pebbles or played simple board games. Checkers was always a favorite. As they recovered their energy, the children played bocce ball on a flat spot on the lawn, tug of war, hide and seek, or hopscotch. Those children were returned to dell 'Annunziata in hopes of being adopted.

Dolores began bringing Filomena and Mateo to the village market, and on forays into the wild hills and forests on the flanks of Vesuvius. Soon their home-made apothecary was as familiar to them as the lemon scented air, or the glinting waters of the bay below. Their two mothers sent them to the apothecary confident they could retrieve the needed herbals and medicines correctly.

Filomena and Mateo accompanied Esperanza as she made her rounds in the north wing every morning, checking on each sick child, assessing their needs, tracking their progress, changing bedding, and emptying chamber pots. They followed their two mothers on their regular visits to dell 'Annunziata, bringing home sick children and returning them, healthy and happy, to the orphanage. The townspeople stopped whispering behind their backs or gossiping about nefarious goings-on at the villa. Instead, they spread the word that their neighbors, the famous family of healers at the villa, were curing sick children when no one else could.

As their reputation grew, poor, desperate parents knocked on the villa's doors more and more often, offering chickens, eggs, woolen blankets - anything they owned – to get treatment for their sick children.

"Our neighbors told us to bring our babies to the hospital in the villa above Napoli," they'd explain when they arrived. "They said you were miracle workers and could save my child."

The more often the family of healers saved them, the more their reputation spread. When aristocrats began arriving, begging 'The Family,' as they came to be called, to heal their suffering children, they offered more than poultry, and The Family's finances grew along with their fame.

When Filomena was sixteen, and the precocious Mateo was nine, Esperanza introduced them to Adolfo's precious books, manuscripts, and scrolls she had once studied.

"They contain knowledge of the healing traditions of the Greeks, Romans, Arabs, and Hindus. We use elements of all those traditions here at the children's hospital," she said. Mateo imbibed the knowledge of the masters as easily as water, and at times exhibited flashes of brilliance. Filomena had to work harder, but she proved to be a diligent student, thirsty for knowledge and unflagging in her devotion to learning.

By the time Mateo was twelve, he began creating innovative treatments, experimenting with a sponge soaked in opium, mandrake, and hemlock held under the noses of patients to help them sleep if they suffered in pain. Esperanza, very aware of the danger of these treatments, supervised his activities closely, insisting these powerful ingredients be used sparingly and with the utmost caution. Mateo experimented with his remedy until he had calibrated the dosages appropriate for the age and weight of each patient. They worked in shifts as a team, around the clock, so busy they needed to hire kitchen help and a maid to keep the household functioning.

The Family instructed the helpers on the fundamentals of a healthy diet, insisting that their patients eat the freshest vegetables, eggs, and meats. Dolores created a chart matching the type of food best suited to various illnesses, according to the principles of the classic healers.

In the afternoon, when shadows grew long, and the breezes breathed sweet aromas into the air, Esperanza and Dolores drifted to the loggia to enjoy a respite from the rigors of their busy days. They sat side by side, gazing down at the children playing on the lawn below.

"Did you ever think fate would bring us to this point?" Esperanza mused, "with a thriving infirmary, a son and a daughter bringing joy to our lives? I have always craved stability and a family to love." She turned her head toward Dolores smiling, "and a companion to share it with. Do you remember when we met?"

"I certainly do," Dolores scowled. "You were as ferocious as a caged lion."

"Of course! Because that's exactly what I was, a caged lion of a girl, ready to scratch my jailers' eyes out."

"Now, here we are. You did not expect to have a family and I did not expect to have a friend," Dolores said, gazing down on the scene below. "Who would have believed that the Signore, the most unapologetic of rogues, would be the one to fulfill our dreams."

"Do you ever wonder what the future will bring for Filomena and Mateo? In only a few years, Mateo will be old enough to attend Salerno Scola Medica."

"He is so bright" Dolores pronounced, "and is already showing a great talent for healing and improvising new treatments. I have no doubt he will be a brilliant student. And Filomena," she looked down at the girl supervising the children. "She has the makings of a very competent manager."

Sitting companionably in the quiet of late afternoons, they conjured up the final scene.

"I can easily see us fading out like the memory of a long-ago dream." Esperanza whispered. "Soon it will be Mateo and Filomena standing side by side as we are now, looking down from the loggia with the sun glinting off the bay below, the scent of lemon and olive trees filling the air, and children playing in the grass as the bells of Santa Maria waft up from the village. The circle will be complete, our dreams fulfilled and their dreams just beginning."

EPILOGUE

1300

"It's getting late." Filomena's forehead crinkled with concern as she pulled her stained apron over her head. Mateo, would you go out to the loggia and see what's keeping our mother? She's late for dinner."

When Mateo did not return, Filomena's stomach clenched with an amorphous foreboding, and she hustled to the loggia. Mateo knelt next to his mother's chair, arms flung across her body, his face buried in her tunic, moaning pitifully. Filomena had seen enough death to recognize the ashen pallor of her skin, the slack jaw, and her unearthly stillness to realize she was gone.

She sent one of the older children to dell'Annunziata with a message informing the new Mother Superior that Esperanza had passed away. The sisters would know what to do. Filomena knelt next to Mateo, encircling his shoulders with her arm, and joined him in mourning.

Within two days, the sisters of dell 'Annunziata had arranged everything. They washed Esperanza's small body, combed her hair, now grey and frizzy, her smokey grey eyes closed forever, dressed her in her best clothing, and laid her in a casket before the altar at Santa Maria's. For two days people from the village and beyond filtered through, crossing themselves, kneeling with bowed heads murmuring prayers, and lighting votive candles, assured that the soul of this saintly woman was now sitting at the feet of the Lord, surrounded by angels. They gathered in small groups exchanging stories of the old pirate in his ominous villa on the flanks of Vesuvius, and how this orphaned slave girl transformed the place into a renowned sanctuary where the children of the wealthy and the poorest alike received the best medical care in the land.

When the visitation period ended, the strongest men lifted the coffin, spread with a simple undyed linen funeral pall, and bore her to the church cemetery. There they laid her to rest next to the grave of her dear friend and partner, Dolores. Dolores' stone read:

"Dolores (last name unknown), was laid to rest here this 20th day of November, in the year of our Lord, 1290."

Their deaths did nothing to reduce the number of parents who wanted the best care for their children and who continued to bring them to the hospital. The villa now had the words, 'Sanctuario di guarigione per bambini', 'Healing Sanctuary for Children' engraved over the front door, and the children's hospital continued to welcome all the sick bambini.

1305

A frizzy-haired child of three toddled through the village streets, his somber parents close behind him. When they reached the cemetery, Mateo and Filomena handed the boy two bouquets, one with irises and one with tansys. He placed one on each of the graves as reverently as a toddler can and returned to stand between his parents watching as they wept silently. "No cry," he said. "No cry."

The End

About the Author

Cindy Burkart Maynard is passionate about history, and the natural world, a passion that adds rich detail and context to her historical fiction novels. Her characters come to life on the page as they portray what it was like to live in another time and place. She weaves compelling, dramatic stories based on strong characters facing daunting challenges. She has co-authored two nonfiction works about the Colorado Plateau and the Desert Southwest and contributed articles to Images and Colorado Life Magazines. She has been a Volunteer Naturalist for Boulder County for more than twenty years, and served as a Docent at the Sonora Arizona Desert Museum in Tucson, AZ.

Awards:

Colorado Authors League Award Winner for Western literature

Women Writing the West Award Finalist

WILLA Literary Award finalist for soft cover fiction.

Readers' Favorite Five Star Author

Winner of the Marie M. Irvine award for Literary Excellence

Professional Affiliations:

Historical Novel Society of North America

Lighthouse Writers

Women's Fiction Writers Association

Colorado Authors League

Rocky Mountain Fiction Writers

Authors Guild

Acknowledgments

I would like to thank my long-suffering husband, Bob Maynard, my first reader, staunch supporter, and moral supporter. I owe so much to Julian De La Motte, developmental editor and medievalist par excellence, who kept my depiction of medieval Europe accurate and helped hone a very rough draft into a coherent story. My beta readers, Pat Gustafson and Jane Watermolen, patiently listened to my ramblings and provided practical suggestions and helpful advice. I can't imagine what I would have done without all of you.

Bibliography

Doubleday, Simon R. *The Wise King: A Christian Prince, Muslim Spain, and the Birth of the Renaissance*. New York, Basic Books, 2015.

Green, Monica H. *The Trotula: An English Translation of the Medieval Compendium of Women's Medicine*. Philadelphia, University of Pennsylvania Press, 2002.

Hildegard Von Bingen. *Hildegard's Healing Plants*. Beacon Press, 11 May 2002.

Lancaster, Jordan. *In the Shadow of Vesuvius: A Cultural History of Naples*. Great Britain, Tauris Parke, 2019.

Lowney, Chris. *A Vanished World*. Free Press, 2005.

Origo, Iris. *The Merchant of Prato*. New York Review of Books, 14 July 2020.

HISTORIUM PRESS

www.historiumpress.com